MRS. JEFFRIES and the Yuletide Weddings

Berkley Prime Crime titles by Emily Brightwell

THE INSPECTOR AND MRS. JEFFRIES
MRS. JEFFRIES DUSTS FOR CLUES
THE GHOST AND MRS. JEFFRIES
MRS. JEFFRIES TAKES STOCK
MRS. JEFFRIES ON THE BALL
MRS. JEFFRIES ON THE TRAIL
MRS. JEFFRIES PLAYS THE COOK
MRS. JEFFRIES AND THE MISSING ALIBI
MRS. JEFFRIES STANDS CORRECTED
MRS. JEFFRIES TAKES THE STAGE
MRS. JEFFRIES QUESTIONS THE ANSWER
MRS. JEFFRIES REVEALS HER ART
MRS. JEFFRIES TAKES THE CAKE
MRS. JEFFRIES ROCKS THE BOAT
MRS. JEFFRIES WEEDS THE PLOT
MRS. JEFFRIES PINCHES THE POST
MRS. JEFFRIES PLEADS HER CASE
MRS. JEFFRIES SWEEPS THE CHIMNEY
MRS. JEFFRIES STALKS THE HUNTER
MRS. JEFFRIES AND THE SILENT KNIGHT
MRS. JEFFRIES APPEALS THE VERDICT
MRS. JEFFRIES AND THE BEST LAID PLANS
MRS. JEFFRIES AND THE FEAST OF ST. STEPHEN
MRS. JEFFRIES HOLDS THE TRUMP
MRS. JEFFRIES IN THE NICK OF TIME
MRS. JEFFRIES AND THE YULETIDE WEDDINGS

Anthology

MRS. JEFFRIES LEARNS THE TRADE

MRS. JEFFRIES and the Yuletide Weddings

Emily Brightwell

BERKLEY PRIME CRIME, NEW YORK

THE BERKLEY PUBLISHING GROUP
Published by the Penguin Group
Penguin Group (USA) Inc.
375 Hudson Street, New York, New York 10014, USA
Penguin Group (Canada), 90 Eglinton Avenue East, Suite 700, Toronto, Ontario M4P 2Y3, Canada
(a division of Pearson Penguin Canada Inc.)
Penguin Books Ltd., 80 Strand, London WC2R 0RL, England
Penguin Group Ireland, 25 St. Stephen's Green, Dublin 2, Ireland (a division of Penguin Books Ltd.)
Penguin Group (Australia), 250 Camberwell Road, Camberwell, Victoria 3124, Australia
(a division of Pearson Australia Group Pty. Ltd.)
Penguin Books India Pvt. Ltd., 11 Community Centre, Panchsheel Park, New Delhi—110 017, India
Penguin Group (NZ), 67 Apollo Drive, Rosedale, North Shore 0632, New Zealand
(a division of Pearson New Zealand Ltd.)
Penguin Books (South Africa) (Pty.) Ltd., 24 Sturdee Avenue, Rosebank, Johannesburg 2196, South Africa

Penguin Books Ltd., Registered Offices: 80 Strand, London WC2R 0RL, England

This book is an original publication of The Berkley Publishing Group.

FIRST EDITION: November 2009

Library of Congress Cataloging-in-Publication Data

Brightwell, Emily.
Mrs. Jeffries and the yuletide weddings / Emily Brightwell. —1st ed.
p. cm.
ISBN 978-0-425-23046-6
1. Jeffries, Mrs. (Fictitious character)—Fiction. 2. Witherspoon, Gerald (Fictitious character)—Fiction. 3. Police—England—Fiction. 4. Housekeepers—England—Fiction. 5. Weddings—England—Fiction. 6. Murder—Investigation—Fiction. I. Title.
PS3552.R46443M643 2009
813'.54—dc22 2009029943

PRINTED IN THE UNITED STATES OF AMERICA

10 9 8 7 6 5 4 3 2 1

This book is dedicated to Blake Michael Fredericks
with great anticipation of all of his years to come;
and to Jim Andrews, in grateful remembrance
of all of his marvelous gifts.

MRS. JEFFRIES
and the
Yuletide Weddings

CHAPTER 1

Agatha Moran didn't consider herself a cruel woman, merely a determined one. She collapsed her umbrella and stood in the darkness staring through the drizzle at the house. She put her bare hand on the top of the wet wrought iron fence surrounding the courtyard to steady herself and gather her courage. She'd been in such a state this afternoon, she'd forgotten her gloves. Even with her umbrella, she'd gotten soaked to the skin, and she'd stomped through so many standing pools of water, her feet were freezing as well. But she ignored her discomfort. She had more important concerns than her own misery. All she cared about was making sure it was stopped.

All the way here, she'd wondered if she'd have the courage to go through with it. Agatha laughed harshly, amazed she'd ever had any doubts about her own course of action. No matter how difficult, it was a task that had to be completed. Too much was at stake to give up now.

Across the expanse of the tiny cobblestone courtyard, she could see straight in through the window. The drawing room was packed with guests. She smiled grimly. Good. This was perfect; an audience was just the weapon she needed. If she knew her quarry, and she was sure she did, then her appearance at this particular tea party should be enough to stop this madness. She hadn't wanted to do it this way, but she had no choice. Some people were simply too stupid to be reasonable.

She closed her eyes, took a deep breath, and reached for the latch on the gate. A gloved hand grabbed her arm and jerked her backward with such force, she stumbled but managed to grab on to the railing to keep from falling.

Her assailant whirled her around, but before she could utter so much as a sound, the knife plunged straight into her heart. She gasped as the blade was yanked out and thrust back in again and then again. As her knees buckled, she looked down, surprised to see a long wooden handle jutting from her torso.

By the time she collapsed onto the pavement, she didn't see anything at all.

The home of Inspector Gerald Witherspoon was very quiet. Though it was late afternoon, at this time of year it was already dark outside. In the kitchen, the housekeeper, Mrs. Jeffries, and the cook, Mrs. Goodge, were enjoying a cup of tea as they waited for the others in the household to come home.

Wiggins, the footman, was out on some mysterious errand of his own, which both women were sure was buying Christmas presents. Betsy, the maid, was gone to the dressmaker's and her fiancé, Smythe, the coachman, was at the stables. The inspector was, of course, at the Ladbroke Road Police Station.

Mrs. Jeffries heard the back door open. She glanced at the household's mongrel dog, Fred, who was sleeping on his rug by the cooker. He didn't move, didn't leap up and race for the back door. He simply lay there. "It must be Smythe returning," she laughed. "Fred's just thumping his tail."

"Humph," Mrs. Goodge snorted. She was a portly, elderly woman with gray hair which she bundled neatly under a floppy cook's hat. She wore a clean white apron over her dark blue dress and sensible high-topped black shoes. She pushed her wire-framed spectacles back up her nose. "That dog is gettin' so lazy he barely gets up when Wiggins comes in, either. Smythe should count himself lucky he gets a tail wag or two."

Smythe stuck his head in the kitchen. "Is it safe to come in? Is she here?"

"She's at the dressmaker's," Mrs. Jeffries said with a smile.

He sighed in relief and stepped into the room. He took off his heavy black overcoat as he walked, pausing just long enough to toss it onto the coat tree. Smythe was a tall, muscled man closer to forty than thirty. His features were harsh, his complexion slightly ruddy, and his black hair had more than a few strands of gray. But the hardness of his features was softened somewhat by his ready smile and deep brown eyes. "Good, it'll give us a chance to 'ave a bit of a natter." He pulled out the chair and sat down.

"She'll not be gone long," Mrs. Goodge warned. "She's only havin' the weddin' dress fitted. The rest of the trousseau is already finished and ready to be delivered this Saturday."

"I'll keep my ears open for the door," he replied. He turned his attention to the housekeeper. "Have you had a chance to speak to the inspector?"

"I discussed the matter with him before he left for the

station this morning." She poured him a cup of tea and put it in front of him. "I was going to tell you but you were out the door before I had a chance."

"I had to meet the plumber at the flat before eight. He was worried that gettin' that new kitchen sink in is goin' to be an all-day job so I had to get there before he started pullin' out the old one," he replied.

"Yes, well, I hope everything went according to plan," she continued. "But in answer to your question, the inspector is quite happy to come to a new arrangement about your and Betsy's living situation. However, he did want me to make it very clear that just because you're getting married, there's no reason you must leave the house. We can turn the attic into a flat for the two of you." She had suggested that to the inspector; truth to tell, she really did hate the idea of the two of them leaving. Even if they'd both be here every day, it wouldn't be the same.

Smythe smiled gratefully. "That's kind of him, but I think it's best if we move into our own flat. It'll make Betsy feel good to have a home of her own."

"She has a home," Mrs. Goodge said before she could stop herself. "Both of you do. This is your home and movin' into that flat is goin' to cost such a lot of money. And what about our cases? What if we get one early in the mornin' or late at night? What'll we do then? You'll not be here. You'll be livin' somewhere else."

Mrs. Goodge was referring to the fact that their employer was now the most famous police detective in London. Before he'd inherited this house, Witherspoon had been quite happily working in the records room at Scotland Yard. But when he'd hired Mrs. Jeffries as his housekeeper, she'd put a stop to that nonsense. She'd seen his true potential and made sure his talent wasn't wasted on putting old cases away in file boxes.

In the years since then, Inspector Witherspoon had solved more murders than anyone in the history of the Metropolitan Police Force. His superiors were amazed by his uncanny ability to unravel even the most complex of cases.

Gerald Witherspoon was as surprised by his newfound ability as anyone else, but that was only to be expected. He had no idea his entire household helped him on each and every investigation. They'd come together from a variety of diverse backgrounds and grown to be a family as they'd investigated the inspector's cases. Now with Betsy and Smythe set to marry and move out, Mrs. Goodge was terrified that everything would change.

Smythe smiled at her. "Now you're not to be frettin', Mrs. Goodge. We'll always be here for our cases. You know that. We'll only be around the corner so even if we get a case in the dead of night, Wiggins could nip round and fetch us."

"But livin' in a flat is so expensive," she protested. She'd been in service since she was twelve and couldn't imagine living in a house one had to pay for oneself. The very idea filled her with dread.

"I've saved my wages for years. We'll manage just fine." He looked away as he spoke, unwilling to meet her eyes. Truth was, he was richer than most aristocrats and he'd been hiding it from some of the people he loved for far too long.

Smythe's connection to this house started long ago, when he'd been hired as a young coachman by Inspector Witherspoon's aunt, Euphemia Witherspoon. Then he'd had a chance to go to Australia to seek his fortune. He'd gotten lucky and actually made a huge amount of money, all of which he'd invested wisely. When he'd returned to England, he'd stopped to pay his respects to his old employer and found her dying.

It was then that he'd met Wiggins. Of all Euphemia's

servants, the young lad had been the only one trying to take care of the poor woman. Smythe had taken charge; he'd sacked all the other servants, sent Wiggins to find a good doctor, and hired a domestic agency to bring in cleaners to disinfect the house.

But despite his efforts and the best medicine money could buy, Euphemia Witherspoon continued to deteriorate.

Yet as she lay dying, she set into motion the circumstances that led to Smythe's current dilemma. She'd made him promise he'd stay on and see that her nephew, Gerald Witherspoon, was settled in properly, and more importantly, wasn't taken advantage of the way she had been.

As fate would have it, by the time he'd fulfilled his promise, it was too late. He'd gotten involved with all of them and he didn't want to go. From the first evening Mrs. Jeffries had presided over the servants' supper table, he'd been impressed with her good humor, insight, and intelligence. When Mrs. Goodge had first come along, she'd been a bit of a snob, but she'd cooked the most mouthwatering meals he'd ever had. And then there had been Betsy. She'd been a mere slip of a lass but he'd fallen half in love with her on sight.

Then they started solving murders, and he'd realized that Betsy, despite the difference in their ages, had feelings for him as well.

But his biggest mistake had been in not telling all of them how much money he had right from the beginning. He'd let them think he was simply a coachman. Eventually, as he and Betsy had gotten closer and fallen in love, he told her the truth. He'd not start their life together by keeping secrets from her. That wasn't right. Mrs. Jeffries had figured it out as well. But Mrs. Goodge and Wiggins had no idea he was wealthy. And he hated the idea they'd think he'd deliberately kept it from them, when it hadn't really been that way at all. Now he couldn't very well tell the cook that not only was he not in the least concerned about paying the rent on his new flat, but that he'd bought the entire building. But despite all the changes coming their way, he was determined that he and Betsy would still help with the inspector's cases.

Mrs. Goodge leaned toward him, her expression earnest. "But it will be lonely here without you and Betsy."

Smythe reached over and patted her hand. "We'll be here every day. It's not goin' to be that different except that in the evenin', instead of goin' upstairs, we'll go around the corner to our flat."

Mrs. Goodge stared at him for a moment and then sat back in her chair. "Don't mind me; I'm just behavin' like a silly old woman who's scared everythin' is goin' to be different once you two leave."

"You're not silly," Smythe said quickly. "You're not old and nothin's goin' to change."

"Of course not," Mrs. Jeffries interjected. "All of us, including Betsy and Smythe, will still do our parts in our investigations."

"And we'll all still be together," he added.

Mrs. Goodge smiled but said nothing. Yes, they all did their parts, and her contribution wasn't going to be altered by a wedding. Her sources, as she called them, would still troop through the kitchen on a regular basis. With every case they had, she had an army of delivery lads, chimney sweeps, fruit vendors, laundry boys, and tinkers sitting at this very table. She plied them with tea and treats and learned all sorts of useful information. All she had to do was mention the names of their victim and suspects; if there was gossip to be had, she'd get it all.

That didn't always work, but one of the few advantages

of getting old and having had to work for your living was that you had many other places to go for help. She'd scul-leried and cooked in some of the finest houses in the king-dom and now had a vast number of former associates she could call upon for information.

She did her part, and she intended to keep on doing it until they laid her in the ground. Helping the cause of jus-tice had given her long and sometimes bitter life a genuine sense of meaning. She'd wasted far too many years doing what society had told her was right and proper: never step-ping out of her place and making sure that no scullery maid or kitchen gardener dared step out of theirs, either. But in these last years of her life, she was profoundly grateful she'd been given a chance to atone for being such a foolish old snob. Oh, she wasn't frightened about her place in their in-vestigations changing; she was scared that despite all their best efforts, the family they'd made would drift apart.

They heard the back door, and this time, Fred leapt up and raced toward the hallway.

They heard Betsy say, "Close your brolly, Wiggins. We're in the house now and an open one is bad luck."

"Ruddy thing is stuck," Wiggins muttered. "There, got it. Cor blimey, it's late. Do you think they've started with-out us? Hello old boy, glad to see me, are you?"

Wiggins and the dog came into the kitchen first. The animal was butting his head against the footman's knees, demanding a bit of attention. He reached down and stroked the dog's back with one hand while taking off his gray flat cap with the other. He was a good-looking young lad in his early twenties. Brown hair fell forward on his face; his cheeks were round and pink from the cold, and he was grinning broadly. "Hello. Sorry to be late, but it's awful out there. One minute it's pourin' it down and the next it stops. Lucky for Betsy we met up at the omnibus stop. She forgot her umbrella. Is that seed cake? Cor blimey, we've not 'ad seed cake in ages."

"Hello, everyone." Betsy came in at a more sedate pace and went toward the coat tree. She took off her outer garments and hung them on the peg next to Smythe's overcoat. She was a slender blonde in her midtwenties with blue eyes, porcelain skin, and lovely features. "It's so cold out there. I meant to be home much sooner but the dressmaker took ages to do the fitting." She slipped into the chair next to Smythe. Under the table, he grabbed her hand and gave it a squeeze.

Mrs. Jeffries, who'd already poured two cups of hot tea, handed one to the footman and one to the maid. "I'm glad you're both back safely. It is getting very cold out there. Is it still raining?"

"It let up just as I was leaving the dressmaker's." Betsy reached for her cup with her free hand.

"Are you all fitted out, then?" Smythe asked. "All ready for the big day? It's less than a fortnight now."

Betsy gave him a reassuring smile. His words had sounded light and casual, but his tone couldn't disguise the flash of anxiety that had flitted across his face. She didn't blame him for being concerned. They'd been trying to get married for well over a year now.

Their original date had been last June. But a few days before their wedding, Smythe had been called away to Australia on a life or death errand to help an old friend. She'd been very put out by his leaving and vowed never to speak to him again. But that was impossible—she loved him. So when he finally returned, they worked out their differences. They set their second wedding date for this past October.

Then Smythe had been shot on the inspector's last case and she'd realized how fast life could change. If that bullet had been a bit higher, he'd be dead and not just carrying around a scar. Betsy wanted them to marry immediately. So he had to tell her about his big surprise, his wedding gift to her. He'd tracked down her long-lost sister in Canada and she and her husband were coming to the wedding. There was nothing for it but to wait until October. But nothing seemed to go right. Instead of getting married when they'd planned, their second wedding date got pushed back.

Norah and Leo, her sister and brother-in-law, had been delayed by Norah's sprained ankle, and then the ship sailing was delayed by the worst Atlantic storms in fifty years. The earliest her family could get here was mid-December.

Betsy was disappointed, but she decided to make the best of it. They'd have a Christmas wedding, and no matter what happened, on December eighteenth, Inspector Witherspoon would walk her down the aisle of St. Matthew's Church. As her dear friend Luty would say, come hell or high water, she and Smythe were going to get married in eight days.

"Of course I'm all ready." Betsy grinned. "Let's just hope we don't get us a murder right now."

"Don't even joke about that," Mrs. Jeffries warned. "It's been a long time since our last one, and as you've got family coming all the way from Halifax, we need to have plenty of free time."

"Indeed we do," the cook agreed. "You might be all ready, but the rest of us have plenty to do before we're ready for the big day. Then we're right into Christmas."

"But a case would be nice," Wiggins put in eagerly. He shoveled the last bite of his seed cake onto his fork. "Just polishin' brass and doin' the 'ousehold chores is right borin'. Even with this weather, I'd not mind bein' out and about. It's been ages since I've been 'on the hunt' so to speak."

Wiggins hadn't told the others about his newest plan; he was saving his wages to open his own private inquiry agency and frankly, he was eager to get out on the hunt again. It would be a few years before he had enough money to seriously pursue his dream, but he'd decided that now that Betsy and Smythe were getting married, he ought to think a bit about his own future. He wasn't a conceited person, but he knew that everything he'd learned while helping with Inspector Witherspoon's cases had given him just the right experience he needed to run a successful private inquiry agency. He was good at finding out information. He'd honed his skills on tweenies and housemaids, but he was sure his ready smile, cheerful disposition, and the occasional bit of slyness would work equally well on anyone else.

He glanced at Smythe, hoping his comment hadn't caused offense. He knew how much Smythe wanted to get that ring on Betsy's finger. But the coachman grinned good-naturedly.

"We've got enough on our plates right now." Smythe laughed. "If we had an investigation, I don't know what we'd do with our visitors from Canada. They'll be here tomorrow."

"We'd manage just fine." Betsy put down her cup. "Norah and Leo are staying at a hotel. I mean, I'm not saying I want us to have a case, but if it happened, we'd figure out a way to handle everything properly, and, well, it has been a long time since we've had a good investigation to sink our teeth into." She was delighted to finally be getting married, and she was even more excited about seeing her sister, but she'd never turn her back on helping the inspector.

Gerald Witherspoon had taken her in when she'd collapsed onto his doorstep. Even though she was completely untrained, he'd offered her a position as a housemaid so she'd have a roof over her head. She'd do anything for him. Of course, if she were truly honest, she'd admit that she loved the hunt as much as Wiggins. She was proud of the skills she'd developed. She'd trot along to a suspect's or a victim's neighborhood, step into a greengrocer's or a butcher's shop, flash a wide smile at the clerk, and start dropping names. Before you could blink your eyes, they'd be talking a blue streak.

She was also good at following people, a skill she didn't mention too often in front of Smythe. He tended to be a bit overprotective, and she was certain he wouldn't approve of some of her activities.

"Of course we'd be up to the task," Mrs. Jeffries demurred. "But nonetheless, it would make life a bit more difficult." As much as she hated to admit it, Betsy was right. It had been far too long since they'd had a nice, interesting investigation. Solving crimes was certainly a lot more appealing than domestic work. She was also rather proud of what they'd accomplished. Because of their efforts, numerous murderers had been brought to justice, and more importantly, a good many innocent people had been saved from the gallows.

After the death of her late husband, a policeman in York, she'd come to London looking for a change of scenery. She'd had his pension and a bit of money of her own. But within days she'd been bored to tears.

Shopping made her feet hurt, the theater was interesting but one couldn't sit through a play every evening, and even the day trips to the south coast had convinced her that travel often left one with a headache and a nasty case of indigestion. Luckily, she'd seen an advertisement for a position as a housekeeper to a policeman. That had piqued her interest.

She'd come along here to Upper Edmonton Gardens, chatted with the inspector, and been offered the position. It hadn't been too long before they were actively helping solve the inspector's cases. Each of them made their own special contribution. She was the one who generally put it all together. Nature had gifted her with the capability of taking seemingly unrelated facts, ideas, or gossip and coming up with the right solution. She wasn't overly proud of her special skill; after all, all of them were equally skilled in different ways. That was one of the reasons they worked so very well together.

"I don't think we'll be gettin' us a case today," Wiggins declared. "It's too wet and cold out there even for a killer."

"We've not moved the body, sir," the constable said proudly. "And even though the rain has stopped, I've had the lads standing over it with their brollies to make sure no more evidence gets washed away by the mist."

"Excellent, Constable," Inspector Gerald Witherspoon replied. He surveyed the street while he waited for Constable Barnes to pay off the hansom driver. Chepstow Villas was a street comprised of a long row of semidetached white stucco homes. Even in the darkness, he could tell they were all at least four stories high.

The body was directly in front of the home at the very end of the row. The rain had stopped, but the cobblestone street was wet and deep puddles filled the potholes along the side of the road.

"It's a posh area," Constable Barnes murmured as he joined the inspector. He was a tall man with a ruddy complexion and a head full of iron gray hair underneath his policeman's helmet. "And I'll bet my pension that no one saw or heard anything."

Witherspoon sighed heavily. "I daresay, you're probably right. More's the pity."

The constable glanced at his superior and noted that the inspector's thin, bony face wasn't unduly pale. A few drops of rain were sprinkled over his spectacles and his lips were set in a grim line, but he didn't look as if he were going to lose his lunch. Barnes was one of the few people who knew that the famous Gerald Witherspoon was squeamish about corpses. And from the report that came into the station, this wasn't going to be a pleasant one. Stabbings were usually very messy. "Would you like to examine the body, sir?"

"Yes, of course." Witherspoon swallowed heavily, took a deep breath, and moved to the cluster of constables standing by the wrought iron gate. "Who found the victim?" he asked as they drew near.

"A passerby saw the woman lying there and went and fetched Constable Hitchins." He pointed to one of the policemen by the corpse.

"Did you get the passerby's name?" Witherspoon asked as he forced himself to move closer.

"Yes, sir. It was a Mr. Yates. He owns the Angel Arms, the pub just around the corner. We let him go along as he had to open up. Constable Hitchins vouched for him and this is Hitchins' patch."

They'd been crossing the cobblestones as they walked and were now at the body. All three of the constables stood back respectfully while simultaneously still trying to hold their umbrellas over the victim.

"You've done a good job, lads," the inspector said. "But the rain has stopped and your arms must be aching. So stand at ease. I don't think the damp will wash away any evidence."

"Thank you, sir," the constable closest to him said as he and the others lowered their arms.

"Which one of you is Constable Hitchins?"

A tall, dark-haired constable standing on the far side of the body stepped forward a bit, stopping just short of the dead woman's arm. "I am, sir."

"What time was it that you were called to the scene?"

Witherspoon glanced down at the body and then quickly looked away. Something appeared to be growing directly out of the woman's chest.

"It was about five forty-five, sir. I'd just turned down the road when Mr. Yates, he's the one that spotted her, comes running up saying he's seen a dead woman lying in front of number seventeen," Hitchins explained. "I know Mr. Yates. He's a sensible sort of fellow, not one to exaggerate, so I took him at his word. I knew we'd need assistance. I blew my whistle and kept blowing it as I followed him here. A few minutes later, the other constables arrived. As I'd already seen the body by then, I immediately sent Constable Mackie off to the station for a superior officer."

"I expect you could tell right away that it was a murder," Barnes murmured. "What with the knife sticking out of the poor woman's chest."

"That I could, sir," Hitchins admitted. "When I got here she was on her side, and I know you don't like us to move the body, but I did roll her onto her back to make sure she was really gone—even with that wicked-looking blade in her chest. I've seen some people survive the most awful wounds and I didn't want to leave the poor lady lying here if there was any chance of saving her life."

"You acted correctly, constable." Witherspoon knelt down, and all three of the constables turned their policeman's lanterns toward the dead woman. He forced himself to take a good look at her. She'd most definitely been stabbed. His gaze shifted away from the handle protruding from her chest. Dark stains, probably blood, soaked the front of her black and gray checked waistcoat and bled onto the edges of her cape. She was plump, with a round, pale face and short, puffy fingers clutching a cloth handbag. A tendril of dark blonde hair slipped from beneath her black bonnet. A closed umbrella, also dark in color, was lying about a foot from her right hand. Witherspoon nodded toward the umbrella. "Has this been moved?"

"No sir," Hitchins replied. "Your methods are quite well-known, sir, so we didn't touch anything."

Witherspoon nodded. He felt a bit guilty taking credit for what was and had been standard police procedure for the past fifteen years. But correcting the young officer would only embarrass the lad, and he had no wish to do that. "Has the police surgeon been called?"

"He's been sent for, sir," one of the other constables volunteered.

"Do we know who the lady might be?" Barnes asked as he knelt down on the other side of the body. He plucked the handbag from her lifeless fingers, opened it, and poured the contents out onto his palm. "A pound note, two shillings, and tuppence." He popped the money back inside, closed the top, and waved at Hitchins. "Enter this into evidence, please." He handed him the purse.

Witherspoon rose to his feet and surveyed the area. A small crowd had gathered at the corner and across the road. He could see people standing in the doorways and peeking out from behind drawing room curtains. He looked at the house just in front of them. Over the front door, light poured out of the transom window, but the drapes on the front windows on all four floors were tightly drawn. "That's odd. You'd think whoever lived here would be a bit curious about what was happening right outside their front door."

"Maybe no one is home, sir," Barnes suggested.

"They're home." One of the other constables stepped forward. "I went to the door, sir. The butler said the family was having high tea in celebration of some event and please not to bother them. That's when they pulled all the drapes closed, sir. The fellow came out again a few minutes later and asked if we'd be gone by half past six. I told him I'd no idea how long we'd need to be here. He seemed quite annoyed."

Barnes crossed his arms over his chest as he looked at the house. "They must not want their fancy party interrupted by something as common as murder."

"Well, I'm afraid that can't be helped," Witherspoon said. He looked at Hitchins. "Can you show me exactly how you found the body?"

Hitchins nodded and scurried to the other side of the corpse. "She was lying exactly where she is now, sir, only she was on her side." He thought for a moment. "No, wait a minute, that's not right, her right arm was on the bottom of the gate. It was almost like she'd been holding on to the railing as she fell."

"Which railing?"

"The one running down from the latch," Hitchins explained.

The inspector stared at the house for a long moment. It was the last one on the row, and he noticed that unlike the others on the street, it had a glass conservatory attached to one side. It was too dark to make out much detail of the structure, but it looked a bit unfinished. He shook himself and turned to Barnes. "Her umbrella was closed, Constable."

"And you think she might have collapsed the thing in preparation for going in there?" He jerked his thumb toward the house.

Witherspoon nodded. "Unfortunately, I believe we're going to have to interrupt the tea party." He broke off as a hansom cab, followed closely by the mortuary van, rounded the corner. "Ah, good, the police surgeon has arrived. Constable Barnes, can you organize a house-to-house up and down the street. Perhaps we'll get lucky and someone will have seen or heard something. As soon as I've had a word with the surgeon, we'll go inside there and have a chat with them," he instructed, pointing across the small courtyard to the house. "Frankly, I find their behavior most peculiar. On second thought, go in and see if you can get someone to come out and have a look at our victim. If we're very lucky someone might be able to identify her. It would certainly save us a great deal of trouble if we could find out who she is."

Barnes grinned broadly, pushed open the gate, crossed the courtyard, and banged the brass knocker. A few moments later, the door opened and a man stepped outside. He and Barnes began to talk, but their voices were so low, the inspector couldn't hear what was being said.

The hansom and mortuary van pulled up and stopped on the other side of the road. The doctor got out of the cab and hurried toward the body. Witherspoon smiled in recognition as he saw it was Dr. Amalfi coming toward him. "Good evening, Doctor." He nodded respectfully. "Sorry to have to call you out on such a miserable evening."

"All in a day's work, Inspector," Amalfi replied. He waved the mortuary attendants and their lamps toward the body, knelt down, and began his examination.

From behind him, the inspector could hear voices raised in argument, but knowing that Barnes was well able to handle even the most recalcitrant of witnesses, he kept his attention on the doctor.

"All I can tell you is that she's not been dead long," he finally said as he rose to his feet. "The postmortem should give us more information." He glanced at the two attendants. "Get the gurney and let's load the poor woman up—"

Barnes interrupted. "Just a moment, Doctor. We'd like this gentleman to take a look at the body and see if he recognizes the woman." He turned to the man from the house and nodded toward the corpse. "Go ahead, sir, have a look."

"This is nonsense," the man snapped, turning to the inspector. "I'm Jeremy Evans. I own this property and I must say, being dragged out of my home in the middle of a social occasion has been most inconvenient."

"I'm Inspector Gerald Witherspoon, and I assure you, sir, we've no wish to disrupt your lives, but this poor woman was found dead right in front of your home so we must ask you and your household a few questions." He noticed that Mr. Evans hadn't looked at the dead body lying inches away from his booted foot.

"Good gracious, why? We've nothing to do with this unfortunate person," Evans protested.

"How do you know?" Witherspoon asked calmly. "You haven't looked at the victim so you can't possibly know she has no connection with your household."

Evans' eyes widened. "Just because she happened to die in front of my home, doesn't mean you should bother myself or my household."

The doctor stepped forward. "Are you going to have him try to identify her or not? I'd like to get her back to the mortuary."

Witherspoon looked directly at Evans. "Can you please take a look at the victim, sir?"

Evan sighed irritably and glanced downward.

"Get some lanterns on her, lads," Barnes called out to the constables. Three police lanterns were immediately directed onto the victim.

"Take your time, sir," the inspector instructed. "Take a good look. Have you ever seen this woman before?"

Evans stared at her for a long moment. Just then, the front door opened and footsteps pounded across the courtyard. They all turned to see a young woman racing toward them.

Jeremy Evans grabbed her just as she reached them. "Go

back into the house, Rosemary," he ordered harshly. "This is no place for you."

But she shook him off and plunged onward, stumbling over her long skirts. Barnes grabbed her arm, steadying her.

She stared down at the victim, her eyes widening in horror. "Oh no," she cried. "It can't be. It simply can't be. It's Miss Moran. What's she doing with that thing in her chest? Oh no, she can't be dead, she simply can't be."

"Rosemary! Go back to the house!" Evans cried.

But she ignored him and dropped to her knees next to the body, tears running down her cheeks.

Witherspoon knelt down next to her. "Miss, do you recognize this woman?" he asked gently.

She nodded and swiped at her cheeks with the back of her hand. "She's my old governess. Her name is Agatha Moran."

"And were you expecting to see her today?" the inspector pressed. "Had she been invited to your home?"

"I've not seen her in years. Not since I was sent off to school."

"And she certainly hadn't been invited here," Evans snapped. "Now come along, Rosemary, you're making a spectacle of yourself."

The inspector stood up. He reached down, grasped the weeping woman under the elbow, and gently helped her to her feet. He pulled her back and nodded at Dr. Amalfi. "Go ahead and take her away."

"Now see here, sir," Evans began, but the inspector cut him off.

"Mr. Evans, if you don't mind, I'll escort the young lady inside," he said. "Constable Barnes and I have some questions that we must ask."

"This is most inconvenient," Evans muttered as he fell in step behind them.

Barnes lingered a moment to speak to Constable Hitchins. "You'll be in charge of the scene. Make sure the house-to-house is completed and that you get the lads doing a thorough search of the area." Then he turned and hurried after the others.

Before the small group reached the house, the front door opened and a rather surprised-looking butler came rushing out. He skidded to a halt in front of Jeremy Evans. "May I be of any assistance, sir?" he asked.

"Have you seen our guests out the back way?" Evans snapped. He stepped around the inspector and started into the house. The others followed.

"Yes, sir, just as you instructed." The butler spoke loudly as he was now at the rear of the procession entering the house. "Sir Madison is the only one left. He's in the drawing room with the mistress."

Evans stopped in the foyer and turned to Witherspoon. "When I found out there was a dead woman outside and that the police had arrived, I had the butler see our guests out the back way. Today was supposed to be a happy occasion."

"That's unfortunate, sir." Witherspoon released the young woman's arm. "You'll need to provide us with a list of your guests. One of them may have seen something useful."

"Is that really necessary?" Evans asked irritably. He cast a quick glance at his daughter.

"I'm afraid so, sir," the inspector said. "Now, if you'll just let us speak to whoever else is in the household, we'll ask our questions and be on our way."

"If you must, Inspector. Let's go into the drawing room." He moved to a set of double doors on the other side of the foyer, opened them, and motioned for the others to follow.

As Witherspoon and Barnes crossed the threshold, a short, plump woman with brown hair piled high in an elaborate style leapt up from her chair. Her blue eyes narrowed and her mouth turned into a thin, disapproving line. She was dressed in a blue silk tea gown with high-necked lace collar and wide white lace cuffs. "Jeremy, what is the meaning of this? What are these policemen doing here?"

"You'd best sit down, my dear," Jeremy Evans replied. "I'm afraid this situation is no longer merely an inconvenience to us."

"Oh Mama, it's horrid, absolutely horrid. Poor Miss Moran has been murdered," Rosemary blurted. "She was stabbed right in front of our house."

Witherspoon knew he needed to gain control of the situation. "I'm Inspector Gerald Witherspoon," he said politely. "This is Constable Barnes. I'm afraid we're going to have to ask you some questions.

In the small room on the third floor that had been turned into a cozy sitting room for the staff, Betsy put her hands on her hips and gave Smythe a good glare. "I'm not being silly," she protested. "I know you've said it's to be a surprise, but I would like to know where we're going to live and where we're going to spend our wedding night."

He grinned wickedly and started toward her. Betsy took a step backward, holding up her hand to ward him off. "Now you're not getting round me that way," she charged. "I'll not have you being all sweet and charming and then not telling me a blooming thing."

He stopped. He could tell by the dangerous look in her eyes that she wasn't going to be distracted with a bit of teasing or a kiss. But he didn't want to tell her his plans. Not yet. He wanted it to be a surprise, and truth be told, he was just the tiniest bit nervous that maybe she'd not be so pleased to be moving into their own flat. "You want to know where we're goin' to live."

"That's right."

"Holland Park," he replied. It was the truth, barely.

"So we're staying here," she pressed.

He shrugged. "Maybe. Maybe not. Besides, you promised you'd not nag me about it. You know I'll take care of you . . ."

"I'm not nagging," she cried. Suddenly, her eyes filled with tears. "I'm upset and nervous and my whole world has changed." She put her hands over her face, backed up another step, and flopped down on the old settee. "My sister, who I haven't seen in years, is arriving tomorrow; every time we try to get married something awful happens; and, to top it off, I don't even know where I'm going to live."

He flew across the room and pulled her into his arms. "Oh love, I'm so sorry, I'd 'ave never wanted it kept a secret if I knew it was goin' to hurt you like this. But once the surprise of Norah and Leo comin' to the weddin' was out of the bag, I wanted to do somethin' to make our marriage special. If knowin' where we're goin' to live will make you feel better, I'll tell ya. I've—"

She put her hand over his lips before he could finish the sentence. "I'm the one who should be sorry. I'm carrying on like a silly twit. Don't tell me—I do trust you and you've gone to a lot of effort to do something wonderful for me. I'll not ruin it because I'm having a fit of nerves."

He stared at her intently. "Are you sure, love?"

"I'm positive." She smiled brightly. "I'm just being silly. It's just wedding nerves and the thought of seeing my sister again after all these years."

"Don't you want to see her?"

"More than anything," she assured him. She'd not have him think she wasn't grateful for all he'd done to get her relatives here. "But you know how it is with family, and besides, Norah always was a bit of a bossy boots. I guess part of me is wondering what she'll be like after all these years. But I expect that she's changed. After all, most of us do."

Mrs. Jeffries paused as she closed the drapes of the drawing room window. A police constable stepped off the curb in front of the gas lamp across the road and crossed toward the house. She jerked the curtains closed and went to the front hall, opening the door just as the constable arrived.

"Good evening, Constable." She smiled pleasantly. She wasn't sure whether to laugh or cry—there was only one reason a constable would be here at this time of day.

"Good evening, ma'am." He nodded politely. "I'm Constable Markham. Inspector Witherspoon sent me around to let you know he's been called out on a case and he'll be quite late tonight."

"Oh dear," she replied. "How unfortunate. Would you like to come in and have a cup of tea? It's very cold out there."

"Thank you, ma'am, but no, I'm just on my way home. That's why the inspector asked me to stop in. I was getting off duty and this is on my way."

"Yes, of course." She was desperate to find out more information. "I do hope he didn't get sent off too far away. I don't think he took his umbrella with him and it looks like there's more rain on the way."

"He should be fine, ma'am." The constable smiled indulgently, as the young do toward older people. "He's only gone to Notting Hill. A woman was found stabbed in front of a house on Chepstow Villas. Once he conducts the preliminary investigations, a hansom can have him home in fifteen minutes."

"Oh that does make me feel better." She leaned forward conspiratorially. "He doesn't like me to fuss, but a man his age simply shouldn't spend too much time out in the wet. I hate to think of him being miles away and then having to come home in the dead of the night."

"Yes ma'am." He smiled politely, turned, and headed down the short staircase to the pavement. Mrs. Jeffries stood at the open doorway, watching until he disappeared down the street, then she closed the door, took a deep breath, and raced for the kitchen.

Mrs. Goodge had just put supper on the table. Smythe and Betsy had taken their seats and Wiggins was pulling out his chair as she flew into the kitchen. Everyone looked up. "Hurry and eat," she charged. "We've got a murder."

CHAPTER 2

The elegantly dressed woman ignored her husband and turned her full attention on Witherspoon. "I'm Arabella Evans," she snapped. "And I would appreciate an explanation as to what is going on here."

A tall, blond man who'd been sitting on the settee put his teacup down on a side table and rose to his feet. He said nothing, merely looked curiously at the two policemen.

"I've just told you, Mama," Rosemary said, "Miss Moran's been killed. She's been stabbed to death right outside our house. Did you send her an invitation to tea? She must have been on her way here."

"Of course I didn't invite her." Mrs. Evans stared coldly at her daughter. "Don't be absurd, why would she be coming here? None of us have seen the woman in years."

"But Mama, that's not true," Rosemary persisted. "She was here the day before yesterday. I heard you talking with her. I tried to get downstairs to say hello to her, but she'd gone before I got here."

"That is ridiculous." Arabella pursed her lips. "You haven't spoken to her since you were eight and you certainly wouldn't recognize her voice."

"But I would," Rosemary insisted with a shake of her head.

In the bright light of the drawing room, the inspector noticed the young woman's hair was the same color as her mother's. But she was slender rather than plump and her eyes were hazel, not blue. Just then, the blond fellow stepped toward the girl.

"Rosemary, darling"—he took her hand—"you must be mistaken. I'm sure your dear mama would know if this person had been visiting the house."

Rosemary jerked her hand back. "But I heard them . . ."

"You heard me arguing with the dressmaker." Arabella waved her off dismissively. "Now go and sit down while your father and I sort this mess out."

Rosemary opened her mouth as if she wanted to disagree, but then thought better of it and said nothing.

Witherspoon tried again. "As I said, ma'am, we must ask you and your staff some questions. Apparently, the victim was connected to your household in some fashion. Now I'd like Mr. Evans to go with Constable Barnes into another room so we can take his statement. If the two of you wouldn't mind excusing yourselves, I'll stay here and speak with Miss Evans. If everyone cooperates, we'll be able to get this matter sorted out as quickly as possible."

Arabella Evans' mouth gaped slightly in surprise. "I'll remind you, Inspector, to be careful giving orders. You're in my home."

"We are aware of that, madam, and I didn't mean to sound disrespectful, but a murder has been committed less than fifty feet from your front door," Witherspoon replied. "Naturally, we don't want to inconvenience you more than necessary so the sooner we get our questions answered, the sooner we'll be gone."

The tall blond fellow, who the inspector thought must be the "Sir Madison" the butler had mentioned earlier, thrust himself in front of Rosemary. "I'd like to be present when you speak to my fiancée. She's very upset."

Rosemary glared at his back and shoved past him. "Of course I'm upset. Someone I once loved a great deal is lying outside with a knife in her chest."

"What is your name, sir?" Witherspoon asked.

"Sir Madison Lowery," Arabella answered for him. She emphasized the "sir" as she spoke.

"Miss Evans and I are to be married soon." He smiled modestly, revealing a row of even, white teeth. "Surely your questions can wait until tomorrow? Can't you see my fiancée is very distressed?"

"Murder is a distressing business," Witherspoon responded politely. "Especially for the victim. But in the interests of justice, it's very important that we take witness statements as close to the time of the crime as possible."

"But we're not witnesses. We had nothing to do with her being killed," Jeremy Evans protested. He'd moved to stand next to his wife.

"Nonetheless, we're obliged to ask our questions."

Evans sighed irritably and then walked to the door. He rang the bellpull. Almost immediately, the butler entered. "Yes sir?"

"Bring up a bottle of brandy and some glasses. Take it into my study," he ordered. As soon as the servant disappeared, he turned to his wife. "Arabella, you and Madison wait in the study. I think a drink of brandy will help to calm everyone's nerves."

She stared at him for a moment and then shrugged. "As you wish."

Lowery hurried over and offered her his arm. "Come along, my dear lady. Your husband has the right idea. A glass of his excellent French brandy will do both of us a world of good."

When they'd gone, Evans motioned for Barnes to follow him. He crossed the room to a door on the left of the fireplace. "We'll go into the library. It's just through here."

It took a few moments for everyone to go to their respective spots, so the inspector used the time to study his surroundings. This was a rich man's home.

The huge drawing room was opulently furnished with walls papered in pale gold silk and patterned in an elaborate fleur-de-lis design. Two couches upholstered in gold and burgundy striped satin faced each other in the center of the room, flanked by carved side chairs of gold velvet. Love seats, corner chairs, and tables covered with fringed shawls and lace runners filled the rest of the enormous space. A fireplace with a carved ebony mantel and plated by pink marble was on the other side of the room. A gilt-framed portrait of Arabella Evans hung above the mantelpiece.

"Please sit down, Inspector." Rosemary Evans gestured at one of the gold and burgundy couches. He nodded his thanks, waited till she'd settled on the one opposite him, and then took his seat.

"This must be terrible for you," he began. For a moment, his mind went completely blank, then he caught himself. Gracious, he was acting like a green boy. He knew the basics of his job.

"It's been horrible," she replied. Her lips trembled. "When Papa first came in and ordered Stevens to close the curtains, I'd no idea it was because poor Miss Moran was out there lying in the rain. I'd never have let her just lie there if I'd known."

"Can you tell me what time you found out there had been an . . . incident?" Witherspoon asked.

She took a deep breath. "We had tea scheduled for a quarter to five, and Papa was supposed to be home but he was late." She smiled sadly. "Papa works far too hard. But you don't want to hear about our domestic trials. Most of the guests had already arrived, but we couldn't serve because Mama had disappeared. It became a bit awkward; there were people milling about everywhere, and I was just about ready to sit down and do the pouring myself, when Mama finally came back—"

Witherspoon interrupted. "Where had your mama, er, Mrs. Evans gone?"

"Mama had gone to fetch a footman. She was going to send him to look for Papa, but just then Papa arrived and we had tea. Odd, really. Mama usually never leaves her guests unattended." She sighed and looked down at the floor. "Poor Miss Moran, I hope she didn't suffer very much."

"How long was your mother gone from the drawing room?"

Her brows came together thoughtfully. "I don't really know. The only reason I noticed her absence in the first place was that several people were staring rather pointedly at the tea trolleys. But I'm certain she wasn't gone long; as I said, she isn't one to leave her guests to fend for themselves."

He made a mental note to have a quick word with the footman. Perhaps the lad would remember the exact time the mistress of the house spoke to him. "Miss Evans, what made you come outside this evening?"

She glanced toward the windows. The heavy gold curtains were still firmly closed. "I knew something was wrong. The drapes are usually drawn at dark so I wasn't surprised that Papa ordered Stevens to close them during the tea. But when I went up to my room to get a fabric sample to show to one of the bridesmaids' cousins, I noticed the curtains were closed up there as well. The maids usually don't draw those until the household retires for the night."

He looked at her and his expression must have been a bit skeptical, because she leaned toward him, her expression earnest, and said, "But it wasn't just that, though. There's been a strange tension in the air all afternoon. Something just wasn't right. I could feel it. I finally managed to get away from Sir Madison and I followed Papa into the hallway. I overheard him telling Stevens that when the guests left, they were to leave through the back, not out the front door. He insisted they be shown out through the garden."

"You found that a bit odd?"

"Of course," she replied. "But when I asked Papa what was going on, he told me to go back into the drawing room and attend to my guests."

Witherspoon thought for a moment. He was desperately trying to get a sense of who was where at what time. A timeline always came in handy when it came to solving a homicide. "Who greeted the guests when they arrived this afternoon?"

"Mama and I," she replied. "We were right here in the drawing room when Emma and Mrs. Stabler arrived. They were the first."

"What time was this?"

"I didn't look at the clock, but I think it must have been a quarter to five because Mama commented that they were right on time." She pulled a white handkerchief out of the tight lace cuff of her dress and dabbed at her eyes.

"Are you alright, Miss Evans? Would you like a glass of water?"

"I'm fine." She smiled self-consciously. "It's just that every time I think of us in here laughing and having a pleasant time while poor Miss Moran was lying out there dead . . ." She broke off and looked away, but not before the inspector had seen the tears welling up in her eyes again.

She was either a great actress or was terribly distressed about the murder of her old governess, he thought to himself. "Four forty-five was when the tea was due to start?"

She took a deep breath. "That's correct."

"How many guests were there?"

"I'm not certain. I'm not very good at the social aspects of this wedding. I let Mama handle all those details. But the tea was for my wedding attendants and their families. It's a very large wedding party. I've four bridesmaids. When you add in all the parents and siblings, the house seemed quite full. Stevens brought in extra chairs from the morning room."

"When is your wedding?" he asked kindly.

"At ten o'clock on December eighteenth at St. John's Church in Kensington Park." She looked away again. "It's not long now."

Witherspoon realized her wedding was the same day as Betsy's. "It's unfortunate your wedding has been marred by this terrible crime," he said softly.

"It's worse for poor Miss Moran than for me." She looked at him and smiled sadly. "It's been years since she was part of my life, but I have such fond memories of her. She wasn't like most governesses, she was fun and filled with joy . . . we used to have such a nice time together. Oh dear . . ." Her voice broke and tears sprang into her eyes.

Witherspoon looked toward the courtyard so she could have a moment to regain her composure. "If the curtains aren't drawn, you can see straight out to the street," he said. "Is that correct?"

She sniffed and swiped at her cheeks before she answered. "That's right, even with the courtyard being there, because of the gas lamp on the far side of the road, one can have a direct view of the street. I've always rather liked that." She smiled wistfully. "I like watching people. Mama says that's very common and I'm not supposed to do it. She was always after Papa to find us a house in the country. But he loves London, and though he usually gives her whatever she wants, he refused to leave."

"Do you recall noticing anyone lurking about in the front of the house before the curtains were drawn?" He thought that a good question.

"No, but I was late getting ready so I wasn't paying attention."

"Were you late for any particular reason?"

"I'd taken some books back to Mudies Lending Library. I meant to come straight back but they had some new books and I wanted to have a look at them. We've a library here, of course. It came with the house. But there aren't any modern novels. Papa doesn't approve of them, but he does allow me to have a subscription to Mudies. I lost track of time and it was almost half past four when I got home. That gave me just enough time to change and get downstairs before the first guest arrived at the door. Luckily, Mama was in the kitchen having a word with Cook, so she didn't know how late I arrived home." She giggled. "By the time she came into the drawing room, I'd changed and gotten downstairs."

In the library next door, Constable Barnes sat in an uncomfortable straight back chair next to the unlit fireplace. His little brown notebook was open and resting on his knee. Jeremy Evans sat across from him.

"What time did you arrive home today, sir?" Barnes asked.

"It was almost five thirty," he replied. "My wife was annoyed. I was supposed to be home at a quarter to so I could greet our guests."

"And where had you been, sir?"

"At my offices on Fenchurch Street," he explained. "I own quite a large import/export firm."

"When you came home, was that when you saw the victim?" Barnes asked.

"No, actually, I came in through the kitchen. It was Stevens who alerted me that there was something rather unusual going on outside our front door. I went and had a look out the window. That's when I saw the woman on the ground and the two police constables." He closed his eyes and shook his head. "It must have been dreadful for that poor woman, but frankly, Constable, all I could think of at that moment was protecting my wife and daughter. I didn't want their party ruined by such ugliness. So I instructed Stevens to pull the drapes so the guests wouldn't be disturbed by the commotion."

"Weren't you curious, sir?" Barnes watched him carefully.

"Of course I was, but I've just told you, my main concern was my family. It never occurred to me that the dead woman was connected in any way with us. Perhaps if I'd come in the front door, if I'd gone past her, I might have recognized her, but even that is doubtful. I've not seen Agatha Moran in years."

"Yet she ended up stabbed right outside your house," Barnes said, his expression thoughtful.

Evans said nothing for a moment, and then he gave an almost imperceptible shrug. "Be that as it may, Constable, the woman had nothing to do with me or my household."

"You think her being murdered only a few feet from your front door is a coincidence?"

"It's possible she was coming to see us," Evans admitted. "Or perhaps it was just a coincidence. They do happen, you know."

Barnes nodded. "Why were you late home, sir? You mentioned your wife was expecting you at a quarter to five, yet you didn't arrive here until almost half past."

Evans cocked his head to one side and stared at Barnes. "My daughter got engaged six months ago, and ever since then, it's been one social event after another. There's been engagement balls, engagement dinners, engagement galas, and now an engagement tea for all her bridesmaids and their mothers and sisters. Frankly, I didn't see why I should be expected to be here for the ruddy thing. I've done my duty and attended every other function, but honestly, I didn't think I was up to sipping tea among a bunch of giggling girls." He sighed audibly. "Besides, the end of the year is approaching and I wanted to go over my ledgers. End of year is when I make certain all my accounts are in order."

"What time today did you leave your office?" Barnes asked.

"It was past four," he answered. "I walked part of the way home."

Barnes regarded him steadily. "You walked? But it was raining."

"It wasn't raining the whole time and I had my umbrella." He smiled. "I started out in a hansom but I had them drop me off when the rain let up a bit. Surely you can understand. I'd spent the afternoon going over ledgers and my head hurt. I wanted a bit of time to myself before I had to come home and play the gracious host. I've been doing it for months now, and I didn't think my wife would really begrudge me wanting an hour or two to myself."

"Yet you crept in the back way so your wife wouldn't know what time you really arrived." Barnes smiled sympathetically.

"Absolutely." Evans looked amused. "Are you married, Constable?"

"For over thirty years, sir."

"Then as a married man, you'll understand that what we hope for in our spouses isn't always what we get. My wife is a good and generally a reasonable woman. However, I considered it prudent not to parade my tardiness in front of her."

"And you were hoping that by the time the tea party was finished, she'd be over her temper." Barnes grinned. There wasn't a married person on the face of the earth who didn't understand that principle.

"Precisely, Constable."

Smythe wasn't sure if he should laugh or cry. He and Betsy were getting married in less than ten days, her family was due in to London tomorrow, and their flat wasn't anywhere near finished. This was no time for a murder. Yet if he were truly honest with himself, he was delighted they finally had another case.

Oh, they'd had one in the summer, but it hadn't lasted long, as twenty-four hours after the body had been discovered, the victim's wife had confessed she'd clouted her husband with an iron. These thoughts flashed through his mind in a heartbeat. He looked down at his plate, shoved a last bite of potato into his mouth, chewed, swallowed, and got up. "Do we have an address?"

"Chepstow Villas in Notting Hill." Mrs. Jeffries smiled in relief. She hadn't been sure of how Betsy and Smythe would react to the fact that the inspector had another homicide case, but both of them looked quite pleased by the prospect of going "on the hunt." "Sorry, I wasn't able to find out the exact address."

"Not to worry, it can't be that long a street, so the house should be easy to find. There'll be constables everywhere." He started toward the coat tree. "I'll find out what's what."

Wiggins leapt up as well. "I'll come, too," he declared.

"But what about Luty and Hatchet?" Betsy looked from Wiggins to Mrs. Jeffries. "Shouldn't Wiggins get over there and put them on notice that we've a case? You know how upset they get if they're not told right away that we've a murder."

Luty Belle Crookshank and her butler, Hatchet, were good friends of the household. They helped on all the inspector's investigations.

Mrs. Jeffries nodded in agreement. Betsy had a point. She glanced at the carriage clock on the pine sideboard and saw it was already past eight. "Oh dear, I fear we're already too late. They've probably already gone out for the evening. You know how sociable Luty is these days. I can't recall the last time she mentioned spending an evening at home. No, I think it'll be more useful for Wiggins to go with Smythe. Tomorrow he can nip over bright and early and fetch them. We've got to get this investigation started. There's much to do and very little free time."

Wiggins raced to the coat tree. Fred got up and charged after him, his tail wagging a mile a minute.

"Sorry old boy"—he slipped his coat on and reached down to pet the dog's head—"but I can't do walkies now; I'll take you out when I get home."

Fred's tail thumped even faster at the word "walkies."

"I'll take him out," Betsy volunteered. "You two might not be home until midnight, and we don't want any accidents."

Smythe paused in the act of wrapping his scarf around his neck. "I don't want you walkin' around alone at night," he said to Betsy.

"Don't be silly, I'll not be on my own. Fred will be with me." Betsy picked up Smythe's plate and then Wiggins' and turned toward the cooker. "This is a safe area and I'm just going for a short walk around the corner. I'll stop by and see if Lady Cannonberry is home. We're going to need her help as well."

"We're goin' to need everyone's help," the cook muttered softly.

Betsy smiled prettily at her fiancé. "I'll put these plates in the warming oven and you can have them when you get back. Now, go on, get moving. As Mrs. Jeffries said, we've a lot to do so there isn't a moment to waste."

Smythe sighed and gave up the fight. He knew he'd lose. He contented himself with saying, "Mind you be careful," gave her a wink when she giggled, and started for the back door. Wiggins was right on his heels.

Witherspoon closed his eyes and rested his head against the back of his seat while he waited for Sir Madison Lowery to join him. The interview with Miss Evans had been quite exhausting. The truth of the matter was that he rather liked the young woman, yet as a police officer, a homicide detective, he understood all too well that just because she was sympathetic in her demeanor didn't mean she was innocent of involvement in Agatha Moran's death. When investigating a murder, it was important to view everyone as a suspect.

The door opened and he turned to see Stevens enter. He was carrying a silver tray. "Miss Evans thought you might like a cup of tea, sir."

"That would be lovely," he replied eagerly. "That was very thoughtful of Miss Evans."

"She also sent tea in to your constable, sir." Stevens set the tray down on the side table, picked up the pot, and poured the tea into a delicate china cup decorated with a pattern of pink tea roses. "Sugar or cream, sir?"

"Two sugars and a little cream," he replied. His spirits

brightened as he saw there was also a plate of ginger biscuits on the tray. Good—it was hours past his dinnertime and he was hungry enough to eat a horse.

"Here you are, sir." Stevens handed him his tea. "Do help yourself to some biscuits as well," he offered as he left.

Witherspoon took a quick sip of his tea and sighed in pleasure. He reached for a biscuit, crammed it into his mouth, and chewed hungrily, swallowing just as the door opened and Sir Madison Lowery stepped inside the room.

"Do try and make this quick, Inspector." Lowery frowned irritably as he sat down across from Witherspoon. "It is getting late and I'd like to get home. I've a very full day tomorrow."

"What time did you arrive here this afternoon?" Witherspoon took another sip. Delicate cups were beautiful, but they certainly didn't hold very much tea.

"I don't recall the exact time." Lowery crossed his arms over his chest.

"But surely you've some idea of when you got here?" The inspector glanced longingly at the plate of biscuits. "Was it dark outside or was it still light?"

"It was already dark"—he lifted his hand to his mouth to cover a yawn—"the tea started at a quarter to five. I arrived here shortly afterwards."

"Did you see anyone out front when you came inside?" Witherspoon asked.

Lowery hesitated. "Actually, I didn't come in the front way."

The inspector stared at him. "How did you get into the house?"

"I came in through the garden."

The inspector wondered if anyone at this ruddy tea party had come in the front door. "Is it your habit to come in through the garden?"

Lowery raised an eyebrow. "Of course not, Inspector. But

I was late, you see, and I didn't want my fiancée realizing how late I actually was, so I crept in the back way. I came through the kitchen."

"Did any of the kitchen staff see you come in?" he asked.

"Why? Do I need to account for my whereabouts?"

"In a murder investigation, everyone needs to account for their time," Witherspoon replied.

Sir Madison gave him a tight smile. "One of the maids saw me come inside, and I daresay several of the guests spotted me coming in as well. I didn't want Rosemary to be cross with me. Surely you understand, Inspector. You know how women can be about social engagements."

Witherspoon wasn't in the least sure he understood anything about women or social engagements. His relationship with his wonderful neighbor, Lady Cannonberry, was such that if she asked him to be at her home at a specific time, he would do so if it were at all in his power.

"So I take it you had no idea that there was something odd happening right in front of the house?" he ventured.

"Absolutely not," Lowery retorted.

"Were the drapes open when you came into the room?"

Lowery's forehead wrinkled in thought. "I think the butler might have been closing them when I came into the drawing room. Yes, that's right, Stevens was at the window untying the cords. A moment later, he pulled the panels together. But I didn't think anything of it at the time. It was already dark outside and I know the family values privacy. The drapes are always closed in the evenings."

"Have you ever met Miss Moran?" Witherspoon asked.

"No." He shook his head. "Rosemary has mentioned her, of course. She has very fond memories of the woman. But I've not made her acquaintance."

"When you were coming through the back garden to the house—"

"I didn't come through the back garden," he interrupted. "I nipped around the back of number fifteen and slipped in through the conservatory."

"The conservatory door was unlocked?"

"There would be no point in locking the door, Inspector," he explained. "The structure hasn't been finished as yet. It was supposed to be completed before the bad winter weather set in, but there have been a number of delays. Usually, the inside door between the house and the unfinished part is locked, but I knew it wouldn't be locked this evening. Arabella, Mrs. Evans, had mentioned that she was keeping it open to show her guests the new table and chairs that she'd ordered from Spain."

"So you came through an unlocked outside door—"

"No, the outside door hasn't arrived from France. I pushed one of the oilcloths over the lower back windows aside and came in that way. With all this rain, the workers have oilcloths up everywhere."

Witherspoon couldn't quite see what the fellow was talking about, but that didn't matter; he'd insist on being shown the "conservatory" before he and Barnes left.

"I'll wager that's the place." Smythe pointed across the road to the house where a constable stood at attention in front of a wrought iron gate. He and Wiggins were standing behind the trunk of a tree at the end of the street. Their hiding place wasn't very good as the tree wasn't very large, and even a cursory glance in their direction would reveal the two of them. But as they weren't the only ones out having a good look at the police activity, Smythe figured as long as they avoided any constables who might recognize them as members of Witherspoon's household, they should be alright.

Just then, the door of the house directly behind where

they were standing opened and two constables stepped out the front door.

"Cor blimey," Wiggins hissed. "They must be doin' the house-to-house." He cast a quick glance over his shoulder. "Oh no, what rotten luck. It's Constable Griffith."

"He knows us. We've got to get out of 'ere."

Slowly, so as to not draw attention their way, Smythe turned and started to walk back the way they'd just come. Wiggins followed suit. "Is he watchin' us?" he muttered to Wiggins.

"Nah, he's goin' on to the next house." He swiveled around and grinned at the coachman. "What are we goin' to do now? We can't 'ang about 'ere. If Constable Griffith is 'ere, there's a good chance a couple of the other lads from the inspector's station 'ave come to 'elp. Most of them know who we are. They's seen us lots of times."

Smythe hated going home with nothing to show for their efforts. Yet Wiggins had a point. Their faces were too well-known to take the risk. "There's a pub just over there." He pointed up the road as they rounded the corner. "Let's see if we can find out if the gossip has gotten around the neighborhood."

"That'd be a bit fast." Wiggins laughed. "We don't even 'ave the name of the victim."

"True." They'd reached the pub. Smythe pulled the door open. "But we've seen a bunch of coppers over on Chepstow Villas, and that and a few pints should be enough to loosen a few tongues."

"The study is just through there, Inspector." Sir Madison Lowery pointed to a door off the hallway. "Now if you'll excuse me, I must see to my fiancée before I go." He nodded curtly and swung around toward the front of the house.

Witherspoon knocked once, opened the door, and stepped

inside. Across from the doorway, Arabella Evans sat behind a large desk, holding a glass of brandy. Two formal armchairs with carved backs and gold and burgundy striped upholstery were stationed in front of the desk. An elaborate console table with a marble top was on one side of the room, and on the other stood a secretary in the same wood as the desk.

"Please be brief, Inspector," Arabella said flatly. "I have a headache and I'd like to retire. This has been a dreadful ordeal."

"Yes, ma'am, I'll be as quick as possible," Witherspoon replied. He noticed she hadn't invited him to sit down. He had a strong suspicion she wasn't going to, either. "Did you happen to have occasion to look out the window before the butler closed the curtains?"

"No, Inspector, I was attending to my guests." She took a sip of her brandy.

"Did any of your guests happen to mention they'd seen any strangers lurking about the neighborhood when they arrived?" He wished he could take the words back as soon as they escaped from his mouth. The question was foolish: It was unlikely any visitors to the house would notice anything of the sort.

"What an absurd question! My guests would hardly be in a position to know if someone out on the pavement was a stranger or not. As to anyone lurking, I can assure you, I've no idea what that even means."

"I'm sorry, I'll endeavor to make my questions clearer. Did your servants mention they'd seen someone suspicious hanging about the area this afternoon?"

He and Constable Barnes would interview the staff separately, but it never hurt to find out if anyone had made comments about strangers to the mistress of the house.

"It was a formal tea, Inspector"—she sniffed—"and of

course, I insist that it be done perfectly. The servants were all too busy attending to their duties to be loitering about staring out the windows."

"When was the last time you saw or had any communication with Miss Moran?"

"She was Rosemary's governess. We've not seen or heard from her since my daughter was sent off to school when she was eight," she replied.

"Mrs. Evans, I understand you were absent from the tea for quite a long period of time this afternoon. Where did you go?"

"Where did I go?" she repeated. She stared at him incredulously. "What a silly question. I went to fetch a footman. My husband was late and I wanted to find out if he was still at his office—"

Witherspoon interrupted. "You were going to send a footman all the way to Fenchurch Street?"

"Yes." She took another drink. "What of it? That's why I pay my servants, Inspector, to do my bidding. I was very annoyed with Mr. Evans. Sometimes he loses track of time or he falls asleep in his office. But luckily, just as the boy was leaving, Mr. Evans came in the back door."

"Did Miss Moran live here in London?" Witherspoon's knee began to throb. He really wished she'd invite him to sit down.

"I've no idea where she lived." She glanced pointedly at the clock on the wall next to the secretary. "Why would I? I've just told you we've not seen or heard from the woman in years."

"Yet Miss Evans was sure she heard Miss Moran speaking to you on Monday afternoon," he pressed.

"My daughter was mistaken. She heard me speaking to the dressmaker."

"Do you have any idea why Miss Moran might have been in front of your home?"

She shook her head. "None whatsoever."

"Are any of the knives missing from the kitchen?" He watched her carefully and was rewarded with seeing her eyes widen in surprise.

"What an odd thing to ask. How on earth should I know something . . ." Her voice faltered as she realized the implication of his question. "I find this line of inquiry very offensive, Inspector. I shall make sure your superiors hear about this."

"I meant no offense, ma'am," he replied. "But a woman has been stabbed by what appears to be a common kitchen knife, and as far as I can tell, the only kitchen she had any connection to was the one in this house." He'd no idea if the knife was a common one or not, but it had had a plain brown handle and looked very much like the ones he saw Mrs. Goodge use.

Outraged, she leapt to her feet. "Are you deaf? I've told you we've not seen the woman in years. How dare you ask such a question? We've nothing to do with Agatha Moran and none of my kitchen knives are missing. Now I'll thank you to leave."

Mrs. Jeffries stifled a yawn and put more water on to boil. Smythe and Wiggins had come home, but they'd learned very little, only the name of the family who lived in the house near where the victim was found. Betsy had reported back that Lady Cannonberry was delighted to help and would be over tomorrow for their morning meeting. Smythe had then reminded Betsy that her family was arriving on the eleven fifteen train from Liverpool and wouldn't it be a good idea if Luty or Lady Cannonberry took over some of Betsy's tasks in the investigation. Betsy had taken umbrage at his remarks that just because she was getting married and had family coming to the wedding would be reason to shirk her duties. A row had been averted by Mrs. Goodge's quick thinking wherein she reminded everyone that there were plenty of people to share the load.

She yawned again and glanced at the clock. It was almost midnight and she was tired, but she was determined to stay awake and get what information she could out of the inspector. This might very well be the last case they could do together in their present circumstances. Oh, she wasn't worried that Betsy and Smythe would give up their investigations; it was too important for both of them. But she also knew that once the two of them had left the house, things wouldn't be the same. Perhaps it wouldn't be noticeable at first, but life at Upper Edmonton Gardens would most definitely change.

In the quiet night, she heard the clip-clop of a horse's hooves and the jangling of a harness as a hansom cab pulled up in front of the house. She picked up a tea towel and pulled the hot plate out of the warming oven. Putting it on the tray, she covered it with a lid, checked to make sure everything else was at the ready, and went upstairs. She reached the dining room just as the inspector unlocked the front door and stepped inside.

"Oh dear, Mrs. Jeffries, I didn't expect you to wait up for me." He put his umbrella in the stand by the coat tree and took off his bowler hat. "It's terribly late."

"I wanted to make sure you had a bite to eat before you retired for the night, sir." She nodded at the tray. "We've kept this warm for you. Shall I put it on the dining table?"

"That would be perfect. I'm famished." He smiled gratefully as he shrugged out of his heavy overcoat and hung it up.

She went on into the dining room. He followed, rubbing his cold hands together. "It smells lovely."

She'd set the table earlier so all she had to do was put his food in front of his chair. "It's lamb stew," she replied. "With a treacle tart for pudding. I know it generally isn't done, sir, but would you care for a sherry with your meal?"

He laughed, pulled out his chair, and sat down. "I don't care if it's done or not, that sounds wonderful."

She went to the sideboard where she'd earlier put a bottle of Harveys and two sherry glasses. Opening the bottle, she poured out the deep amber–colored liquid.

"If your intention is to stay up and keep me company, then please pour one for yourself." He flicked his serviette open and put it on his lap. "Not that I want you to stay up . . . oh dear, that isn't what I meant. I meant, I know it's late and you're tired . . ."

"I know what you meant, sir." She laughed and brought their drinks to the table and sat down. "And you mustn't tease me, sir. You know good and well I shan't rest a wink tonight until you tell me about your case."

She wasn't afraid she was being presumptuous; it was very much their custom for him to discuss his work with her. Over the years, she'd developed a number of ways to insure she learned all the pertinent facts of a murder, and if she couldn't get the information out of the inspector, Constable Barnes was always an excellent source.

"Oh, it's quite a dreadful case." He speared a piece of lamb. "The victim was stabbed to death on a public street, but so far, we've not been able to find anyone who saw or heard anything."

"How terrible." She took a sip of her sherry. "Did it happen in broad daylight?"

"No, as near as we can ascertain, the murder occurred sometime between five fifteen and half past the hour." He reached for the butter pot.

"That's a fairly short time period, sir."

He speared a slab of butter onto his bread. "Luckily,

there was tea party at the house where the body was found, and the victim was literally right outside their front gate. The home is owned by a Mr. and Mrs. Jeremy Evans. Most of the guests went into the house between half past four and five fifteen. So, since no one mentioned seeing a dead woman in front of the place when they arrived, we've deduced the victim was murdered after everyone was inside. At five thirty, a passerby spotted her lying in the street and alerted the constable."

"So that's how you came up with your timeline," she mused. "Was the victim connected in any way with the household?"

"We think so." He took another bite of stew, chewed, and swallowed before he continued speaking. "A member of the Evans family recognized the body. The victim's name was Agatha Moran, and it turns out she was once a governess to Miss Rosemary Evans. Sad really; poor Miss Evans is to be married the same day as our Betsy and the celebration has been somewhat marred by this murder. Even though she'd not seen her old governess since she was eight, Miss Evans appeared to be very upset when she realized who the victim was."

"Was she coming to see them in particular?" Mrs. Jeffries took another sip.

"Not that any of them will admit." Witherspoon frowned thoughtfully. "But I'm not certain I believe them."

Mrs. Jeffries was surprised. It wasn't like the inspector to be so suspicious this early in a case. "Why do you say that, sir?"

"Well, I think it's because Mr. Evans and his wife were both so adamant that they'd nothing to do with the woman in years." He scooped up more stew onto his fork. "Now I ask you, if someone you'd not seen in years suddenly showed up dead on your front doorstep, how would you react?"

She thought for a moment. "I suppose I'd be more curious than anything else," she finally replied.

"Precisely." He smiled triumphantly and then sopped his bread in the gravy. "Yet neither Mr. or Mrs. Evans seemed at all curious about how the woman came to be stabbed right outside their front gate. Their only concern was to make it very clear to me that they'd neither seen nor heard from the woman in years."

"Perhaps they were simply frightened," she suggested. "Murder is rather terrifying."

"Of course it is, and you may well be right, it could be that they were simply scared." He sighed theatrically. "I suppose that in my position, I've rather gotten used to murder. Dreadful, really, that someone could actually get used to such a thing."

Inspector Witherspoon was one of nature's true gentlemen, but he was not without flaws. Occasionally, he allowed his narratives to veer toward the melodramatic. But tonight, Mrs. Jeffries needed facts. "Where does Miss Moran live? Here in London?"

"We're still trying to find that out," he said. "No one at the Evans house seemed to know her exact address, though the butler told one of the constables he thought she lived in Islington."

As he finished his dinner, she continued asking him questions. By the time he'd cleaned his plate, had another sherry, and eaten his tart, she was fairly certain she'd learned everything there was to know.

Nonetheless, she'd have a quick word with Constable Barnes in the morning. It never hurt to make double sure she had all the details.

CHAPTER 3

As they took their places for the morning meeting, Betsy glanced at the carriage clock on the pine sideboard. It was almost eight o'clock and she was getting a bit nervous. She didn't want to say anything, but she did hope they'd get on with it. She needed time to change her clothes and tidy herself up a bit before she and Smythe had to meet her sister's train. Still, she ought to be grateful for small favors; getting everyone here at this time of the morning was quite an accomplishment. She smiled at Lady Cannonberry as the slender middle-aged blonde sat down in the empty chair next to Mrs. Goodge.

This morning's meeting had almost come undone before it even began. Lady Cannonberry had arrived at the back door a split second after the inspector had left the kitchen. They'd almost run into each other. That could have been a tad awkward considering that Inspector Witherspoon had no idea that his "special friend" had helped investigate more than a dozen of his cases.

Ruth Cannonberry was the widow of a peer of the realm and could have easily led the upper-class life of a lady of leisure. But instead, after her husband's death, she'd thrown her time and energy into helping the poor and working to get women the right to vote. She'd been raised the daughter of a country vicar and consequently had taken the admonition to love her neighbor quite seriously. She was the one who insisted that everyone in the household call her by her Christian name, except, of course, in front of the inspector. Ruth was very sensitive to the feelings of others, and despite her social conscience and dislike of the English class system, she knew the staff would be uncomfortable addressing her in such a familiar manner in front of their employer. Betsy admired her greatly.

"Do stand still for a moment, madam," a deep male voice instructed. Betsy turned to see Hatchet attempting to untangle the voluminous green netting trailing from Luty Belle Crookshank's gigantic hat.

"I am standin' still," Luty Belle retorted. She was an elderly, gray-haired American woman who dressed in bright colors no matter what the season of the year. Today she wore a brilliant green overcoat and a matching hat festooned with a variety of multihued feathers and draped yards of veiling that were currently tangled around the brass button of her collar.

The tall, white-haired man dressed in an old-fashioned black frock coat was her butler, Hatchet. He was also her very best friend. "There, that should do it." He unloosed a length of fabric and freed his employer.

Luty and Hatchet had been witnesses during one of the inspector's earliest cases. Luty's elegant Knightsbridge home had shared the same communal garden as the murder victim, and being sharp-eyed as well as nosy, Luty had noticed the various members of the inspector's household asking questions and snooping about the area. Shortly after the successful resolution of that particular murder, Luty had come to them for help with a problem of her own. Ever since, she and Hatchet had insisted on being part of all the inspector's cases. She was rich, eccentric, and kindhearted and egalitarian in outlook. Occasionally, she was blunt to the point of rudeness, but her money gave her access to people out of reach for the rest of the inspector's household.

Luty knew every politician, financier, and aristocrat in London, and she used those connections ruthlessly. She wasn't the only one with useful connections, though. Hatchet had resources of his own that he called upon when the need arose.

Mrs. Jeffries took her place at the head of the table and waited till Luty and Hatchet had settled in their places. "I take it all of you have been told the basics of the case." She reached for her cup.

"Wiggins told us on the way over here," Luty replied.

"And Mrs. Goodge very kindly gave me what details she had," Ruth added.

"Excellent, then we can get right to what I found out from the inspector last night and what I learned from Constable Barnes this morning," she said.

"Lucky for us that Constable Barnes always stops in when they're on a case," Mrs. Goodge murmured. "And all we have to do is give the man a quick cup of tea."

"We are indeed fortunate," Mrs. Jeffries agreed. Constable Barnes had figured out that the inspector's household helped him. But instead of taking offense that "amateurs" were interfering, he tried to aid them and was of great assistance in getting information they'd learned to the inspector. She gave them a quick, concise report on the additional facts she'd found out from Witherspoon.

"Agatha Moran must have been goin' to see the Evans family," Mrs. Goodge said. "It's too much of a coincidence to think she just happened to be passin' by just as a killer wieldin' a knife was larkin' about waitin' for a victim."

"And I don't like the way they shut them curtains." Wiggins nodded vigorously. "Even upper-class people are curious."

"But coincidences do happen." Betsy glanced at Smythe. "We were almost torn apart by one, remember?"

He nodded in agreement, his expression sober. He knew exactly what she meant. Only a few days before their original wedding, an old friend had shown up on their doorstep and he'd had to leave for Australia. "That's true. But this doesn't sound like a coincidence to me. There's somethin' right odd about this murder. The poor woman was killed right in the middle of a public street just after dark. The killer must 'ave been desperate—even lunatics like that Ripper feller waited until it was late before he did his murderin'. Sounds to me like someone didn't want her goin' into that house."

"You may be right," Mrs. Jeffries said quickly. "But as yet, we don't have enough information to form any useful conclusions."

Until they had as many facts as possible, she didn't want any of them forming opinions. On one of their previous cases, they'd come up with ideas and theories early in the investigation and it had almost ended in disaster. Furthermore, she'd observed that once people felt they knew the answer, they stopped looking for possible alternatives and interpreted the facts to fit their own theories. "Now, let me tell you what Constable Barnes said. They found out Agatha Moran's address. She lived on Thornley Road in Barnsbury, at number seven. That's over by Islington, I think. The constable says she owned a small residential hotel. Unfortunately, that's the only other bit of information I was able to obtain."

For the next fifteen minutes, they discussed the few facts they had about the murder. Finally, Luty said, "I think I'm goin' to set my sights on findin' out what I can about the Evanses' financial situation. Nells bells, we've got to start somewhere and they're as good a place as any."

"But what if they've nothing to do with the murder?" Hatchet asked. "What if Agatha Moran being stabbed in front of their home really is one of those awful coincidences that happen?"

"Then I'll have wasted my time," she replied. "But somehow, I don't think that's goin' to be the way of it. Besides, if they own one of them big houses on the edge of Bayswater, they've got to be rich, and we all know that money and murder often walk hand in hand."

"I agree," Mrs. Jeffries said.

"I'll 'ave a go at the hansom cab drivers," Smythe offered. "If she came all the way from Islington, she might 'ave taken a cab. It was rainin'."

"Right then." Mrs. Goodge got up. "We've a couple of names to start with, the Evans family and Sir Madison Lowery. I've got half a dozen sources comin' through the kitchen this mornin'. Maybe one of them will have heard some gossip that'll prove useful. Mind you, I've only got a bit of seed cake and some treacle tarts left to feed them, but I'll get some more bakin' done. Too bad the inspector didn't bring the list of guests home with him."

"Yes, I was disappointed about that as well," Mrs. Jeffries mused. "But I'm sure Constable Barnes will keep us informed if it appears that any of the guests had a connection to the dead woman."

Wiggins grinned broadly. "Maybe I'll see if I 'ave more luck than the constables 'ad on findin' us a witness. Even if it was dark and miserable last evenin', it weren't that late that the poor lady got murdered. Someone must 'ave seen somethin'. There's bound to be servants and such millin' about."

"As soon as I get my sister and Leo settled in their rooms," Betsy said, "I'll do the shops in the Evanses' neighborhood."

"Betsy, there's no need for that," Mrs. Jeffries protested. "It's been years since you've seen your family. You must spend time with them. We've plenty of help."

"I'll try speaking to the shopkeepers," Ruth volunteered. "I'm sure I won't be as clever as you are." She smiled at Betsy. "But I'll do my best."

Betsy wasn't sure what to say. On the one hand, she did want time with her family, but on the other, she didn't want to be left out. Despite Smythe's assurances to the contrary, once the two of them married, their lives were going to be different. The people around this table were her family as well, and this might be their very last case together while they all lived in the same house. "Alright, I'll spend the day with Norah and Leo. But if they're tired from the journey and I have a chance to nip out, I'll see what I can find out as well. After all, we've a lot of territory to cover." She reached across and patted Ruth's arm. "You'll do fine getting those shopkeepers to talk. Just smile a lot and act as if every word they say is pure gold."

Constable Barnes paid the driver and turned to see Witherspoon frowning at the home of the late Agatha Moran. It was a tall, four-story structure of brown brick with a painted white façade on the ground floor. The tiny front garden was enclosed by a wrought iron fence, and just inside the gate, a set of steps led down to the lower ground floor. "Is anything wrong, sir?"

Witherspoon shook his head. "Not really, I'm just surprised. The house is so large. From what little we know of Miss Moran, she wasn't a wealthy woman. She was a former governess."

"So you're wondering how she could have bought a place like this on a governess's salary." Barnes started up the short walkway. "Perhaps she inherited it, sir." He raised his hand and banged the brass knocker against the brightly painted green door. "However she got the place, she's done a decent job keeping it up. The door lamps are polished, the walkway is properly paved, and the fence has been newly painted."

The door flew open and a middle-aged woman wearing a cook's cap and an apron appeared. Her eyes widened in fear and her lips started to tremble. Then she slumped against the doorframe. "Oh, dear God in heaven, something's happened to her, hasn't it? That's why she didn't come home last night." Slowly, she began to sink toward the ground.

The two policemen moved simultaneously, leaping forward and grabbing the woman before she collapsed. Witherspoon grabbed her from one side, getting his arm under her elbow and around her middle, as Barnes did the same on her other side. As gently as possible, they hauled her backward into the house.

The small foyer contained an entry table and a formal armchair. Moving together, they eased her onto the seat. "Are you alright, madam?" Witherspoon asked. She'd gone very pale. "Should I fetch the doctor? You don't look well."

She raised her hand palm up, shook her head, and took a deep gulp of air. "No, just give me a moment and I'll be fine."

"Can I get you something?" Barnes glanced toward the drawing room opposite them. "A brandy or a whisky?"

"No, I'm alright. Just give me a few seconds," she gasped.

They stood waiting for her to regain her composure, and finally she took a deep breath and looked at Witherspoon. "I'm Jane Middleton, Miss Moran's cook and housekeeper. Something has happened to her, hasn't it? Something awful." Her hazel eyes filled with tears.

"I'm afraid she's dead," Witherspoon affirmed softly. "She was stabbed yesterday evening in front of a house in Notting Hill."

Barnes studied the distraught woman. "You don't seem surprised by this. Was Miss Moran worried that someone was trying to do her harm?"

Jane Middleton stood up. "Let's go into the kitchen. I don't want the others hearing what I've got to say."

"What others?" Witherspoon glanced around the small space. The drawing room was empty and there was no one in the hallway or on the stairs. As far as he could tell, they were completely alone.

"This is a residential hotel, Inspector." She started down the hall toward the back of the house. "And take my word for it, you can't see up the stairwell, but there's at least three sets of ears hanging about on the first-floor landing. As you'll need to be speaking to all of them yourself, it's best if they don't hear my statement. Now come along."

As they trailed after her, the two men exchanged glances. When she'd addressed him, Jane Middleton had used Witherspoon's rank, yet neither man had introduced himself.

When they reached the kitchen, she hurried to the cooker, struck a match, and put the kettle on. Witherspoon started to introduce himself. "I'm Inspect—" but she cut him off.

"I know who you are. You're Inspector Witherspoon." She smiled slightly and then jerked her chin toward the constable. "And you're Constable Barnes. Gracious, does my boy envy you. Mind you, from the way he tells it, every constable in the force would give their eyeteeth to work with the famous Inspector Witherspoon." She flicked her gaze back to Witherspoon. "My boy Roddie talks about you all the time. He's a constable in Marylebone Division and he pointed the two of you out to me just last week. You were coming out of the Marylebone Magistrates Court. That's how I knew to get you away from all those listening ears before I made my statement. If Miss Moran's been murdered, you'll need to interview everyone in this house. My Roddie is always going on and on about police procedures and what should and shouldn't be done. Now you two sit yourselves down and I'll make us a nice cup of tea. I was fixing myself one when you knocked on the door."

Bemused and a bit embarrassed by her comments, Witherspoon did as ordered, pulled out a chair and sat down. Barnes took the empty seat across from him.

"Are you sure you're alright, ma'am?" he inquired. Her color had improved, but she was still very pale.

"Of course I'm not alright," she muttered as the kettle began to whistle. "My friend's been murdered and I've no idea what's going to happen. But that's life, isn't it. All sorts of odd things happen and none of us has any idea what the eventual outcome will be, do we. I've been worried about her ever since she got back from her holiday. She was right as rain when she first come in the door last Sunday evening. But that didn't last long."

"Miss Moran had been away?" Witherspoon asked softly.

"Yes, for the last six months. She took one of those grand tours of the continent. You know, one of those fancy ones from Thomas Cook. She's wanted to go for ages, and she finally decided that she better do it while she was fit enough to see everything she wanted to see." She sniffed and dabbed at her eyes.

"Miss Moran was in good spirits when she returned home

last Sunday evening?" Barnes inquired. He glanced at Witherspoon, who gave him an almost imperceptible nod. They had to make sure Miss Moran's murderer hadn't followed her home from her travels.

"She was a bit tired, perhaps, but certainly not depressed or upset or worried about anything." She poured the boiling water into a waiting teapot as she spoke. "She said the trip was the most wonderful time she'd ever had in her life and even said she might take another trip in the spring."

"She didn't make any mention that anyone had bothered her or that she'd had any trouble on the trip?" the inspector pressed.

"She said everyone was very nice and that she'd made some new friends. Mind you, she got right back to work the very next day and didn't give herself any time to rest. The next morning she took all the correspondence and receipts and even the old newspapers into her office. When she came out later that afternoon, I could see something had upset her. But she wouldn't tell me what was wrong." Her voice broke and she turned her back on them and went to the drying rack by the sink. She got down three mugs and, still keeping her face averted, pulled a tray off the worktable shelf and put cream and sugar on it.

Neither man spoke. Jane Middleton was a proud lady who'd had a deep shock, and it was only right to give her a few moments to get her emotions under control.

She sighed, loaded the tray up with the rest of the tea things, and came to the table. "Help yourselves to cream and sugar," she commanded as she handed them their mugs. She took the seat next to the inspector. "Then you can ask your questions."

Barnes reached for the cream. "How long has Miss Moran owned this place?"

"Thirteen years." She smiled wanly. "I started to work

here the day the workmen left. Miss Moran was smart; she'd bought this old place and done the rooms up nicely so they could be let to ladies. She's run it all on her own since she opened the doors for business. This trip she took was the first holiday she's had in all these years."

Witherspoon knew he ought to start asking questions, but as sometimes happened when he learned new facts, his brain needed a few moments to comprehend the information. Agatha Moran had been out of the country. What, if anything, did that mean?

"As I said earlier, ma'am, you weren't surprised when we arrived on the doorstep." Barnes took out his notebook and flipped it open. "You were shocked and upset, but not surprised."

"I was afraid something terrible was going to happen. But Miss Moran wasn't one to be told what to do. But she was in such an awful state yesterday afternoon; she went to the window in the front parlor so often she liked to have walked a hole in the hall carpet. When she finally left the house, I was afraid."

"Why were you frightened?" Witherspoon picked up his mug and took a sip. He watched her carefully over the rim.

"Because she'd been acting odd since Monday." Jane clasped her hands together and pressed them under her chin as she spoke. "She wasn't eating. She would go out for hours, and when she'd come back, she'd either be pale as a ghost or so angry she could barely speak. I tried to get her to tell me what was wrong, but she wouldn't, and I couldn't press her. Yesterday afternoon was the worst of all; she was like a woman possessed. She'd jump every time there was a noise out front and then run to the door."

Barnes stopped scribbling. "Was she expecting someone?"

"She didn't tell me that specifically, but it was obvious from the way she kept watching out the window of the front parlor. She wasn't ordinarily one to waste time in such foolishness. Finally, as it got later and later, she got very calm and told me she was going out—"

Witherspoon interrupted. "What time was this?"

"I'm not sure," Jane replied. "I was in such a state, I didn't notice the time. But it was past three; I know that because the afternoon mail had come. Miss Moran had been standing by the door waiting for it. When the postman finally shoved it through the slot, she snatched it up like a madwoman. But whatever she was looking for wasn't there, because she threw it on the table and told me she was going out and not to wait dinner for her. I knew something awful was brewing. I tried to get her to stay in, but as I said, she wasn't one to be told what to do. As she put on her hat and coat, she just kept muttering that she'd make them see reason no matter what the cost."

"It sounds as if she was expecting either a visitor or a letter," Witherspoon murmured.

Barnes reached for his mug of tea. "Do you know who she was referring to when she was talking about making them 'see reason'?" he asked.

She smiled grimly. "Of course I do—she was talking about Arabella and Jeremy Evans."

"Are you nervous?" Smythe took Betsy's hand and pulled her close as they stood at the barricade of the number ten platform waiting for the train from Liverpool. Around them Euston Station bustled with activity as people rushed from the platforms to the street. On the huge arrivals board, shuttles clattered as the board changed, announcing the arrival of the London Northwest Express from Liverpool.

"I've got butterflies in my stomach. I was just a child when I last saw Norah and Leo. People change." Betsy tightened her grip on the bunch of flowers they'd stopped and bought on their way into the station. "What if I don't recognize her?"

"No matter how much she's changed, you'll recognize your own sister," he promised. He turned his attention to the platform as the train chugged to a stop. The carriage doors opened and passengers poured out of the compartments. The ticket collectors opened the barricade.

The trickle of passengers soon turned into a torrent surging for the gate. Betsy rose up on her tiptoes and craned her neck as she tried to spot her relatives. "There, there, I see her." She pointed to a couple at the back of the queue. "Oh my gracious, it's her. It's my Norah."

Smythe stared at the woman who would soon be his sister-in-law. She looked like his Betsy, only a bit plumper and older. She wore a dark green traveling suit with a fitted jacket and carried a carpetbag. Her blonde hair was tucked up under a sensible brown and green bonnet, and the expression on her face was one he'd seen many times on his beloved Betsy's. She was anxious and just a bit worried. The man walking beside her was of medium height and wore a dark navy blue suit, a black overcoat, and a bowler hat. His complexion was ruddy, his build stocky, and his face apprehensive as he scanned the crowd. He carried two brown suitcases.

Betsy grabbed Smythe's hand and pulled him toward the barrier just as Norah and Leo came through. Norah's eyes widened as she spotted Betsy coming toward them. For a moment, no one said anything, and then Betsy gave a squeal of delight. "Oh my goodness, I didn't think I'd ever see you again!" she cried as she hurled herself at her sister.

Norah dropped the carpetbag and held out her arms, her blue eyes, so like Betsy's, filling with tears. "I thought you were dead," she said in a voice that trembled as they fell into each other's arms. The two women held each other tightly, and without warning, both of them began to cry.

Smythe looked at Leo. The fellow did the sensible thing and put the cases down and then stepped around the two sisters. "Let's give them a minute," he said softly as he edged away.

Smythe didn't have to be told twice; watching Betsy cry, even tears of happiness, was about his least favorite activity on the face of God's green earth. He followed his soon-to-be brother-in-law, and when they were a few feet away, he stuck his hand out. "I'm Smythe . . ."

"I know who you are." Leo extended his own hand and they shook. "And I'm very grateful to you for arranging all this. I don't know that I can ever pay you back . . ."

"Pay me back," Smythe repeated. "There's no need for any talk like that. This is Betsy's weddin' present. Your comin' is a gift to the both of us, so let's not have any talk of payin' back. I 'ad hoped that lawyer had made that clear."

Leo cocked his head and studied him, and then he broke into a wide grin. "I thought the lawyer was completely daft. It took him two visits to convince me this wasn't someone's idea of a strange joke. I'm glad to meet you, Smythe. Is that your first or your last name?"

Smythe laughed. "I'll let you find that out at the weddin'. Oh look, I think they've quit their tears. What do you say we get the ladies to your lodgin's? I think a nice hot cup of tea is in order."

"We kept in touch by letter," Jane Middleton explained as she led the two policemen out to the foot of the stairs. "It was very easy, actually. It was a tour, you see, so I always knew where to contact Miss Moran. Besides, this place practically runs itself. We've five permanent residents at the moment, but two of them have gone to visit relatives for Christmas."

"How long have they been gone?" Witherspoon asked.

"Miss Grant left at the end of November to stay with her family in Wales and Miss Beddowes left two weeks ago to visit her sister in the Lake District," she replied. "But both departures had been planned for quite some time, and Miss Moran was well aware that there would only be three tenants here when she got back from her trip."

They'd arrived at the foot of the staircase. Jane looked up. "Miss Farley and Mrs. Crowe, could you both come down here please, the police would like to have a word with you," she called.

Though they couldn't see around the wall of the first-floor landing, they could hear the shuffle of feet and soft murmur of voices.

"I told you they were all listening," she hissed softly. "Miss Farley, Mrs. Crowe, did you hear me?"

"We were just coming down for our morning tea."A middle-aged woman appeared at the head of the stairs. She was tall and slender and wore a black dress with a yellow shawl around her shoulders. Directly behind her came another woman, this one a good deal younger, dressed in a blue and gray plaid suit and wearing spectacles.

"Yes, of course," Jane said as they reached the bottom of the staircase. "I'm afraid I've some bad news." She glanced uncertainly at Witherspoon and then plunged on when he gave a nod. "Miss Moran is dead and the police are here to talk to you."

"Dead?" the woman in black repeated. "But that's ridiculous. She was in perfect health when I saw her yesterday afternoon."

"I don't think the police are here because she died of natural causes," the other lady said dryly. She turned her attention to the inspector. "I'm Helen Farley. I've lived here for three years. This is Ellen Crowe; she's been here for twelve years."

"I'm Inspector Witherspoon and this is Constable Barnes. And as you've correctly surmised, Miss Moran's death wasn't natural. We do need to ask you some questions." He glanced at Jane Middleton. "May I use your parlor?"

"Of course." She pointed to a door down the hallway. "The constable can take Mrs. Crowe into the dining room and you can use the parlor for Miss Farley. If you want to speak to Miss Bannister, you'll need to go up. The stairs are difficult for her."

"They are not," a voice snapped from upstairs. "I've got my cane. I can get down quite easily and I've got plenty I'd like to tell those policemen."

"I'm sure you do, Miss Bannister," Jane called back. "But the policemen aren't ready to speak with you just yet." She smiled ruefully at Witherspoon. "She's getting a bit childish, but that doesn't mean she doesn't have something useful to tell you."

"She spends most of her day listening at the top of the staircase," Mrs. Crowe added. "She might have heard what Miss Moran and that man were arguing about yesterday."

"What man? What argument?" Jane Middleton demanded.

Mrs. Crowe gave her a condescending smile. "A man came to the door when you went out yesterday morning to do the shopping. Miss Farley had gone to the lending library, so as I was on my way out, I answered the door. I had to go to the post office. The fellow was very rude. He barged in and demanded to see Miss Moran. She came out of her office and seemed to know who he was so I went on my way."

Jane eyed her suspiciously. "If you were at the post office, how do you know they were arguing?" Jane asked.

"Because when I got to the post office, I realized I'd left my coin purse on the table, and I had to come back for it so I could buy the stamps. When I returned, you could hear the two of them having a very heated discussion."

"Could you hear what they were arguing about?" Barnes asked.

She shook her head. "No, all I heard were raised voices, but I was in a hurry so I went right out again. Miss Moran's office is directly under the stairs there." She pointed to a doorway. "I should think there's a good possibility that Miss Bannister heard them quite clearly."

Wiggins rounded the corner and wondered if he dared walk up Chepstow Villas again. He'd been up and down the street now twice, and if he wasn't careful, someone was going to notice him hanging about. His luck had been terrible today. He'd not seen so much as a housemaid, a tweeny, or a footman stick their nose outside. For goodness' sakes, didn't these households have any servants? Just then, he spotted a young woman coming up the servants' stairs from the home next door to the Evans house.

She wore a short brown jacket over a lavender housemaid's dress and carried a shopping basket on one arm. She reached ground level and stepped out onto the pavement. She walked toward him.

Wiggins wasn't going to miss this chance. "Excuse me, miss"—he doffed his cap politely as she came close—"I'm lookin' for a family named Evans but I fear I've lost their address. I've got to deliver a note to them." He pulled an envelope he'd borrowed from the inspector's study out of his jacket, flashed it at the girl, and then shoved it back into his pocket. Betsy had recommended that he carry it because people were more likely to believe what they could see with their own eyes.

The girl stared at him without speaking. She was skinny as a rail with reddish blonde hair tucked up under her maid's cap, a sprinkling of freckles over her nose, and blue eyes set in a thin, pale face. "They live just there." She pointed to the Evans home and started on her way.

Wiggins hurried after her. "Please, miss, would you be able to tell me if a Miss Rosemary Evans is receivin' visitors?" He hadn't planned on the girl bolting so quickly and was frantically coming up with ways to keep her talking.

"You mean is she 'at home,'" the girl replied, using the socially acceptable term. "I've no idea, I don't work for them. I work for next door, for Mrs. North, and if I'm back late with the shopping, Cook will have my head on a platter."

Wiggins silently cursed his bad luck. But in a heartbeat, everything changed. The girl suddenly stumbled on the uneven pavement, and as she pitched forward, Wiggins grabbed her arm and pulled her backwards. "Cor blimey, miss, this walkway is bloomin' dangerous. Are you alright?"

"Oh thank you," she gasped. "You saved me from a bad fall." She laughed self-consciously as she regained her footing.

He released her elbow and stepped back, giving her a bit of space. "Don't mention it, miss. By the way, my name is Harry Parkson. Are you sure you're alright, miss?"

"I'm fine." She smiled, revealing a set of uneven teeth. "It was just a silly stumble. The council really needs to do something about these pavements. My name is Margery Wardlow."

Wiggins gave her a wide smile and nodded his head politely in acknowledgment of the introduction. "I'm pleased to meet you, Miss Wardlow. If you don't mind my sayin' so, you're still a bit pale. May I buy you a cup of tea? There's a very respectable café just around the corner." Wiggins always took care to find the local cafés when he was on the hunt.

"Oh, I don't know." She hesitated and lowered her lashes coyly. "I really should get on with the shopping."

He sighed regretfully. "I wouldn't like you to get into trouble with your mistress, Miss Wardlow."

"Oh, she'll not be home for ages, and Cook was sneaking off to have a lie down when I left, so I've time for a quick cup of tea, and please call me Margery. I didn't mean it when I said she'd have my head if I was back late. I'm not used to young men speaking to me like you did, and sometimes I say things without thinking when I'm a bit nervous."

"I do the same thing myself, and I'm sorry if I made you nervous," he apologized.

"Oh no, not nervous in a bad way," she said quickly. "Oh dear, I'm doin' it again. Rattling on without thinking."

"You're not rattlin' on at all. Please allow me to escort you to the café, Margery." He took her arm and led her toward the corner.

Wiggins wasn't a vain person, but he knew he was considered handsome by some of the fair sex, and he could see by the change in her expression that she was having a closer look at him. He wasn't above flirting to obtain a bit of information, but sometimes, he wondered if it was wrong to pretend an interest in a young lady when all you really wanted to do was find out who might or might not be a killer. Then he realized he was being foolish; he wasn't deliberately playing with anyone's feelings.

A few minutes later, she was sitting with her back to the window at a small table in the café. Wiggins put her tea and a plate of buns in front of her. "I took the liberty of orderin' us some pastries," he said, using the proper terms he'd learned from Mrs. Goodge and taking pains to pronounce all the words correctly. He had the feeling that Margery was the sort of girl to feel comfortable with good manners.

"Oh how nice," she exclaimed. "But you didn't have to get me a treat. The tea would have been enough."

"It's my pleasure. After all, you did show me where the Evans family lives so I can deliver my note." He gave her a friendly smile as he took the seat opposite. He hoped she'd start talking about the murder. "There's no hurry, though. I'm not expected back until lunchtime. How long have you been at your household?"

She took a sip of tea. "About three months. It's a nice enough place, I suppose. They're not stingy with the food and Mrs. North doesn't make us pay for our own tea and sugar like some households."

"My master is right decent as well." He picked up a bun, split it in half, and put the pieces down on either side of his cup. "I heard there was some trouble at the Evans house?"

"Trouble?" she repeated as she helped herself to a bun. "Oh, you mean that poor woman getting stabbed right in front of their house?"

Finally, he thought. Now maybe he could learn something. "I think that's what I heard my guv say," he murmured. He wasn't sure how much he should reveal.

"Oh, it was absolutely terrible. Someone murdered Miss Evans' old governess just as they were having a tea party. It happened right out on the public street as well." Margery popped a bite of pastry into her mouth.

"That is awful." He shook his head. "I expect she must 'ave been on her way to the party then?"

"Oh no, they'd not seen the woman in years." Margery leaned forward eagerly. "I overheard Mrs. McBain and Mrs. Walters, that's our cook and housekeeper, talking about it this morning. Cook's been working for Mrs. North for years and she knows everything. She was telling Mrs. Walters that the governess had been let go when Miss Rosemary Evans had been sent off to school and that was years ago. She remembers it quite clearly because she said it was scandalous the way the woman carried on when she got the sack."

"What did she do?"

Margery frowned thoughtfully. "I'm not really sure. Mrs. North came thumping down the stairs just then to have a word with Cook so they stopped talking. But the governess must have done something or Cook wouldn't have remembered it all these years."

Wiggins wasn't sure what to ask next. Luckily, he didn't need to say anything, as Margery started talking again.

"This morning I overheard Mrs. North complaining to Mr. Sutton, that's her fiancé, that the murder was going to ruin Miss Evans' wedding plans."

He feigned surprise. "But why should it? I mean, surely it wasn't the poor lady's fault that one of her old servants got murdered outside her house."

"It might not be her fault, but it's certainly got everyone in the neighborhood all upset." Margery smiled smugly. "When they were talking about the murder, Mr. Sutton raised his voice to Mrs. North, and he's never done that before."

Betsy sat in the comfortable overstuffed green chair and waited for Norah to come out of the bedroom. Smythe had wanted to put Leo and Norah into a fancy hotel, but Betsy had insisted they'd be more comfortable with a suite of rooms over a pub. She'd been proved right as well—Norah and Leo had both visibly relaxed when the four-wheeler Smythe hired had pulled up in front of the Three Swans Pub.

The rooms were beautifully furnished without being so posh that her family would be terrified of moving about and making themselves at home. Even better, the Three Swans was on Holland Park Road, less than a quarter of a mile from Upper Edmonton Gardens.

Norah stepped out of the bedroom and closed the door softly. "The rooms are lovely, Betsy," she said. "But it must be costing your fiancé the very earth."

Betsy shrugged. Smythe hadn't told her not to mention his money, but on the other hand, she didn't feel comfortable talking about his private business. "Don't worry about that." She laughed. "What's important is that you're here."

The men had already left. Leo to the East End to see an old auntie of his, and Smythe to start hunting for clues.

"It's wonderful to see you again." Norah sank down on the sofa next to Betsy's chair. "I was afraid I'd never have this chance. I did send letters to our old address, but there was never an answer."

"We were turned out right after you left," Betsy blurted. "The baby had got sick—"

"I know. Mrs. Collier wrote and told me what happened to Amy," Norah interrupted. "I'm sorry I wasn't able to be there for you and Mum."

"You weren't to know," Betsy said quickly. "I mean, you and Leo had moved to Leeds and, well, you had your own lives."

"I should still have done something." Norah turned her head and stared out the window. "But we had no idea things were so bad. I sent Mum a letter from Leeds when Leo got that job at the shipyard in Liverpool."

"I don't think she ever got it," Betsy said softly. "She wrote to you at the Leeds address but we never heard back. Then Amy took a turn for the worse and Mum lost her position—"

Norah interrupted again. "But I did send her a letter. I swear I did."

"Of course you did," Betsy replied.

"You don't sound like you believe me." Norah's eyes filled with tears. "But I swear it's true. I told her Leo had gotten a job at the shipyard in Liverpool and that we were going there."

"I'm sure you did."

"I promised I'd send her our address as soon as we were settled."

"Norah, don't get upset. I know you sent the letter." Betsy laughed uneasily. She'd hoped her first hours with Norah would be filled with joy and laughter, that she'd be able to talk to her about marriage and men and life and all the other things that one could only ask a sister. Oh, she knew the mechanics of what happened on a wedding night—no one who'd been raised in their old neighborhood could be unaware of what went on between male and female. She just wanted a cozy chat. She didn't want to waste what little time they had together with going over old territory that didn't matter one whit anyway. The past was over and done with, and she aimed to keep it that way. They both had built good, decent lives for themselves, and that was that. "Old Mrs. Larson downstairs probably grabbed the letter and kept it. You know how she and Mum didn't get on. She was always playing mean tricks on us."

Norah took a deep breath and got ahold of herself. She laughed self-consciously. "Oh don't mind me, I'm just being silly. You're right. I'll bet that's exactly what happened. Mrs. Larson was a nasty old crone, wasn't she? Now, tell me about that fellow of yours. Are you going to be staying on at the inspector's house after the wedding?"

"I don't know," Betsy admitted. "Smythe told me it's to be a surprise."

Norah looked askance. "You don't know where you'll be living?"

"Well, in all fairness to Smythe, I'm sure it'll be something nice, and it might even be at the inspector's home. The attic could easily be converted into a small flatlet." She broke off with a sigh. "I know, it's odd. But he's a good man and I love him dearly."

"He must love you as well," Norah smiled broadly. "He's certainly spent enough coin getting your family here for the wedding."

CHAPTER 4

Constable Barnes waited until Ellen Crowe took a seat at the long oak table before pulling out a chair and sitting down. He pulled out his pencil and notebook. "Mrs. Crowe, what did the man who came to the door yesterday look like?"

"I wasn't really paying attention, Constable. As I said, I was in a rush to get to the post office. But I'll do my best. He was tall."

Barnes interrupted. "What do you mean by tall? Was he my height?"

"About your height," she replied.

"What color hair did he have?"

"He wore a hat"—she frowned—"but I think his hair might have been reddish brown, and he was wearing a black overcoat. I remember that. That's not very useful, is it? Half the men in London have black overcoats. Oh, I do recall one aspect of his appearance. He was quite pale."

"You're being very helpful, ma'am," he assured her as he scribbled down the description. He finished writing and looked up at her. "How long have you known Miss Moran?"

She drew back slightly, as though she were surprised. "Surely you heard Miss Farley tell the inspector I've been here twelve years."

"Indeed I did, ma'am," he said. "But that doesn't mean you've only known her for twelve years."

Mrs. Crowe cocked her head to one side and stared at him. "What makes you think I was acquainted with her before I came here to live?"

He met her gaze squarely. "Were you?"

She remained silent for so long that he thought she wasn't going to answer, then she sighed and said, "Agatha Moran and I were at school together in Winchester. When she was nineteen, she left to accept a post as a governess and I stayed on as a teacher. No one here knew about our past acquaintance. Both of us preferred it that way."

"Why was that, ma'am?" he asked.

She sat up straighter in the chair. "Miss Moran gave me a substantial discount on my rent. It would be awkward for me if the others knew what I was paying for my room. Though what's going to happen now that she's dead is anyone's guess. I expect it'll take a few months to settle her estate, but even so, I'd better start looking for another place to live."

Barnes had been a policeman far too long to be overly shocked, yet he was taken aback by her words. "Were you fond of Miss Moran?"

"Not really." She gave him a rueful smile. "I know that sounds callous, Constable, but it's the truth. We weren't close friends when we were at school, and after I moved in here, she was my landlady, nothing more."

"Yet she gave you a substantial discount on your rent," he prompted as he grabbed his pencil. "If you weren't good friends, why would she do that?"

"Because she felt guilty, Constable," Ellen Crowe retorted. "You see, the governess position she took all those years ago should have been mine. As I said, Constable, we were at school together. We were the two oldest students and both of us were seeking employment. I'd seen an advertisement for a position with a family in Portsmouth and I'd written to them asking for an interview. The wife, a Mrs. Collins, replied to my letter telling me that as the family was in need of a governess right away and that as she was going to be in Winchester the following week, she'd stop by the school to see me." As she spoke, her voice got harsher and her eyes narrowed as the old, unforgotten resentment resurfaced.

Barnes, who'd been trying to write and watch her at the same time, stopped and gave her his full attention.

"I told Agatha about the interview," she continued. "I was so excited to finally have a chance at a position, and of course the worst happened. On the day I was supposed to meet Mrs. Collins, I came down with the measles. Passing along a nasty disease to one's prospective employer isn't a good idea, so I couldn't risk speaking to her in my condition. I'd given two of my teachers as references, so I asked one of them to please explain the situation to Mrs. Collins." She broke off and laughed. "What a fool I was. My old teacher didn't stand a chance; Agatha Moran met Mrs. Collins at the front gate, and two hours later, she had my position."

Barnes stared at her curiously. Didn't she realize she'd just given him a motive for murder? It wouldn't be the first time someone had waited years to avenge an old wound. "And you stayed on at the school as a teacher?"

"That's correct. Oh dear." She smiled suddenly and shook her head. "You must think me awful. It sounds as if I hated Agatha, but I didn't. If I'd taken the position in Portsmouth, I'd never have met my husband."

"You did sound as if you still resented her." Barnes grabbed the pencil.

"When I think about it, I can still get agitated," she admitted. "But honestly, it was years ago. Even though we weren't friends and hadn't been in touch for years, Agatha did me a great kindness, and she more than made up for what she'd done."

"How did you end up living here?" he asked. He wasn't sure he believed her. She'd certainly sounded more than "agitated" to him.

"When my husband died, I was left with only a small pension," she explained. "One day I happened to run into Agatha at Victoria Station. Odd, but we recognized one another instantly. We went to the café there and had a cup of tea. I told her about my husband and our life together. She told me about the families she'd worked for in Portsmouth and the Isle of Wight and then mentioned she owned a residential hotel for ladies here in London. One thing led to another, and soon enough, I found myself living here at a much more favorable rent than I had been paying. I was happy and grateful to have a decent roof over my head."

He nodded. "Where were you yesterday afternoon?"

"You mean after I left the post office." She gave him an amused smile. "I went to visit a friend in Putney. Her name is Olivia Whitley and she lives at number five River Road in Putney. We spent the afternoon together, and I took the train home. I got here in time for supper."

Hilda Bannister was sitting in a wing chair next to the sofa when Witherspoon got to the landing on the second floor.

His interview with Miss Farley had been very short, as she claimed she'd neither seen nor heard anything suspicious yesterday. He hoped that Constable Barnes was having better luck with Mrs. Crowe.

"There's naught wrong with my hearing," Hilda said as she spotted him. "I might be old, but I'm of sound mind and strong limb." Her face was as wrinkled as a raisin, her eyes watery, and the few wisps of hair she had left were pure white.

"I'm sure you are, Miss Bannister," he said as he sat down on the sofa. "That's why I'm so very anxious to speak with you."

"It took you long enough to get up here," she charged. "I've been waiting."

"I had to speak with Miss Farley," he replied. "I didn't mean to keep you waiting. Now, do you recall what time it was that the man came to speak to Miss Moran yesterday?"

She thought for a moment. "I don't recall exactly what time it was; my clock is in my room and I was out here. But it was sometime in the morning when I heard someone knocking loud enough to wake the dead. Usually Mrs. Middleton takes care of the door, but she was gone to do the shopping, so I guess one of the others must have opened up."

Witherspoon gave her an encouraging nod. "And you were sitting right out here when he was let into the house?"

"That's right, I was sitting here in my usual spot."

"Could you hear what was being said?"

"Not exactly, but I could tell it was a man." She chuckled. "So as I was alone here, I got up and scurried out onto the top step so I could have a listen. Life's awfully boring when you get to be my age. My eyes are weak so I can't read as much as I'd like"—she tapped the cane propped against her cushion—"and with my rheumatism, getting about is a little hard, so whenever there's a bit of excitement in the house, I like to take an interest."

"Yes, of course you do," he answered quickly. He rather admired her willingness to confess to being an eavesdropper. He'd observed that wanting to overhear what others said without being seen was a very common desire, yet very few people would actually admit to such an activity. "Did you hear what the man said?"

"I just heard him yelling that he had to talk to Agatha Moran," she said. "Miss Moran must have heard him shouting as well, because she came out of her office and told him to come with her. They went back inside and she closed the door, more's the pity. It's a very thick door, Inspector, but not thick enough to keep everything quiet. After a little while, I heard her screaming at him like a common fishwife."

"Were you able to make out any of the words?" he asked hopefully.

"She called him names." She grinned, revealing a surprisingly even set of white teeth. "None of the ones I heard were very flattering, either."

Witherspoon wondered if it would be indelicate if he asked her to repeat what she'd heard. He started to speak and then thought better of it. For a lady of her advanced years, perhaps it would be best to get some paper and ask her to write the words.

But before he could suggest that course of action, she continued. "She called him a coward. I heard that one very clearly. I suspect the entire neighborhood heard it, she was shouting it loud enough."

Apparently, she wasn't the least embarrassed to repeat what she'd heard.

"Then she called him a craven, spineless excuse for a man

and told him that if he wasn't going to do anything about it, he should stop wasting her time and just go."

"This is very useful, Miss Bannister," Witherspoon said eagerly. "Please go on."

"They had come out of the office by then and were in the hallway just below. That's why I was able to hear them so clearly."

"How long was the man here?"

She tapped her finger against her chin. "Not long. Certainly not more than ten or fifteen minutes. They were in the office talking quietly for a good part of that time and then she started screaming at him. By the sound of it, he got out of here as fast as possible." She laughed. "I think he was making a run for it, if you know what I mean."

"Did you happen to hear any sort of a response from the man? Did he say anything when Miss Moran raised her voice?"

"Not too much," she replied. "But when he reached the front door, he said something like—" She broke off with a frown. "I want to make sure I repeat what he said correctly."

"I'm sure you'll do just fine." Witherspoon gave her another encouraging smile.

"He said, 'You've no right to ask such a thing of me. The years haven't been kind to me, either, and now that I've a real chance at happiness, I'm not going to risk it for someone I don't even know.' Then he opened the front door and left. He must have not closed it properly, because I heard her run down the hallway, and a second later, she slammed the door shut." Her eyes grew troubled and she looked away. "I think she was crying by then. No, I tell a lie. I know she was. I could hear her sobbing." She sighed. "I felt really awful for her, but I knew she wouldn't appreciate any words of comfort. She wasn't one to show her feelings. That's what was so surprising about the whole incident. Agatha Moran has been my landlady for years, and this is the first time I've ever heard her raise her voice. It was frightening, Inspector, very frightening."

Witherspoon reached over and patted her hand. "I'm sure it was, Miss Bannister. Something had upset Miss Moran dreadfully, and I suspect that whatever trouble the poor woman had found had much to do with her murder. But you must take comfort in the fact that we'll do our very best to find the person who took her life. Are you certain you didn't catch a glimpse of the man? It would be useful if we had some sort of description of him." He knew that Barnes would be able to get a description from Ellen Crowe, but it never hurt to have more than one.

She shook her head. "I tried to move farther down the stairs to get a peek at him, but I wasn't fast enough to see his face. All I saw was a tall, dark blur as he left. These eyes of mine are old. I'm sorry, Inspector. I wish I could help you."

"That's quite alright, ma'am," he said quickly. "Your statement is very useful, and I'm sure it'll help us in our inquiries."

"Good. I liked Agatha Moran. She was decent to me and to everyone else in this house."

Smythe put his hand in his pocket and jingled some coins together as he stepped out of the small shed used by the hansom cab drivers for having a quick cup of tea and taking a break. He'd been all over North London, and so far he'd not found out a blooming thing. He'd questioned all the drivers, but none of them had picked up a woman matching Agatha Moran's description. But as there was also an omnibus stop two streets over from her house, it was likely she might have used the omnibus and not a cab.

He pulled his coat tighter against the chill wind and started across the road. As he dodged past a cooper's van, he spotted a pub and decided to try his luck. There was always gossip to be had in a pub.

He pushed through the door of the Angels Arms Pub, paused just inside, and surveyed the area. It was a good, working-class establishment: plain whitewashed walls, wood floors scratched and scarred with age, and wooden benches along the walls. A small fire burned in the fireplace on the far side of the room, and people crowded up against the bar as all the tables and benches were full. He worked his way through the crowd to the bar and wedged himself between a lad in a porkpie hat and an elderly woman.

The pub was busy, so it took a few minutes to get the barman's attention, but he was in no hurry. He leaned slightly to his left trying to hear what the young man next to him was saying to his companion, a young woman wearing an overcoat and a maid's cap.

Their voices were so low, he couldn't hear a word.

He leaned to his right, trying to hear what a white-haired old dear on that side was talking about, and as Luty would say, he hit pay dirt.

"Eddie Butcher claims that she was being followed. He was outside cleaning the Morrisons' gutters yesterday afternoon when she came out her front door. It had stopped raining for a bit, and Eddie was trying to get the job done so he could be paid. Anyways, he said there was a man that ducked out of the stairwell at the Hogart place, that's the empty building just next to hers, and he trailed after her," the woman said to her companion, a younger dark-haired woman with a basket containing a few wilting flowers on the counter in front of her.

"Don't be daft," basket lady scoffed. "Half the roughs in Barnsbury have been dossing in that stairwell. Besides, you can't believe a word he says. Eddie lies. He makes up tales as easy as water chucks down a drainpipe. Who would possibly want to follow Agatha Moran? The woman was an old stick if there ever was one. My Daisy goes in and cleans at the hotel every month or so when they do the heavy work, and she says the woman is so proper she wouldn't raise her voice if the ruddy room was on fire. She got murdered because she just happened to be at the wrong place at the wrong time. These days, crime is getting terrible."

"What'll you have, sir?" The barman's voice pulled his attention away from the women.

"A pint of bitter," he said quickly.

"I'd not be so sure of that," the other woman shot back. "She was murdered in Bayswater, and that area has more constables than a dog has fleas. Posh areas always get better patrollin' than the rest of us. Besides, the Moran woman might be a proper old stick now, but have you ever wondered where she got the money for that hotel?"

"She saved it up from her wages," basket lady snapped impatiently. "She used to be a governess—"

"Rubbish. No governess makes enough money to buy a house that size and turn it into a moneymakin' business," the other woman retorted. "You didn't live here when Agatha Moran come along, but I did. She bought that property freehold and then spent thousands of pounds makin' the place habitable. Believe me, there was plenty of gossip about her then. The place is huge and it's got a big garden in the back. A place like that doesn't come cheap."

"Maybe she inherited money from her family." Basket lady picked up her glass and drained it.

"Agatha Moran didn't have any family." The elderly woman smiled maliciously. "I told you, my friend cleans for her neighbor every now and again. She said she heard Miss Moran herself say that the reason she opened the hotel was so women like her, women with no family to fall back on, could have a decent place to live."

"That doesn't mean she didn't have family at one time," basket lady insisted as she slapped her empty glass onto the counter. "And I liked her. She was always very pleasant when she came into the shop. She never got impatient when I was servin' other customers and always treated me with courtesy. I'm sorry she's dead."

"Well I'm sorry she's dead, too." The white-haired woman sniffed disapprovingly. "But I think there was someone followin' her that day. You're not the only one who knows someone. My friend Mary Thompson works in the house next door and she told me that there's been two men showin' up at the hotel in the last week. Both of them were nicely dressed—"

Basket lady interrupted. "They were probably bankers or lawyers. Agatha Moran was a businesswoman."

"And a proper businesswoman would have gone to the bank or a solicitor's office," the other woman argued. She suddenly stopped speaking and stared straight at Smythe. "What are you lookin' at?"

Smythe started in surprise. Blast a Spaniard, he really had forgotten how to handle himself when he was on the hunt. He shouldn't have been caught openly eavesdropping. But he recovered quickly. "Forgive me ma'am"—he doffed his cap politely—"but I wasn't meanin' to listen to your conversation, it's just that when I 'eard you speakin', I realized you were talkin' about Miss Agatha Moran's murder."

"So what?" She stared at him suspiciously. "That's no reason for you to be listenin' to someone else's private conversation. Are you a policeman? You don't look like a policeman."

"I'm not a policeman, ma'am." He smiled apologetically. "But I do 'ave a special interest in that particular case. That's why I'm here. I didn't mean to be rude by eavesdroppin' on a private conversation, but I've not had much luck findin' out what I need to know, and if I don't go back with somethin' useful, my guv'll 'ave my guts for garters. Please excuse my bad manners and let me make it up to you by buyin' the both of you a drink." He waved the barman over. "What'll you 'ave?" he asked

He was hoping they'd be so distracted by the prospect of a free drink they wouldn't think to ask what his "special interest" might be.

Basket lady grinned broadly and held up her empty glass to the barman. "Another of these, Alf." She turned to Smythe. "Ta, that's right gentlemanly of you, sir."

"I'll have the same," the elderly lady said quickly before turning her attention to Smythe. "I've never seen you 'round here."

"I don't live in the neighborhood," he replied honestly. "I'm here on business."

"And your business concerns that poor woman who was stabbed to death?" She watched him as she spoke.

"Let's just say I've been hired by an interested party to find out a bit of information about the late Miss Agatha Moran."

"What kind of information?" she asked. She nodded her thanks as the publican put their drinks on the counter.

Smythe handed him a ten-shilling piece. "Keep the change." He waited till the barman turned to serve other customers and then answered her question. "All I'm wantin' is just a bit of information about Miss Moran."

"Are you one of them private inquiry agents?" she asked.

"Don't be daft, Stella," basket lady scoffed. "Can't you see how he's dressed? He's not a private inquiry agent. They always wear them checkered suits with the funny caps."

Smythe had no idea what she was talking about, but he forced himself to laugh. "You're a sharp one, ma'am. I'm not one of them; I'm just hired to do a bit of checkin', that's all."

"Who hired you?" the elderly lady asked as she took a drink.

"I'm not at liberty to say." He smiled to take the sting out of the words. "That's confidential."

"You must be workin' for a newspaper, then," she guessed. "But I've never 'eard of them payin' anyone to find things out. Usually they just print what they like and not give a toss if they get it wrong."

Smythe had no idea whether newspapers did or didn't pay informants, so he just continued smiling at her. "As I said, ma'am, my employer is confidential. But I would appreciate knowin' where I could meet this Eddie Butcher. I'd like to have a chat with him."

Both women stared at him. Basket lady spoke first. "Well now, I'm not sure that Eddie would appreciate me tellin' anyone where he lives. Likes his privacy, he does."

Smythe could take a hint. He reached in his pocket and pulled out a half crown piece and waved it under her nose. "Would this buy me his address?" he asked softly.

"It'll buy it from me." The older woman shoved herself in front of basket lady and stuck out her hand.

"Here, that's mine." Basket lady elbowed her friend aside and snatched the coin out of Smythe's hand. "Eddie dosses at number three Stone Lane. That's in Islington. He's got a bed there."

"Thank you, ma'am," Smythe grinned widely. "Your 'elp is much appreciated."

"Hey, what about me?" the elderly woman complained. "I'm the one that told you about 'im."

Smythe reached back in his pocket and drew out another

coin. Life had been good to him—he could afford to be a bit generous to an old woman. "Of course you did, ma'am," he said as he handed her the coin. "And I appreciate your help." He glanced at the other woman. "I'd also be obliged if both of you would keep this little visit of mine to yourselves."

"What are you doing here?" Mrs. Jeffries put the teapot down next to a plate of brown bread and stared at Betsy. "We didn't expect you to come to the afternoon meeting. You're supposed to be visiting with your sister."

Betsy untied the ribbons of her hat, pulled it off, and hung it on a peg. "We visited for most of the morning, then I realized she was getting tired." She began to unbutton her cloak. "So I decided to come home. I'll see her early tomorrow morning—I'm going there for breakfast with her and Leo. Am I the first one back?"

"Not quite. Wiggins is here. He's gone to wash his hands, Mrs. Goodge is getting another tin of tea out of the larder, and I think I just heard Luty and Hatchet's rig go around the corner," she explained as she unobtrusively took a good look at the maid. Betsy's cheeks were overly bright and her smile a bit forced. But perhaps that was to be expected: A wedding, visiting relatives one hadn't seen for years, and a murder were enough to put a strain on anyone's nerves.

"I'll give my hands a quick wash then as well." Betsy crossed to the sink on the far side of the room. She was glad Smythe wasn't home yet. He'd know in a heartbeat that she was a bit upset. Her time with Norah had been good, but still, after the first few hours, it had suddenly gotten just a little bit awkward between them.

Betsy pumped the handle and shoved her hands under the stream, wincing as it came out cold. She and Norah had been nattering away, asking each other questions, catching up on all the details of their respective lives when they'd suddenly seemed to run out of things to talk about. She shook the water off her hands and reached for the tea towel. But surely that was normal? They'd not seen each other in years. Surely it was natural to be just a little uncomfortable after the first round of questions were all answered. She was startled out of her reverie by the sound of footsteps coming from every direction. Mrs. Goodge shuffled out of the pantry, Wiggins thudded down the back stairs, and it sounded as if half a dozen people were coming along the hallway from the back door.

Smythe came into the kitchen first, shedding his coat and tossing it onto the coat tree before slipping into his seat. He was followed by Luty, Hatchet, and Ruth.

It took a few moments for everyone else to settle down, so Smythe used the time to reach over and plant a quick kiss on Betsy's lips. "Did you 'ave a good day, love?"

"Wonderful." She gave him a wide smile. "And tomorrow, they want us to have breakfast with them. I told Norah it would have to be very early, but she said that's fine; she's asked the pub kitchen to have it ready at half past seven."

He nodded, gave her hand a squeeze under the table, and then turned his attention to Mrs. Jeffries, who took her place at the head of the table and started pouring the tea. The others slipped into their seats.

"If no one has any objection, I should like to go first," Ruth announced. "I've a guest coming in less than half an hour. It's a friend who might know something about our case so I don't want to keep her waiting."

Mrs. Jeffries handed her a cup of tea. "By all means, go right ahead."

"Thank you. I went along to the shops closest to Chepstow Villas and had a word with some of the clerks." She looked at Betsy. "I must say, I don't know how you manage to learn so much. I didn't hear anything useful whatsoever. I don't think I'm very good at getting shopkeepers to talk. Every time I mentioned Agatha Moran's name, either they'd never heard of her or another customer came into the place. It was most discouraging."

"Now you mustn't think that way and you mustn't give up." Betsy smiled sympathetically. "But I do know what you mean. Sometimes it's very hard. There have been lots of times when I couldn't find out anything, either. It just happens that way sometimes. But you get better at it with practice."

Ruth reached for the cream pitcher. "Well, I shall endeavor to do my best tomorrow. I won't have it said that I've let you all down."

"We'd never say such a thing," Mrs. Goodge exclaimed. "Even if you can't get a word out of those shopkeepers, you do your fair share. You've helped us lots of times."

Ruth gave her a grateful smile. "That's very kind of you, Mrs. Goodge."

"Bein' as Ruth has to leave soon, maybe I'd better say what I heard today," Luty said. "Not that I'm implyin' the rest of you didn't learn things worth tellin', but there does seem to be a bunch of long faces around this table . . ." She looked pointedly at Hatchet.

"I'll have you know, madam," he told her, "I am being polite and waiting my turn."

"Go ahead, Luty," Mrs. Jeffries said quickly. "What did you find out?"

"The Evans family has got plenty of money, and from the gossip I heard, Mrs. Evans is usin' their fortune to improve her social standin'." Luty grinned. "Gossip is that Arabella Evans has been huntin' for a titled husband for her daughter for the past two years. She almost gave up before she found Sir Madison Lowery."

"What took her so long?" Mrs. Goodge asked. "There's no shortage of impoverished aristocrats in this country."

"Apparently Sir Madison was on the continent for a time, then he was married, then a widower," Luty explained. "Luckily, he came back on the marriage market about a year ago. He was introduced to Rosemary Evans at a dinner party given by Margaret Porter Hains."

"I know her," Ruth interjected. "We met at a dinner party last summer. I can't say that I liked her very much. She seemed to think trying to get women the right to vote was a waste of time."

Mrs. Jeffries didn't want them distracted by a debate on the merits of women's suffrage. "What else did you learn, Luty?"

"Not too much. Sir Madison doesn't come cheap, though. My source told me he insisted on a cash settlement before he'd make Rosemary Evans his bride."

"A cash settlement." Smythe frowned. "You mean he took money for proposin' to the girl?"

"Sir Madison isn't doin' anythin' plenty of other poor aristocrats haven't done," Mrs. Goodge pointed out. "These people don't marry for love, Smythe."

"I know that," he protested. "But 'e sounds a right callous sort."

"I don't think he's quite as bad as I'm makin' out," Luty admitted. "My sources told me he was right open and aboveboard about what he wanted."

"And what would that be?" Hatchet helped himself to another slice of bread.

"He asked for and got a marriage settlement that gives him a house and a bit of cash once the vows are said." She paused. "Strange, isn't it? What the newly rich will do to climb up a rung or two on the social ladder. It ain't as if Sir Madison was any sort of prize."

"What do you mean?" Betsy asked.

"Well, my source said that Sir Madison is a very minor aristocrat. As a matter of fact, there was some gossip that he had no right to use the 'sir' in front of his name, and what's more, it's his second marriage."

"His first wife died," Mrs. Goodge added. "Oh sorry, I didn't mean to interrupt you." She smiled apologetically at Luty. "I'll wait my turn."

Luty waved her hand. "That's alright. I was finished."

Mrs. Jeffries looked at the cook. "Why don't you tell us the rest of what you learned?"

"It wasn't much. I just happened to stumble across that information about Sir Madison Lowery when I was tryin' to find out a bit about the Evans family, and I was only askin' questions about them because no one who came through this kitchen today knew anythin' about Agatha Moran." She sighed and reached for the teapot. "Honestly, I'm no snob, but it is so much easier when the victim is from the upper classes. There's always plenty of gossip about *them*." She poured herself another cup.

"Now Mrs. Goodge, you mustn't get disheartened," Mrs. Jeffries warned. "We never know what information is going to be useful at this stage of the investigation."

"I know that." She added milk to her tea. "But gettin' a bit of old gossip doesn't seem like much of a contribution."

"Gossip is always good," Ruth interjected. "It's certainly helped on lots of our other cases. So, what else did you hear?"

"Supposedly, Sir Madison inherited the house he lives in now from his first wife," Mrs. Goodge said. "She was one of the Birmingham Trents."

Mrs. Jeffries raised her eyebrows. Death was always a detail of interest. "How did the first wife die?"

"My source didn't know"—Mrs. Goodge took a quick

drink and swallowed—"but I've got other sources comin' through tomorrow, so I should learn a bit more fairly soon."

"Did you find out anything else?" Mrs. Jeffries asked.

"Only that Lowery hadn't gotten much of a marriage settlement from his first wife's family, only the house and a bit of money. Rumor has it that he's gotten through the money and that he was lookin' for a rich woman to marry when he met Rosemary Evans."

"Do we know if Sir Madison had ever met Agatha Moran?" Wiggins asked.

"My source didn't seem to think so," the cook replied.

"So if he'd never met the woman," Wiggins continued, his expression thoughtful, "he'd not have a reason to murder her."

"But we can't possibly know that," Betsy argued. "It's too early to make any assumptions about who does or doesn't have a reason to have killed Agatha Moran."

"I agree, Betsy," Mrs. Jeffries said. "We can't possibly know what relationships people might have with one another or what information will turn out to be important."

"When are they getting married?" Betsy asked.

"The same day as you," Wiggins said quickly. "They've been engaged for over six months."

Betsy looked at the footman. "Are you sure? I thought the inspector told Mrs. Jeffries the family was celebrating the engagement yesterday afternoon when the murder happened."

"They've been celebratin' ever since the couple got engaged," Wiggins supplied. "I had a chat with one of the housemaids from the house next door and I found out a few things." He told them about his encounter with Margery Wardlow.

As was his habit, once he'd escorted the maid to the

shops, he'd found a quiet spot, pulled out his little brown notebook, and written down everything she'd told him. It wasn't that he didn't trust his memory, but he knew from painful experience the importance of details and didn't want to forget even the smallest or most insignificant fact.

"Now that is interesting," Mrs. Jeffries muttered. "Agatha Moran's parting with the Evans household was not a happy one. Years later, she ends up stabbed right in front of their house."

"I know that coincidences happen," Luty said. "But I don't think this is one. There's a reason she was murdered right in that spot."

"Maybe she was on her way to the Evans house," Smythe speculated. "Maybe someone didn't want her goin' inside."

"That certainly sounds like a reasonable assumption," Mrs. Jeffries agreed, but then she caught herself. "No, no, we mustn't start speculating until we have more facts." She glanced at Wiggins. "Anything else?"

"Not really," he replied.

"What did you mean about the Evanses celebrating ever since the couple got engaged?" Betsy asked. She was more curious than anything else.

"Sir Madison Lowery and Rosemary Evans have been officially engaged since June. They've had one social occasion after another in celebration of the upcomin' nuptials." He grinned. "Leastways that's what Margery told me. She said there's been balls, teas, dinners, and everythin' else you could imagine. She also said that her mistress, Mrs. North, had been complainin' to her fiancé that the murder was going to ruin the weddin' and that seemed to upset the fellow so much he started yellin'. Margery said she'd never heard him raise his voice before."

"Is this Mrs. North engaged as well then?" Mrs. Goodge

asked. When the footman nodded, she continued, "Good gracious, is everyone in London gettin' married?"

Mrs. Jeffries went on full alert. Any behavior exhibited by someone in the vicinity of the murder was cause for them to take a second look. "Did Margery Wardlow have any idea why Mrs. North's fiancé would get upset over a neighbor's wedding being ruined?" she asked.

She was careful to keep her tone calm and even. She didn't want the others giving this particular tidbit of information too much importance. Everyone, including herself, was prone to speculation, and at this stage in the investigation that could lead to disastrous consequences.

"I asked her the very same thing," he answered proudly. "But she'd no idea why Mr. Sutton got so upset."

"Sounds like we ought to broaden our inquiries a bit," Smythe said. "You know, include the neighbors and see if any of them had a reason to want Agatha Moran dead."

"That's a good idea," Mrs. Jeffries said. She looked at Wiggins. "Do you know where this Mr. Sutton lives?"

Wiggins was ready for that question. "He lives on Marsdale Street in Shepherds Bush, but he spends most of his evenin's with Mrs. North. She's in the house right next to the Evans place."

"What does he do durin' the day?" Luty asked.

"He's a barrister," Wiggins replied. "He tripped over a crack in the pavement and went sprawlin' at Mrs. North's feet. That's how the two of them met. Margery thought it very funny, seein' as how she only went and had tea with me because she tripped over the very same crack and I saved her from a bad fall."

"Sounds like that pavement crack has a lot to answer for," Ruth murmured as she rose to her feet. "I'm afraid I must go. My friend will be at the front door any minute now, and

I think she might be a good source of information. She knows everyone in London." She waved the men, all of whom had started to get up, back into their seats and grabbed her coat off the peg.

"We'll give you a full report of everything you miss," Mrs. Jeffries promised.

"And I'm finished," Wiggins said.

"I'll see you all tomorrow," she called over her shoulder as she hurried to the back door.

"May I have another cup of tea?" Hatchet pushed his empty cup toward the housekeeper.

"Of course." Mrs. Jeffries poured him more tea. "Would you care to go next?"

"This pains me greatly, but I must admit, I learned nothing today about our case." He sighed and reached for his cup. "But I've several sources to see tomorrow, so I'm sure I'll be able to make some sort of contribution to the cause of justice." In actuality, he planned on seeing two excellent sources of gossip.

"Of course you will, Hatchet," Mrs. Jeffries assured him.

"Some days are like that," Luty said. "No matter how hard we try, we jes don't have much luck in findin' out our bits and pieces."

"I'll go next then," Smythe volunteered. He gave Betsy a quick smile and saw that she was staring off into the distance. "I had a bit of luck today."

"With the hansom cab drivers?" Wiggins asked eagerly.

Smythe shook his head. "No, I talked to half a dozen and none of 'em recall droppin' a fare anywhere near Chepstow Villas." He glanced at Betsy again and saw that she was looking at him with interest. "I think Miss Moran must have taken an omnibus to Notting Hill, not a cab. Anyways, I noticed there was a pub just around the corner from her hotel so I went in and had a listen. I got lucky.

Two women were havin' a nice old natter about Agatha Moran."

"What did they say?" Mrs. Jeffries flicked a look at the clock. Time was getting on and the inspector might be home any minute now.

"One of them was dead certain that Agatha Moran was bein' followed yesterday. The other lady was equally certain the bloke that reported seein' Miss Moran bein' trailed told tales as easily as most people breathe. But I managed to get his name and address and I'm goin' to find out tomorrow exactly what it was he saw," he said. He went on to give them a full report of his conversation in the pub. Like the others, he took great care to recall every detail, no matter how small.

"Why didn't you have a word with this Eddie Butcher before you came home?" Mrs. Goodge asked.

"He wasn't home," Smythe explained. "One of the other boarders in the room told me Butcher makes his livin' doin' casual labor. But he's usually in his room early of a mornin' . . ." He trailed off and looked at Betsy. "Oh no, I forgot we're havin' breakfast with your family tomorrow mornin'."

"Not to worry, I'll come up with an excuse for you," she said. "Finding Butcher is more important than a family breakfast. You'll have lots of time to get to know Norah and Leo."

He smiled gratefully and squeezed her hand. "Thank you, love." He turned to the others. "That's all I've got."

"Then I suppose it is my turn," Mrs. Jeffries announced. "I went and had a look at the area where Miss Moran was stabbed."

"You were takin' an awful chance." Mrs. Goodge clucked her tongue. "What if the inspector had seen you?"

"I took care that he didn't. Besides, Wiggins, Smythe, and Ruth were all in that neighborhood today."

"But we're used to dodgin' our inspector and the constables that know us on sight," Wiggins interjected.

"As I said, I took great care not to be seen." Mrs. Jeffries tried not to be offended, but nonetheless, her feelings were a tad hurt. Just because she didn't go out on a regular basis didn't mean she wasn't up to the game. "And I had a good reason for going there. I wanted to see precisely where the woman had been killed and more importantly, who could possibly have been a witness." She reached for her cup. "I examined the area thoroughly. From what I could tell, there were two or possibly three houses directly opposite where anyone looking out the window might have seen the killer. Additionally, someone on the upper floors of the house next to the Evans home could also have been a witness."

"But it was dark," Mrs. Goodge pointed out.

"And there is a perfectly good streetlamp less than two feet from the Evanses' gate, so there would have been plenty of illumination," Mrs. Jeffries replied.

"So what are you thinkin', Hepzibah?" Luty asked curiously. "I know you've come to some conclusion or you wouldn't have brung this up."

"You're correct," she said. "I know I'm always warning that we mustn't come to any conclusions too early in the case, but I think that in this instance, some of our earlier speculation might be correct." She knew she was treading on dangerous ground here, but she'd suddenly decided that in this case, they were right.

"What does that mean?" Mrs. Goodge demanded.

"It wasn't even late in the evening when she was murdered. There were half a dozen places where witnesses might have seen the murderer."

"In other words, the killer took a huge risk," Betsy muttered.

"This leads me to believe one thing." She smiled at Smythe and Wiggins. "Your earlier assumption was correct. Whoever murdered Agatha Moran needed her dead before she went into the Evans house."

CHAPTER 5

"I'm so glad you were able to come on such short notice," Ruth said as she gestured for her guest to sit down. They were in the formal drawing room, the one she rarely used because it was quite uncomfortable. The French Empire–style furniture was upholstered in heavy red and gold striped satin, there weren't any decent carpets large enough to completely cover the cold, gray slate floors, and the ceilings were so high that even with fires roaring in both the marble fireplaces, the room was as icy as a tomb. But Ruth didn't think that Lady Mortmain was the sort of woman who would appreciate the warmth and coziness of the small sitting room. From what she knew of the woman, she was a stickler for social etiquette.

Lydia Mortmain was a woman of medium height. She was slender and her every movement was executed with grace and precision. She wore her lustrous black hair pulled back in a large knot at the nape of her neck. The style was severe, but it suited her very well in that it focused attention on her brilliant blue eyes. Her features were in perfect proportion, her skin was porcelain, and even though Ruth knew she was well into her forties, she appeared a good ten years younger.

Like Ruth, she was a widow, but that's where the similarity between them ended. On the very day the mourning period for her late husband ended, Lady Lydia had gone on the hunt for another spouse. Rumor had it that the late, unlamented Lord Elwood Mortmain, like so many of his class, had a title and not much else. Ruth had some sympathy for Lady Lydia's plight. It wasn't as if the woman would have any success in finding employment. Like most of her class, she'd been educated in every aspect of social decorum and protocol, but not much else.

"I was free because Count Medrano broke his leg and had to cancel tonight's dinner party." Lydia smiled slightly. "I was surprised to get your note." She expertly smoothed out the overskirt of her elaborate blue day dress as she sank onto the couch.

Ruth held her breath, hoping the poor woman wouldn't go sliding onto the carpet. That was another reason she rarely used the room: The furniture was dangerous. One false move against the slippery fabric and you'd end up on the floor. But Lydia was apparently skilled in handling such delicate social matters; she dug the heels of her high-topped leather shoes into the slate and slid back onto the seat.

"I'm sure you were." Ruth gave her a friendly smile. "I'm very grateful you were able to come and visit with me. I know how very busy you are." She studied her for a brief moment. She'd spent a good deal of time wondering what approach to take with her guest.

Lydia cocked her head to one side. "Very clever. You've

managed to compliment me and avoid answering my question."

"I need some information," Ruth explained. Among the serious-minded women of the London Society for Women's Suffrage, Lydia was seen as a simpleminded social butterfly. But Ruth realized that simply wasn't true. Lydia was no fool. "And as you know more about the social circles in London than anyone else of my acquaintance, I was hoping you could help me."

Taken aback, she blinked in surprise. "I don't know whether to be insulted or flattered."

"Oh, please be flattered; I meant it as a compliment," Ruth said earnestly. "I've never been particularly good at the social aspect of society. Sometimes the late Lord Cannonberry would be quite cross with me. I was forever forgetting which fork to use or the proper way to address a viscount."

Lydia stared at her for a moment and broke into a wide smile. "I know just what you mean." She rose to her feet. "But if we're going to have a nice chat about who is who in London, can we move to another room? My back is strained from trying not to slide off this settee and I'm freezing."

Ruth got up as well. "Of course, there's a very cozy room right down the hall. I don't like this room, either; it's terribly uncomfortable. But my husband's relatives are always telling me it's the one that must be used for proper social occasions."

As they went down the hall and into the small sitting room, Ruth began to drop the few names they had about the case. By the time they were settling into two overstuffed, comfortable chairs in front of the fire and the butler had brought a small, silver tray with two glasses of sherry, she'd managed to mention just about every name she could recall.

Lydia Mortmain picked up her drink and took a sip. "I've heard of Sir Madison Lowery, of course. He's quite well-known. It's also well-known that he was in the market for a rich wife until he got engaged to the Evans girl. But most people who had any money had the good sense to keep their daughters well away from him."

"Why? Because he wanted to marry well?"

"Of course not." Lydia laughed. "There's nothing wrong in wanting to make a favorable match. I'm looking to do the same myself, but then again, my late husband died of influenza while under the care of a good doctor. He didn't die under mysterious circumstances."

"What kind of mysterious circumstances?" Ruth asked.

Lydia leaned toward her. "Beatrice Trent Lowery died of food poisoning. That isn't particularly mysterious in and of itself. What makes it interesting is the talk that circulated about town when the poor woman died. Apparently, she and Sir Madison had eaten the very same meal, but she was the only one that became *seriously* ill."

"I take it he became ill as well," Ruth guessed.

"Supposedly, but she died and he didn't." She fingered the edge of the crystal glass. "But what really got the tongues wagging was the fact that he took his time in calling for a doctor. As a matter of fact, some of the gossips actually said he didn't call for help at all. His housekeeper became alarmed so she slipped out and fetched the physician. When the doctor arrived, Sir Madison was barely ill while Beatrice was quite literally at death's door."

"How awful," Ruth said softly. "Food poisoning is a terrible way to die."

"Her father wasn't convinced her death was natural," Lydia continued.

"Did he call the police?" Ruth sipped her sherry.

"No." Lydia frowned slightly. "The family friend that

had introduced Beatrice to Lowery managed to persuade her father that the death was one of those tragedies that occasionally happens. Besides, how could one possibly prove it wasn't food poisoning?"

"They could have done a postmortem," Ruth suggested.

Lydia sniffed derisively. "The Trents? You must be joking; they'd have moved heaven and earth to keep their daughter's body from being violated in such a manner."

"But if they suspected foul play," Ruth argued, "surely that would take precedence over their sensibilities."

"If the decision had been up to Mr. Trent alone, he might have allowed it," Lydia said thoughtfully. "But Mrs. Trent had a breakdown of some sort, and I don't think she could have stood anything being done to Beatrice's body. She was their only child, and even though both the Trents were devastated by her death, poor Mrs. Trent almost went out of her mind."

"But that's all the more reason they should have wanted justice for her," Ruth declared.

Lydia raised an eyebrow. "It's not as if there was any real proof that Sir Madison had done anything wrong. He had his defenders as well. Gossip is all well and good, but I don't think anyone, even the Trents, were willing to risk a lawsuit by openly accusing the man of murder."

Ruth tapped her fingers against the arm of her chair. "So what did they do?"

"The Trents went back to Birmingham a few weeks after the funeral." Lydia grinned suddenly. "Yet not before Mr. Trent tried to evict Lowery from the house. But Sir Madison was one step ahead of the family and he brought in the lawyers. Trent probably realized it would be a long, hard-fought battle to get him out."

"Whose house was it?" Ruth asked.

"It had been a wedding gift to both of them," Lydia explained. "But right after they'd married, they'd both done wills leaving the other *all* their property. Her family wasn't pleased when they found this out, but there wasn't anything they could do about it. Then Mrs. Trent's health began to get worse, and the rest of the family, the aunts and uncles and cousins, all put their two pence–worth in and decided it wasn't worth the battle. Besides, the Trents are as rich as cream. Her father only wanted to evict Lowery because he blamed him for his daughter's death. But his animosity toward Lowery was impacting Mrs. Trent's close friendship with Margaret Porter Hains. She's the one who vouched for Lowery's character. She introduced him to Beatrice as well."

Ruth shook her head in admiration. "You are incredibly well informed."

"I have to be," Lydia replied. "The only way a woman like myself can survive is by having the right information at hand. You might as well know that Margaret Hains introduced Rosemary Evans to Sir Madison. That's another catch for him as well. The Evans family is very rich. Gracious, I wonder if she charges a finder's fee—she certainly ought to . . ." She broke off and laughed. "Goodness, I do sound like a catty old thing, don't I?"

Ruth laughed. "Not at all, I find your honesty very refreshing, and you've been very helpful to me."

"Then answer this for me. Is it true you help your friend, that famous policeman who's always in the newspapers, with his cases?"

She thought about denying it, but then realized that was foolish. Besides, Lydia Mortmain had been honest with her. "Is that what people say about me?"

"A few," Lydia hedged. "But it's not really common gossip if that's what you're frightened about."

"I don't help him, at least not in the way one might think," she admitted. "But when he's got a case, I do try to find out what I can about the people involved. Sometimes passing on a bit of chitchat can be very useful to him. But he certainly doesn't ask me to do it."

"But I'll bet he listens to everything you have to tell him, doesn't he?" Lydia said.

"Indeed he does," she replied proudly. "Unlike many of his gender, he has a genuine respect for a woman's words. He's an excellent listener and a dear man who is a very special friend."

"You help him because you want to, don't you?" Lydia regarded her steadily. "Well in that case, I've got another bit of gossip to pass along. Lowery has a lodger living with him. A man by the name of Christopher Selby. He's told everyone that Selby is his long lost cousin or some such nonsense, but his housekeeper told my maid that Selby pays him a very large monthly rent. This means that he is running out of money. I'm not surprised about that, either, because I know that he's been selling off some of the fittings and furnishings they got as wedding presents from her family."

"How did you find that out?"

"I saw him at the same antique shop where I was selling some of my late husband's things so I could pay my dressmaker's bill. Honestly, I don't know what I'm going to do if I can't find another rich husband. This time, I'll make sure he doesn't have a packet of relatives with their hands out."

"Oh dear, you've had to support your husband's family?"

Lydia laughed harshly. "Not voluntarily. Elwood's body wasn't even cold before his mother and brothers charged through our house grabbing everything. They claimed everything of value that we had belonged to the 'family estate' and not to my husband personally. They carted off paintings, porcelains, all of my beautiful carpets, and every piece of silver they could get their hands on. I only managed to keep some of my jewels because my sister had the good sense to grab the jewelry chest and climb out onto the roof until they were gone."

"That's so unfair!" Ruth cried.

"It most certainly was." Lydia nodded in agreement. "But there was nothing I could do about it. They had the law on their side; I couldn't prove the Caravaggio or the Donatello belonged to my late husband. I'm not going to let that happen to me again, that's for certain. The next time I marry it'll be to a nice, ordinary rich man."

"That's very wise of you," Ruth said. "But I still think you were treated abominably. I very much appreciate all you've told me. I'll pass the information along to the inspector. If there's ever anything I can do for you—"

Lydia interrupted. "There is. I'd like you to introduce me to Jonathan March. You do know him, don't you? I saw you with his sister at the Edmondsons' autumn ball and you seemed to be great friends with her. I've been trying to meet him for ages now; he's rich, and the only family he has is a sister!"

Upstairs, the front door slammed shut, startling all of them. Mrs. Jeffries leapt up. "Oh dear, it's the inspector. He's home earlier than usual."

Luty and Hatchet rose to their feet as well. "We'll go out the back," Luty said. Hatchet grabbed their garments off the coat tree and draped Luty's voluminous wrap over her shoulder. "We'll be here for the morning meeting," he called as he hustled his employer toward the back door.

Mrs. Jeffries nodded and ran for the back stairs. The inspector was hanging up his bowler as she stepped into the front hall. "Good evening, sir. We were so busy downstairs we didn't hear your hansom pull up out front."

"That's because I walked home from the station." He unbuttoned his coat and hung it up.

"From Ladbroke Road?" she asked, referring to the local station where he and Constable Barnes were assigned. "But I thought you were going to be in Islington today, at the Moran house."

"I was at the Moran home and Constable Barnes and I were making a good deal of progress when I got a message calling us back to the Yard. By the time I'd finished the meeting with Chief Inspector Barrows, it was too late in the afternoon to go all the way back to Islington, so we went to the station to write up our reports."

"Oh dear, sir. I hope the chief inspector wasn't expecting an arrest this early in the investigation," she said sympathetically. She edged him toward the drawing room. He could do with a nice glass of sherry.

Witherspoon smiled wearily. "The chief inspector isn't quite that unreasonable, but he made it quite clear the Home Office wanted everything cleared up before Christmas." He sighed. "I don't know what it is about politicians that makes them believe setting a timetable to apprehend a killer is remotely possible."

"Of course it isn't, sir. But perhaps as you've had such success in the past, they're of the opinion that you'll come through yet again." They'd reached the open doorway to the drawing room. "Would you care for a glass of Harveys, sir?"

"That sounds wonderful," he agreed. "But only if you'll join me."

She stepped past him and went to the liquor cabinet on the far side of the room. "Of course I will, sir. You know that I want to hear all about your day. Mrs. Goodge says dinner won't be ready for another half hour."

He went to his favorite overstuffed chair and sat down.

She poured the amber-colored liquid into two glasses, recorked the bottle, and picked up their drinks. She handed him his sherry and sank down on the settee next to his chair. "Were you able to find out anything useful from Miss Moran's tenants?" she asked.

He took a sip before he answered. "Actually, as I said, we were making very good progress today. That's what was so annoying about being interrupted and having to go all the way across town. I'd just finished interviewing an elderly lady who had quite a bit to say when the message came. Constable Barnes had learned some very useful information as well."

"Oh dear, that's most unfortunate." She clucked her tongue sympathetically.

"Now, of course, since everyone in the house seems to feel they've already made their statements, my fear is that the ladies will all get together and begin talking among themselves about what they said."

"People do like to talk, sir." She stared at him curiously. "Why shouldn't they speak to one another about the case?"

"Because I've a feeling there was more information to be had," he replied. "And once they all start chatting with each other, they'll influence one another if we conduct more interviews. There was one lady, a Miss Farley, who claimed she neither heard nor saw anything pertinent to the case. Yet after I thought about what I'd learned from Mrs. Middleton and Miss Bannister, I realized that Miss Farley might be mistaken in thinking she'd nothing to say."

"I don't understand," Mrs. Jeffries admitted.

"Agatha Moran came home from a six-month tour of the continent last week. According to Mrs. Middleton, her housekeeper, except for being a bit tired, she was as right as rain when she got in. The next morning, Miss Moran immediately set to work. She took all the hotel receipts, correspondence, and even the old newspapers into her office, and when she emerged a few hours later, her entire demeanor had altered. From that moment until she left the house to go Bayswater and her own death, her behavior was strange and erratic. Everyone in the house noticed."

"So why didn't Miss Farley . . ." Mrs. Jeffries broke off. "I see what you mean, sir."

"Good, I was afraid I wasn't expressing myself very well. I know that sometimes I get a bit muddled—"

She interrupted. "You're not muddled, sir." She stared at him over the rim of her glass. She liked to think that she and the others were one of the primary reasons for his success as a detective, but occasionally, such as now, she wasn't so sure. Sometimes his observations about human behavior were right on the mark, and occasionally she thought he'd have been a success even without their help. "You were very clear and you're right to be concerned. When you do interview Miss Farley again, you don't want her statement to have been influenced by anyone else."

"My point precisely. We took statements from four people today, and I daresay, only one of them will have the good sense not to discuss the matter—she's the mother of a police constable." He smiled proudly. "She recognized me straight away. I didn't even have to introduce myself."

"How very interesting, sir."

"Indeed it was," he agreed. "Jane Middleton is a very intelligent woman. Her statement was very concise and her observations I'm sure will turn out to be important. But the entire episode was a bit strange."

"Strange in what way?" Mrs. Jeffries asked.

He told her about their meeting with the Moran housekeeper.

Mrs. Jeffries listened carefully as he gave her the details of the encounter. "Gracious, it sounds as if she was expecting something awful to happen to Agatha Moran," she observed when he'd finished.

"She was," he agreed as he took a quick sip. "But it was one of those situations where she felt very helpless. She could tell that her employer was terribly agitated and upset about something, but Miss Moran wouldn't tell her what it was."

"You don't think she was holding anything back out of respect?" Mrs. Jeffries pressed. "Women sometimes do that when they think they're protecting a friend's good name or reputation."

He shook his head. "I don't think so. She seemed quite relieved to be talking to us."

"Why hadn't she gone to the police when Miss Moran didn't come home last night?"

"She told me she was afraid that Miss Moran had done something she oughtn't to have done and that by going to the police, she might get her into trouble."

"In other words, she was afraid that Agatha Moran was going to be the one to commit a crime," she mused.

"That was the impression I had," he admitted. "But Jane Middleton isn't a fool. She told us that if we'd not come to the house when we did, she was going to go to the local police station to report her employer missing."

"And she was certain that Agatha Moran's leaving the house yesterday afternoon had something to do with the Evanses?" Mrs. Jeffries wanted to make certain she had understood him correctly.

"Oh yes, she was sure of that. The only connection she knew of between them was that Miss Moran had been the Evanses' governess, but that was years ago. Naturally, Mrs. Middleton's comments will insure that I examine all of them far more closely, but when Constable Barnes gave me the particulars of his interview with Mrs. Ellen Crowe, it became obvious we ought to look in more than one direction. Mrs. Crowe wasn't overly fond of Agatha Moran, either." He finished his sherry, put the glass down, and leaned toward her, his expression earnest. "Naturally, she didn't come out and tell Barnes that she didn't like Miss Moran; as a matter of fact, she said just the opposite. But he told me that as he was taking her statement, he noticed how angry she became as she recalled an incident in their mutual past." He repeated everything Barnes had told him on the hansom ride to Scotland Yard.

Mrs. Jeffries wished she could take notes. There was simply so much new information to absorb. She forced herself to concentrate on what he was saying even though her mind was already churning with new ideas and theories.

"Then I got quite a bit more information out of Miss Hilda Bannister," he continued. "She's a very elderly woman but she's most certainly of sound mind. She's not addled or senile."

Slightly dazed by the barrage of new facts, she stared at him as he told her about that interview. When he'd finished, she said, "Gracious, no wonder you were annoyed when you were interrupted and called to the Yard."

"Indeed, it was very frustrating." He got to his feet. "Just as I'd thought of some excellent questions to ask, Constable Barnes appeared at the head of the stairs and said we had to go, that there was a constable downstairs calling us to the Yard. And for what? For the same nonsensical warnings I get every time I've a case. Honestly, Mrs. Jeffries, you'd think that by this time the chief inspector would understand that I know a December murder has to be cleared up by Christmas."

"I'm sorry Smythe had to leave so quickly." Betsy smiled apologetically and picked up her fork. They were having breakfast in Norah and Leo's sitting room. Smythe had paid extra when he made the booking for private dining facilities to be provided to her family for their meals. "But he does have work."

"It's alright." Leo gave her a friendly smile. "We understand, a man's got to work."

"But he'll be here this evening for dinner," she said quickly. "And we'll all have a chance to spend time together so you can get to know him better."

"You're very lucky in your household." Norah reached for another piece of toast. "Most places wouldn't let a mere housemaid have so much time off."

Betsy's eyes narrowed. She wasn't used to thinking of herself as a "mere housemaid." "Our inspector is very good to us. He wasn't raised in a grand house with servants, so he treats us decently, the way people ought to be treated."

"Of course he does," Leo said. "Your Inspector Witherspoon sounds like a very good man. I'm jolly glad we've all got this opportunity to be together. Norah and I had thought to come back to England sometime for a visit, but we couldn't ever have afforded to come like this. Your Smythe is a generous man—"

"I still can't understand how a coachman can have so much money," Norah interrupted with a sweet smile.

Betsy shrugged. She'd spent half the night wondering if she ought to tell Norah and Leo the truth about Smythe's money. Norah was important to her, and she didn't like having secrets between them, but she'd finally decided to say nothing. Smythe's finances were his business. If he wanted Norah and Leo to know how rich he was, he could tell them himself. "He doesn't talk about his finances with me. He just asked me if I wanted my sister and her family at the wedding. When I said I did, he promised he'd take care of the matter. Mind you, you weren't easy to find, so that cost him a bit as well."

Norah flushed and looked away. "Sorry, I didn't mean to pry."

"That's alright." Betsy laughed. She was suddenly glad she'd not told Norah that Mrs. Jeffries had said the inspector wanted her to take this entire week off to be with her family and get ready for her wedding. She turned to her brother-in-law. "How do you like Canada? Is it very different from England?"

"The difference is like chalk and cheese. Canada's a wonderful country. No one in Halifax judges you on who your ancestors were. There, a man is known by the work he does with his own two hands. It's a good life." Leo grinned proudly. "We're saving up to buy a house. In another year or two, we'll have enough. Norah's a fine little money manager, and I make a good wage."

"It sounds a wonderful place. I just wish it wasn't so far away from here." Betsy forked the last bite of egg into her mouth.

"Perhaps next time you can come see us," Norah suggested. "The inspector would let you both take a holiday, wouldn't he?"

Betsy nodded. "Of course. What are you going to do today?" When she'd walked in this morning and seen Leo wearing a suit and Norah the same traveling outfit she'd arrived in, Betsy was certain they had plans that didn't include sitting in the parlor visiting with her. She'd been relieved, because now she could do her part on this case, and just a little hurt, as she'd have thought her sister would want to spend as much time with her as possible.

"We planned to go out to Reading and visit my grandmother," Leo said. "She'll be ever so pleased to see us."

"I hope you don't mind," Norah added. "Leo and I thought you'd have a lot to do to get ready for the wedding and that you wouldn't mind if we nipped off to see his family. His gran's so old she'd never be able to come to Canada and see us, even if we could afford it."

"Of course I don't mind." Betsy felt petty. "And please invite her to the wedding."

Norah gave her a quick frown. "I wasn't hinting."

"I know that." Betsy stood up. She'd forgotten how easily Norah took offense. "But I'm sure that Leo would like to spend as much time with his family as he can. Besides, there's going to be a wonderful luncheon, music, and even a bit of dancing. His gran might enjoy herself, so she's more than welcome."

"That's kind of you." Leo rose to his feet. "But I've no idea whether or not she'd be up to that sort of an outing. I'll see how she looks, and if she's able, I'll ask her to come."

"That'll be fine." Betsy glanced at Norah and knew that Leo was going to hear it as soon as the two of them were alone. Betsy would recognize that expression on her sister's face no matter how many years they'd been apart. Her eyes had narrowed and her mouth flattened into a thin, angry slash of a line. Norah was fit to be tied. "Oh dear, I'd no idea it was getting so late, I must get back. As Norah said, there's a lot to do before the wedding. Will you be back early this evening or shall I drop back in tomorrow morning?" She loved Norah, but spending too much time with her was trying. Perhaps they'd been apart for too long or she'd forgotten what a right little madam Norah could be.

"I'd like to have supper with Gran," Leo said. "But I don't want to upset your plans—"

Norah interrupted with a quick wave of her hand. "Don't worry about that, Betsy'll not mind. After all, you've a right to see your family, too. Just because her fiancé paid for us to come—"

Betsy interrupted this time. "Of course I don't mind. The two of you can do whatever you like."

"Norah didn't mean to . . ." Leo started.

"You don't have to explain me." Norah glared at him.

"Good, glad that's settled." Betsy hurried to the coat tree and grabbed her hat and cloak. "I'll see you tomorrow, then. Have a wonderful time today, and don't forget to invite your gran," she called as she closed the door behind her and hurried down the narrow staircase. She wasn't certain, but by the time she'd hit the bottom step, she thought she could hear Norah's raised voice.

She grinned to herself as she stepped outside. Maybe she shouldn't have left Leo alone to face her sister's tongue. Then she shrugged and started off. After all these years, Leo ought to be used to her sister.

Arabella Evans stared stonily at the inspector. They were in her drawing room, and she was sitting on the sofa. He was standing in front of her. She didn't invite him to take a seat.

"I don't know why you've returned." She crossed her arms over her chest. "As I told you before, we've had nothing to do with Agatha Moran for years."

Witherspoon sighed inwardly. He'd been in such good spirits when he left the house today. "I'm sorry to intrude upon you, madam, but this is a murder investigation and I do have more questions. I've asked Constable Barnes to have a word with your staff. I hope you don't mind."

"You mean the servants? Are you joking? That's most inconvenient, Inspector." She uncrossed her arms and straightened her spine. "We're having a luncheon today with some very important people. Everything must be perfect. I'll not have you keeping my servants from their duties."

"If that is your wish, madam," he replied with a slight incline of his head, "I'll ask them to come to the station. I can take their statements there." Generally, Inspector Witherspoon tried to be as accommodating as possible, but he was a bit annoyed. After hearing what Jane Middleton had to say, the inspector was sure that both Mr. and Mrs. Evans had been less than truthful about their relationship with the dead woman.

She looked at him in disbelief. "Are you serious? You do understand that all it would take is a word or two from my daughter's fiancé, and your life could be made most uncomfortable."

Witherspoon hated it when people tried to bully him with threats. It was such a foolish waste of his time, and it clearly illustrated their character. "Mrs. Evans, your future son-in-law may do whatever he likes. By all means tell Sir Madison that my superior officer is Chief Inspector Barrows at Scotland Yard. But in the interim, I will get statements from your servants. Agatha Moran, a woman who was connected with this household, was murdered right outside of your front door. Frankly, not only have you and your husband behaved in a very odd manner, but we've statements from other witnesses that lead us to believe you haven't told us everything you know."

Arabella's jaw dropped. She stared at him for a moment and then sagged back against the cushions of the settee. "Ask your questions and get out of here."

"Thank you, ma'am," he said. He didn't like being annoyed. It made for very bad police work. "Now let me ask this again. Have you had any recent contact with Agatha Moran?"

"What do you mean by recent?"

"Anytime this past year, including this past week?" he asked.

She looked away. "I've seen her once."

"Yet when I asked you that before, you insisted you'd had nothing to do with the woman since she left your employment?" He let the question hang in the air to avoid calling her a liar.

"For God's sake, Inspector, she'd just been murdered only a few feet from my front door." She looked at him contemptuously. "What sane person wouldn't have done the same? Of course I lied and said I'd not seen her."

"When, exactly, did you see her?" He kept his tone calm and deliberate. Arabella Evans was irritating, but not any more than many women of her class.

"A few days ago, I received a note from her."

"How did the note arrive? By post or by hand?"

"It came in the second morning post," she replied. "I read it and sent a reply by the afternoon post."

"The one o'clock or the three o'clock post?" Witherspoon did some quick calculating in his head. If she replied by the earlier one o'clock post, Agatha Moran would have received the note by that same afternoon.

"The one o'clock."

"What did the note say?" he asked.

"She wanted to see me, Inspector. I should have thought that was obvious." Her tone was clipped.

"Did you invite her here?"

Arabella waved her hand in a negative gesture. "Of course not, I told her to meet me in town. I had an appointment with my dressmaker the following day. I instructed her to meet me at Lyon's Tea Shop on Oxford Street."

"You met her there? Is that correct?"

Arabella smiled wryly. "Of course, Inspector. There was no reason not to meet with her, but I didn't have a lot of time to spare that day. We had a quick cup of tea together. It was a very amicable meeting."

"What did she want to see you about?" Witherspoon asked.

"She said she'd heard Rosemary was to marry and she had some family silver she wanted to give to her as a wedding gift."

"She wanted to give your daughter her family heirlooms?" the inspector repeated, his expression skeptical.

"They were hardly heirlooms," Arabella explained. "When we employed her, she had a few trinkets that she kept in her room. Rosemary used to love playing with them. Miss Moran thought Rosemary would enjoy them as a gift. They hardly have any real monetary value."

"So the gifts were sentimental in nature," he clarified.

"That's correct. I told her to send them along to the house, and then I excused myself and went to the dressmaker."

"What time did you and Miss Moran meet at the tearoom?" He shifted on his feet as his bad leg began to tire and made a mental note to send a constable to the tearoom. Hopefully one of the staff would recall serving the two women. He wanted to verify Arabella Evans' account of the meeting; she had already misled him once and he was determined she'd not do it again. She was a rather irritating woman.

"I instructed her to meet me at ten forty-five," she informed him. "Miss Moran was prompt. But then, I'd expect nothing less of her. She was always very good at keeping a schedule. She instilled a number of very good habits in Rosemary."

"And afterwards you went right to the dressmaker's?" He moved his weight again as his knee began to throb.

"I've just told you that." She sighed impatiently. "Now look, I really must attend to my household—"

He interrupted, "I'll need the name and address of your dressmaker. Did you walk there or did you take a hansom?"

She glared at him. "As it was just around the corner, I walked. The dressmaker's name is Madame Corbier and her shop is on—"

"I know the establishment," he said, cutting her off again.

He wasn't generally so rude, but he was in a great deal of pain and could feel his knee starting to swell. He'd not seen Lady Cannonberry in over a week now, and he was nervous about Betsy's wedding. He was walking her down the aisle, and it was his duty to insure her nuptials went off perfectly. He had a horrible feeling that uncooperative and untruthful witnesses like Arabella Evans weren't going to help him get this case solved before Betsy's big day.

Downstairs, Constable Barnes wasn't having an easy time of it, either. "Let's try this again, ma'am." He sighed. "What time did the guests start arriving for the tea party?"

Mrs. Grayston, the housekeeper, stared at him as if he were a half-wit. "And I've already told you, I was in the kitchen so I've no idea when the first one got here. But it was probably close to four thirty."

Barnes decided that would have to do. He really wasn't interested in any of the guests; the reports from the constables indicated that to date, none of them were acquainted with the victim. He'd hoped to use the timeline of the arrival of the first guest to get some idea of where each of the individual family members might have been between the start of the tea party and the murder. He tried another tactic. "Who greeted the guests when they arrived?"

"I suppose Mrs. Evans and Miss Evans greeted their guests."

"But you don't know that for a fact," he pressed.

"I've just told you, I was in the kitchen checking on the petit fours. Cook has had some trouble lately with her baking and I wanted to make sure they were acceptable. By the time I got back upstairs, Stevens was at the front door and guests were arriving. I've no idea who got here first."

"Was Mrs. or Miss Evans in the drawing room when you came upstairs?" he asked.

"Where else would they be . . ." Her voice trailed off. "Oh dear, I've made a mistake. Come to think of it, Mrs. Evans wasn't there. But some of the guests had already arrived. I remember now, because I overheard Miss Evans telling Lady Warburton that her mother would be right back and to please make herself comfortable."

"Do you know where Mrs. Evans had gone?"

"I've no idea. But I saw her coming back into the drawing room a bit later."

"You saw her coming down the stairs," he probed. Ye gods, getting information out of this woman was harder than pulling hens' teeth.

"I didn't say that, did I. I saw her coming in from the conservatory." She jerked her thumb up. As they were downstairs in the butler's pantry, the constable assumed she was pointing at the conservatory.

"The conservatory?" he repeated.

"That's right." Some of her bluster had faded. "I assume she'd gone there to check on something. We've had workmen in for the past month and the wretched room still isn't finished. Mrs. Evans wanted it done by this week. She'd planned to host a champagne breakfast there the day before the wedding."

He raised his bushy eyebrows in disbelief. "So she left a social occasion to go and check on how the work was progressing."

"Don't be daft." The housekeeper snorted derisively. "Mrs. Evans wouldn't do such a silly thing. She probably went to make sure the workmen had put up oilcloths to keep the wet out. There's some very expensive furniture in there now, and I imagine she wanted to be certain her new Spanish table wasn't going to be ruined by the rain coming in on it."

Barnes winced. He'd only done a cursory search of the premises and felt foolish now. He should have gone into the conservatory instead of just glancing at the front from the street.

"Like I said," the housekeeper continued, "the wretched place still isn't finished, so Mrs. Evans will not likely be hosting anything there till well after the New Year. The builders have mucked up the job and there isn't even glass in half the frames. Add to it, Mr. Evans wasn't home like he was supposed to be, so he couldn't take care of the problem. I imagine she went to make sure they'd done what she told them. It was very cold and she did have guests coming."

Barnes suddenly went still. He couldn't believe he'd been so derelict in his duty. Blast, why had he relied on the lads to search the house? None of their reports had mentioned oilcloths or open windows. "Were the empty frames at ground level?"

She shrugged. "How should I know? I don't go in there. The workmen are rude. Now, if you're finished, I've a lot of work to do."

He wasn't finished at all, but he wasn't going to waste any more time on questioning her. There had to be other servants who would be more helpful. He looked down at the list of names the butler had given him and selected the next one. "Could you send the downstairs maid to see me, please."

She gave him a curt nod. "Mind you don't keep her long. We've a lot to do before the guests get here today."

CHAPTER 6

"Are you sure you'll not have another cup of tea?" Mrs. Goodge smiled at the young lady sitting across from her at the kitchen table. Phyllis Thomlinson was eighteen, plump as a Christmas goose, and currently unemployed. She wore a navy blue wool hat, high-necked blouse and jacket, both also navy blue, and a fitted gray skirt. The clothes had seen better days, but they were clean, and the rip in the jacket lapel had been neatly mended. Her hair was dark blonde and tucked back in a roll at the nape of her neck; her eyes were brown, her skin a perfect porcelain, and her face as round as a pie tin.

"No thank you, ma'am, I'm fine." Phyllis bobbed her head politely. "I hope you don't mind my coming 'round. But Mrs. Dubay said it would be alright and that you might have a position available now that your housemaid is getting married."

Mrs. Goodge had been surprised when the girl had shown up at the back door with a note from Mollie Dubay, a woman she'd worked with years ago. Out of courtesy to her old colleague, she'd invited the girl inside and offered her a cup of tea. Mollie's note hadn't said much, merely that Phyllis was out of work and might be useful to the Witherspoon household. "Our maid isn't leavin' us," she explained gently. "She's gettin' married but she intends to stay on here."

"Mrs. Dubay told me that'd probably be the way of it, but she suggested I come around anyway," Phyllis said quickly. "She thought your household might need an extra pair of hands because of the wedding and it being Christmas and all."

Mrs. Goodge stared at her, her expression speculative. That actually wasn't a bad idea. All of them were doing their very best, but with the various demands on their time, everyone was falling behind. Mrs. Jeffries hadn't hired the extra staff for the wedding luncheon, Smythe's tailor had sent notes twice reminding him he had to do a final fitting, Wiggins hadn't had a spare moment to polish the big silver trays, and she'd even skimped on the baking for her sources. Perhaps a bit of help would be useful. But it wasn't her place to promise the girl anything. "I'm not the person in charge of hirin'," she said kindly. "That would be our housekeeper, Mrs. Jeffries, and I'm afraid she's out at the moment."

"But you could put in a good word for me," Phyllis pleaded. "I'm a fully trained housemaid and I've got references. I worked for Sir Madison Lowery but he had to let me go—"

"Sir Madison Lowery," the cook interrupted. "You worked for him?" Bless you, Mollie Dubay, Mrs. Goodge thought. Not long ago, she'd done her friend a good turn, and Mollie was returning the favor. She must have heard that Inspector Witherspoon had caught the Moran case and, gossip being what it was, must have learned about the connection between Lowery, the Evans family, and the dead woman.

"He had to let me go," Phyllis explained. "He's getting married as well. He said his new wife would be bringing her own staff with her."

"Nonsense. A new wife might bring along her own personal maid, but she'd not bring an entire new staff," Mrs. Goodge declared. "Are you certain that's why he let you go? Was there, perhaps, another reason?"

"I wasn't sacked because I was lazy or there was anything wrong with my work," Phyllis said defensively. "I worked hard."

"But you were let go, and frankly, I've never heard of a housemaid gettin' dismissed because—"

"He let me go because he couldn't afford to pay my wages," she blurted. "Oh dear, I'm sorry I interrupted, and I shouldn't have said that, should I? We're supposed to be discreet about—" She broke off and turned away, but not before Mrs. Goodge saw the tears in her eyes.

"Don't cry now, it's alright." She reached over and awkwardly patted the girl's arm. "I wasn't implyin' there was anythin' wrong with your work. But before I speak to our housekeeper on your behalf, I need to know as much as possible about you."

Phyllis pulled a clean but tatty handkerchief out of the sleeve of her blouse and dabbed at her eyes. "I'm sorry, I didn't mean to start blubbering; it's just that I so desperately need a bit of work. I live close by and I'd be willing to do anything, anything at all." She teared up again.

"We'll see if there's somethin' for you here," Mrs. Goodge said quickly. "But I'm not makin' any promises. Staff decisions are up to our housekeeper."

Phyllis gazed at her with a hopeful expression. "Really? You'll speak to her on my behalf?"

"I said I would, didn't I? Now why don't you start by tellin' me about your time at Sir Madison's home?" She felt a twinge of guilt. Mrs. Jeffries might be dead set against hiring the girl, so she had to find out as much as she could about Madison Lowery while she had the chance. The housekeeper might very well think that a stranger in the household could cause a number of problems with their inquiries into Agatha Moran's murder. But I didn't make Phyllis any promises, she told herself.

"What do you want to know?" she asked eagerly.

"How long were you there?"

"Four years. I was hired as a housemaid."

"And what were your duties?" Mrs. Goodge knew good and well what a housemaid did, but she wanted the girl talking freely about her former employer.

"As I said, I was hired on as a maid, but I did a bit of everything except for the cooking." She smiled shyly. "You know, cleaning the floors, dusting and polishing the furniture, beating the rugs properly every week. Making the beds, tidying up and airing the rooms regular like."

"You weren't interested in learnin' to cook?" Mrs. Goodge asked, more to satisfy her own curiosity than to find out anything about Lowery. She was always a bit mystified about why others were so uninterested in baking a perfect apple tart or making a tasty lamb stew.

"I'd love to have learned," Phyllis answered. "But he was real particular about his food, and he only let Mrs. Perkins, the cook, make his meals. But I did help with the serving, and I did the clearing up from the dining room."

"What sort of household was it? Formal?"

"Oh yes, very formal. We didn't speak to him unless he spoke to us first," she replied.

"How big a staff was there?" Mrs. Goodge reached for the pot and helped herself to more tea.

"There were four of us. I did the housecleaning, Mrs. Clark is the housekeeper, Mrs. Perkins the cook, and Janie Dempsey the scullery. Mind you, I don't think Janie's there anymore. I ran into her cousin just the other day and she said Janie had been let go as well."

"So he's only got a cook and a housekeeper now?" Mrs. Goodge frowned. "And you say it's a big house?"

"It seemed big when I was doing the cleaning." She smiled. "But it's not as big as this one."

"I imagine workin' for a single man was very uncomfortable," Mrs. Goodge said chattily.

"Sir Madison Lowery wasn't single when I first went there. He had a wife. Lady Lowery was very nice to us, and we were all sad when she passed away."

"How did she die?" Mrs. Goodge asked.

"Food poisoning," Phyllis said. "It was awful. They'd been out to the theatre and had asked Mrs. Perkins to have a cold supper waiting for them when they got home. They both got sick that night. Poor Lady Lowery was ill for days before she finally passed away."

"What caused the food poisonin'?"

Phyllis frowned slightly. "Well, Sir Madison claimed it must have been the roast chicken. But I think it must have been the oysters they'd had for lunch that day."

"Wasn't the doctor able to determine what had caused it?"

Phyllis snorted. "The doctor didn't get there until the poor woman was almost dead, and by then, there wasn't a bit of anything left in poor Lady Lowery. She'd been sick so many times; she couldn't even keep water down."

"What about Sir Madison? Was he ill as well?"

"Yes, but he wasn't near as bad as she was," Phyllis explained. "He vomited a time or two and that was it. But she was in terrible straits. That's why I'm sure it was those oysters and not the chicken. She adored oysters. Sir Madison brought them home that day as a special treat for her. She ate quite a few at lunch. I remember because he kept teasing her and telling her to leave some for him. But I'm sure it wasn't the chicken. She didn't like cold roast chicken."

Constable Barnes put the guest list from the Evans tea party on top of the stack of statements he'd taken from the Evans servants. "They more or less all said the same things they did the first time, sir. The only discrepancy we've got thus far is between Mrs. Evans' first and second statements, and she readily admitted she lied the first time around."

"I know, but I was so hoping someone would recall some little detail they'd not mentioned earlier," Witherspoon said. "Pity no one did. What about the guest list? Anything useful there?"

"We've checked them all, sir, and not one of them will admit to knowing Agatha Moran. I went over the statements myself and the constables did a thorough job of questioning everyone."

"I'm sure they did." Witherspoon closed his eyes and leaned back in his chair. "I went over the statements as well, and you're correct, there's no evidence any of them knew the victim."

"According to both of the butler's statements, most of the guests were already in the house when the murder happened," Barnes added. "So I think we can cross that lot off. We've also not had any luck with the neighbors. The lads have been up and down that street speaking to everyone who might be a possible witness, but no one saw or heard anything."

After they'd left the Evans house, they'd gone back to the inspector's office at the station, as Witherspoon wanted to compare his second interview with Arabella Evans to the second set of statements Barnes obtained from the servants.

"Which leaves us with the Evans family, Sir Madison Lowery, and Ellen Crowe." Witherspoon straightened up.

Barnes bobbed his head toward the open gray folder. "What about Eleanor North, sir? The housemaid is sure she saw her slipping into the house through the back door at twenty past five."

"And Mrs. North's statement says she arrived at the party at four fifty," he murmured.

"That's a good half hour discrepancy, sir," Barnes pointed out. "And the maid was consistent in both my interviews with her."

"I wonder why none of the other servants saw her come in that way?" Witherspoon mused.

"I asked the girl that very question," the constable answered. "She said everyone was busy and she saw the woman because she'd gone to the butler's pantry to fetch the silver cake service."

Witherspoon leaned forward on his elbow and rested his chin on his fisted hand. "That sounds reasonable enough. I wonder why Mrs. North lied? Well, I suppose we shall find out today. Let's go and have a word with her. Afterwards, if we've time, I'd like to go back to the Moran house. We need to have a good look through her office, and I want to speak to Miss Farley again."

"Are we going to try and get to Putney as well?"

Witherspoon winced, caught himself, and started toward the door. "I'd forgotten about that. No, I don't think we need to do Putney. We can send a constable to interview Olivia Whitley and verify Ellen Crowe's alibi. We should also send someone reliable to Lyon's Tea Shop on Oxford Street. I want to confirm that the meeting between Mrs. Evans and Miss Moran was as amicable as she claimed."

"I'll see who's on the duty roster on our way out, sir," Barnes offered as they headed out of the station.

Wiggins looked at the lad with pity. "Do you have to wear that outfit all the time?"

"Nah, they only make me dress up like this when Mrs. Evans is having important people to luncheon," the boy replied. He tugged at the spaniel's lead, pulling the dog away from the base of the tree. He was dressed in an old-fashioned footman's livery, complete with tight white leggings, a sapphire blue surcoat trimmed in gold braid, a matching blue waistcoat that was a bit too tight for his chubby frame, and a white shirt with a frilly collar.

An odd twist of luck had led Wiggins to the boy. He'd spent a good hour walking up and down the road in front of Chepstow Villas when he'd spotted a constable coming toward him. Fearing it was someone who would recognize him as a member of the inspector's household, he'd waited a few seconds until the constable wasn't staring right at him, turned on his heel, and nipped around the corner to Denbigh Road. He'd been cursing his bad luck when he'd found himself directly behind the Evanses' huge back garden, and just about then, the footman and the black-coated spaniel had come out of the servants' entrance. Striking up a conversation with the boy had been easy.

"I didn't think anyone but the Queen made their footmen dress like that," Wiggins said with a shake of his head. He glanced over his shoulder, making sure that the constable hadn't taken it into his head to come this way. But he saw no one except for an elderly gentleman coming down the short stairway of the Wesleyan Methodist Chapel.

"It's not that bad." The boy gave him a friendly grin. His hair was red, his eyes blue, and he had hundreds of freckles covering his broad face. "I just have to stand about for a few minutes making sure that all the guests get a look at me." He nodded toward the dog. "Today's good, though. Lady Warburton brought Inkie here, and she always gives me a sixpence for walking him. He's a real sweet one." Inkie's tail wagged as he heard his name. "Mrs. Evans doesn't have the nerve to tell her to leave him at home. I like dogs, don't you?"

"I do. I've got one of my own; 'is name is Fred. I'm a footman as well, but I've never worn anythin' like that. I do have a uniform, but I've only worn it once." Wiggins wasn't sure the coat and jacket still fit. It had been years since he'd tried the outfit on. "But mine's not a fancy one like yours. It's just a plain brown suit with black leggings. What's your name?"

"Mickey Dobbs." He stopped suddenly and reached down to pet the dog. Inkie gave him a goofy dog smile and tried to lick his hand. "I work for the Evans family. Do you work around here?"

"I'm from Holland Park," Wiggins replied. "The housekeeper sent me down 'ere to deliver a note." The boy seemed chatty enough, but he knew the dangers of asking too much too fast. "My name is John. Do you like it at your household?"

"It's alright, I guess." Mickey straightened and they started walking again.

"'Ow long 'ave you worked there?"

Inkie stopped and sniffed at the leaves of a shrub. Mickey tugged gently on the lead, but the spaniel only shoved his nose further into the branches. "A year, but I'll not be there much longer. My brother's gone to Rhodesia, and once he's settled, I'm to join him. I'm saving my wages."

"You're goin' all the way to Africa? That sounds excitin'!" Wiggins exclaimed. He'd always wanted to travel to that part of the world himself.

Inkie pulled his head out of the bush and they started off again. "We've had the police around," Mickey added eagerly. "A lady got stabbed right in front of the house, and I got to speak to this cranky old copper who asked me all sorts of questions."

"Cor blimey, was the lady someone from your house?"

"Nah, none of us knew her. But I overheard the butler telling the cook that the dead woman used to work for the master and mistress. But I didn't get to hear anything else. But the police talked to me—the old peeler asked me all sorts of questions."

Wiggins didn't think Constable Barnes would mind being referred to as a "peeler." Policemen were often called far worse than that. "What did he ask you?"

"He wanted to know if I'd seen the comings and goings of the guests or the family when the lady was killed. I told him what I knew, but I don't think it was all that helpful." They'd reached the corner. Mickey pulled the lead gently as he turned to go back the way they'd come. Inkie spotted another bush and made a rush for it, dragging Mickey with him. "You silly old thing." The boy laughed but gave the dog his lead.

Wiggins hurried after them. "Maybe you helped more than you thought. You never know what little fact or detail will help the police catch the killer."

"I don't see how." Mickey shrugged. "After I checked that the builders had covered the mistress' new table properly with the oilcloths, I spent the rest of the evening keeping the fire burning in the cooker," he explained. "I didn't even leave the kitchen until all the guests had gone out the back door and the police came. In a way I'm glad it happened."

Wiggins looked at him sharply. He didn't seem like a bloodthirsty sort. "Glad what happened?"

"Oh, I'm not happy the poor lady was stabbed, but I'm awfully happy the police was tramping through the house that night." He grinned. "One of them must have pulled the oilcloth off Mrs. Evans' new table, and the next morning, all that fancy carved wood was soaked. She was furious and she blamed the builders. She was screaming at the foreman that he'd not done his job properly, and he yelled right back at her. He told her they'd covered everything, including her ruddy table, and what's more, them cloths cost good money, and if they all weren't accounted for, he'd add it to her bill. You could hear them shouting at each other all the way down in the kitchen."

He was well into middle age, but when Reginald Manley walked into a room, he was still handsome enough to turn the ladies' heads. A touch of gray brushed his temples, but his black hair was thick and lustrous. He had excellent bone structure, with high cheekbones, a sharp jawline, and a wide, generous mouth. "Would you care for tea or would you prefer something stronger?" he asked his guest. "Oh sorry, I forgot, you never touch alcohol, do you."

Hatchet laughed easily. "Not usually. But sometimes, if there's a special occasion, I'll raise my glass in a toast." He'd given up alcohol years ago, after it had stolen his self-respect and left him for dead in a back alley in Baltimore. But Hatchet wasn't one to waste precious time thinking about his past when he was on the hunt. He'd come to the elegant Mayfair home of one of his old friends looking for information. "I'd prefer tea if you don't mind."

"Please bring a pot of tea and a bottle of Laphroaig," Manley instructed the maid that had shown Hatchet into the conservatory. "And ask my wife to join us."

As soon as the girl disappeared, he waved Hatchet toward a wicker table and chairs. "I'm under strict instructions to send for Myra the moment you appear." Reginald grinned broadly as he sat down.

Hatchet slipped into the seat opposite his host and surveyed his surroundings. They were in a conservatory, the greater part of which was filled with rows of cutting beds laid out on long trestle tables, big tubs of flowers, shrubs and exotic trees in colorful pots. The remainder of the space was given over to a small studio for Reginald's paintings. A canvas on an easel stood a few feet away from where he sat, and next to that was a table with two blue crockery containers holding an assortment of brushes and half a dozen jars of paint.

Reginald Manley was an artist. But he wasn't quite as talented as one needed to be to actually make a living selling his work, so he'd spent most of his adult life using his considerable charm to insure he was in the good graces of a well-heeled female. Manley had learned early that having a special lady friend to help defray one's expenses made life so much easier. But he'd always treated the ladies well, been faithful, and in every case, the liaison had ended with both parties remaining friends. Since taking his marriage vows, he'd devoted himself to his wife's happiness. Hatchet had seen the Manleys together on a number of occasions and was now convinced that whatever the circumstances that might have brought them together, there was now genuine love between the two of them.

Hatchet looked amused. "Lovely. I like your wife. She's a very intelligent woman."

"Yes, but we both know this isn't just a social call. You want information."

Hatchet feigned hurt. "You cut me to the quick. I genuinely want to see you. You're an old friend."

"As are you." Reginald grinned broadly. "And I'm delighted to share a bit of useful gossip with you now and again. Now tell me, are you here about that poor woman that got stabbed in Notting Hill?"

"Don't you dare start speaking until I get over there and sit down," Myra Haddington Manley said from the doorway. "I don't want to miss a word of this." Her long russet-colored skirt swished as she hurried toward them.

Both men started to rise, but she waved them back to their seats. She was definitely middle-aged, her front teeth protruded slightly, and there were more than a few streaks of gray in her brown hair. But her complexion was flawless and there was a lively intelligence in her deep-set hazel eyes. As always, she was beautifully dressed. The bodice of her gown was an intricate fleur-de-lis pattern of black lace and russet over a fitted high-necked white blouse. Onyx earrings dangled from her earlobes and a black cashmere shawl was draped over her shoulders.

"How delightful to see you again, Hatchet," she said as she took the empty wicker chair next to her husband.

"The pleasure is all mine," he replied.

"And I wasn't going to ask him anything until you got here, sweetest," Reginald protested. "I sent Hilda to fetch you."

"Of course you did, darling." She patted his hand. "And I got here as quickly as I could. Now you haven't told him, have you?"

"Told me what?" Hatchet looked at Myra. "He's not told me anything."

Myra glanced at Reginald and raised her eyebrows. "You didn't mention Eleanor North?"

"Of course not, I was waiting for you—" He broke off as the maid came back. She was carrying a silver tray, which she put down on the table. She started to reach for the teapot handle.

Myra raised her hand. "I'll pour, Hilda," she offered.

"Yes ma'am." Hilda bobbed a curtsy and then hurried off.

Myra smiled at Hatchet as she picked up the pot. "Do you take sugar and cream?"

"Both." He nodded his thanks as she handed him a delicate pink and white cup. He waited till they'd picked up their glasses of whisky before he spoke. "Now, what was it about Eleanor North that you wanted to tell me?"

"You know that she lives right next door to the Evans family?" Myra began.

He nodded. "I do."

"But what you might not know is that she came in late to that tea party and that the hem of her skirt was soaked," Myra announced proudly.

Hatchet kept his smile with difficulty. He didn't want them to see how disappointed he was. It had been raining—half of London's hems were wet that afternoon. "That's quite extraordinary."

Myra watched him for a few seconds and then burst out laughing. "How very polite you are. Of course you don't know the rest of it, do you?"

"Stop teasing the poor man, Myra," Reginald admonished. "He doesn't know what we know. No one does."

"Oh don't be so stuffy. I've got to meet with that Ladies Horticultural Society in two hours so I deserve a bit of fun," she said. "Let me start at the beginning. Our housekeeper, Mrs. Parker, is from the Isle of Wight. Her family owned a small lodging house in Ryde. Apparently, she heard Reginald and I discussing the Moran murder, and during that discussion, we mentioned the Evans family and how sad it was that their governess had been stabbed right in front of their house." She paused and took a quick sip of her whisky. "The next morning, when we were going over the weekly expenses, Mrs. Parker happened to mention that Eleanor

North's fiancé, Tobias Sutton, lived in the house next door to where Agatha Moran had a position as a governess when she was employed by a family in Ryde."

Hatchet wanted to make sure he understood. "Let me get this straight; your housekeeper claims that the Evanses' neighbor Mrs. North has a fiancé that knew the victim?"

"That's right." Myra nodded affirmatively. "Mr. Sutton lived in the lodging house her family owned. He's a barrister, and he was well acquainted with Agatha Moran. Mrs. Parker said she remembers seeing the two of them walking along the seaside together."

"How long ago was this?"

"Over twenty years," Myra answered. "But Mrs. Parker remembers it clearly because Agatha Moran was a governess to a family named Hinshaw. They were very proper people, and back in those days, if you were a governess, you most certainly didn't stroll along the seaside with a young man."

"I wonder why Sutton didn't come forward with this information. Agatha Moran was identified in all the newspapers. Surely, he must have realized the police would be interested in his connection to the dead woman," Hatchet murmured.

"Don't be absurd." Reginald laughed. "If Eleanor North found out he had any connection with a murdered woman, she'd break off their engagement."

Hatchet drew back in surprise. "For goodness' sake, why? Sutton can hardly be faulted because someone he once had a connection with was mur—"

"That wouldn't make any difference," Myra interrupted. "Eleanor North is obsessed with propriety, and frankly, even though I think it's a peculiar way to live one's life, I can understand to some extent. Her first husband was involved in one scandal after another. She was constantly humiliated by the man."

"Douglas North was an overbearing bully," Reginald added.

"And mean-spirited as well as having a terrible temper," she said. "I once heard one of her friends say that the happiest day of her life was when he got run over by a cooper's van."

"Her husband was killed in an accident?" Hatchet put his teacup down.

"Don't get so excited." Myra gave him a knowing smile. "It wasn't murder. There were dozens of witnesses. Douglas North was very drunk when he was killed. He wandered out into traffic on Oxford Street and got run over."

"Was the driver charged?" Hatchet asked.

"There was an inquest and the magistrate ruled it an accidental death," Reginald said.

"When Eleanor became engaged to Tobias Sutton," Myra said, "the gossip was that she picked him because he was sweet, amiable, and so boring he'd never cause a scandal. She'd not take kindly to anyone finding out that Sutton had once known Agatha Moran."

Hatchet thought for a moment and then reached for his tea. "I suppose coincidences do happen in life," he remarked. "But I find it very strange. What are the odds that he would end up engaged to a woman who lived next door to a family that had once employed his, er, friend?"

"You're being very polite," Myra chided. "Mrs. Parker hinted that there was more between Sutton and Miss Moran than friendship. I suspect that Sutton found out about the connection, and as Mrs. North is very good friends with the Evans family, he was terrified Agatha Moran's name might come up. He didn't want his fiancée finding out he'd once had a relationship with another woman."

"Now, now, Myra, an old romance is hardly a motive for murder," Reginald protested. "Not in this day and age."

"How did Mrs. North meet Sutton?" Hatchet asked. "Do either of you happen to know?"

"I do," Myra said brightly. "Eleanor tells everyone who stands still for thirty seconds how she met him. Late one afternoon, Eleanor was coming home from shopping, and just as she stepped out of the hansom, Tobias Sutton tripped over a crack in the pavement and went sprawling at her feet. She could tell right away that he was a gentleman, so she took him inside to make sure he wasn't seriously injured." She sighed. "Actually, it is a rather romantic story."

"Humph," Reginald snorted in derision. "I don't believe a word of it. She probably met him at a boring old dinner party."

Smythe stepped into the Dirty Duck pub and stopped just inside the doorway. He'd not meant to come here today, but he'd had the worst luck. He'd wasted half the day chasing all over Islington trying to find Eddie Butcher. But it was as if the fellow had disappeared off the face of the ruddy earth. The other tenants at the doss-house on Stone Lane claimed that Eddie hadn't been back in two days.

"And he's paid in advance for the bed," one of them had told Smythe. "He'd got his wages from the Morrisons and he was afraid he'd spend it at the pub if he didn't pay up." The old man had shook his head in disbelief. "It's not like Eddie to give up a warm bed. Not when he's paid for it."

Smythe had then crossed the fellow's palm with a bit of silver and learned that sometimes Eddie went to visit a sister in Stepney. He'd spent hours in the East End, and passed a bit more silver to Eddie's sister only to learn she'd seen neither hide nor hair of him in months. Then he remembered he'd promised Betsy he'd stop in at the tailors to get his suit fitted, and if his luck held and Blimpey was actually here, he might just be able to get to the tailor shop before it closed. Much as he'd liked to continue investigating on his own, he had too much to do. It was time to spend a bit of money and get help from a professional.

He felt the door open behind him so he stepped to the side and craned his neck, looking for his quarry. When he spotted Blimpey Groggins, the professional he'd come to hire, sitting at his usual spot at a table by the fireplace, he was relieved. Smythe pushed his way through the crowd.

Blimpey saw him, grinned, and waved him over. He was a middle-aged man of sizeable girth with wispy, ginger-colored hair, rosy cheeks, and a broad, welcoming smile. He was dressed in the same clothes he always wore, a brown and white checked suit that had seen better days and a white shirt that was frayed at the collar and cuffs. A bright red scarf was wound around his neck, and a grimy porkpie hat of indeterminate color lay on the table next to his pint of beer.

"So you've finally decided to pay me a visit." Blimpey tapped the empty stool next to him.

"I need your 'elp." Smythe didn't see any point in beating about the bush. Blimpey knew exactly why he was here. On a number of their previous cases, Smythe had used Blimpey's rather unusual services. He charged an arm and a leg, but he was blooming good at his job and Smythe could afford him.

Blimpey had started out in life as a thief. Second-story work had been his specialty, but a narrow escape from a house in Belgravia, coupled with a nasty bite from a mastiff on a very tender part of his anatomy, had convinced him that he ought to find a new profession. Blimpey had an excellent memory and was far more intelligent than the average crook. He was good at putting divergent facts together to come to useful conclusions for the benefit of his clients. By the time the mastiff bite had healed, he'd realized he could make far more money buying and selling information than risking life and liberty climbing trees or running from dogs.

Blimpey now had sources at the police stations, the Old Bailey, the magistrate courts, the financial centers in the City, every shipping line, and all of the insurance companies. He paid his informants top wages and gave them hefty discounts on his services. His clients ranged from bankers looking to see if their managers were honest, to bookies wanting character references on potential customers.

But Blimpey had standards. He wouldn't trade in information that caused harm to women or children, and he didn't get involved in criminal warfare. Violence of any kind was simply bad for business.

"Of corse you do." Blimpey signaled the barmaid to bring a pint. "You're gettin' married, you've got men workin' on yer buildin' and they're needin' one decision after another from you, and you've got yer soon-to-be in-laws 'ere from Canada."

Smythe laughed. "Trust you to be so bloomin' well informed. But then again, that's what you're good at."

"Corse it is," he agreed heartily. "I'm just surprised it took you so long to come see me. The lady was murdered two days ago."

"I thought I could find out a few bits on me own," Smythe muttered.

"You don't 'ave time for that," Blimpey retorted. "Yer weddin' is in a few days and yer guv caught the Moran case. From what I've been hearin', it's goin' to be nigh impossible to solve that one, especially by Christmas."

"You've no business coming here, Inspector." Eleanor North stood in the open doorway of her drawing room and glared at the two policemen. "The maid had no right to let you in the front door—"

Witherspoon cut her off. "It wasn't your maid's fault, Mrs. North; we insisted. It is very important that we speak with you." He didn't want some poor servant losing her position because she'd acted properly. "The only alternative to our coming here was to ask you to come down to the station, and frankly, we thought it more convenient for you if we—"

This time, she interrupted. "Then you thought wrong. I'd have much rather done that than have all and sundry see two policemen at my front door." She flounced into the room and slammed the door shut behind her. She was a tall, slender woman with thin lips, deep-set eyes with dark circles underneath them, and hair that was now grayer than its original color of black. She wore a dark lavender high-necked wool day dress with an overskirt of purple and gray stripes. Amethyst earrings dangled from her ears and a long double string of pearls hung around her neck and dangled against the purple cummerbund circling her waist.

Witherspoon was torn between exasperation and pity. From the expression on her face, he could see she was dead serious. "We didn't know that, ma'am," he explained. "Most people we deal with would rather be interviewed in the comfort of their home than at the station. If you'd like, we can go there now."

She waved him off impatiently and sank down on the sofa. "The damage is already done, so we might as well get this over with." She pointed to the love seat opposite her. "You may both sit."

They sat down and Barnes took out his notebook and glanced at Witherspoon expectantly. He was curious to see how the inspector was going to conduct this interview.

"Oh do get on with it, man," Mrs. North ordered. "I don't have all day."

Witherspoon cleared his throat. He couldn't tell if she

was rude because it was her nature or if she was simply nervous about being questioned again. "Yes, of course. Mrs. North, in the original statement you gave to us, you said you arrived at the tea party at four fifty that afternoon."

She looked down, picked up the bottom strand of her pearls and twisted it gently around her index finger. "That's correct."

"Are you absolutely certain that's the time you arrived at the Evans house?" the inspector asked.

Her head jerked up and she fixed him with a cold stare. "I'm certain."

"Mrs. North, I'm sorry, but we've a witness that contradicts your account," he advised. "Are you sure you don't want to amend your original statement?" He felt it only fair to give her a chance to tell the truth.

The drawing room door opened and a tall man with thinning red hair entered. He stopped, his hand resting on the doorknob. "Eleanor, is everything alright?" he asked, his gaze moving between her and the two policemen.

"I'm fine, Tobias; these men are here about the unfortunate incident that happened during the Evans celebration tea." She gave him a weak smile. "We'll be finished in a few moments. You can wait for me in the morning room."

He inclined his head and began to withdraw.

"Just a moment, sir," Witherspoon called in a raised voice. The man stopped and stared at him. "Were you here on the day the lady was murdered?"

"He was," Eleanor answered for him.

"I'm capable of answering questions on my own." He smiled at her to take the sting out of the words and came toward them, slipping into the seat next to Eleanor and taking her hand. "Dearest, you look very distressed. You shouldn't be here on your own. That's why you've got me."

"Who are you, sir?" Barnes asked.

"I'm Tobias Sutton, Mrs. North's fiancé. Why are you here? She's already made a statement."

"That's why we're here, sir," Barnes replied. "There are inconsistencies in Mrs. North's statement, and we'd like to give her an opportunity to clear them up."

Sutton looked at his fiancé and then turned back to the policemen. "Inconsistencies? Surely there's been a mistake."

"There's no mistake, sir," Witherspoon responded. "Mrs. North's statement says she arrived at the Evans tea party at four fifty that afternoon, but we've a witness that saw her coming in at five twenty."

"That's ridiculous." He laughed softly. "I don't know who you've been talking with, but I assure you they're mistaken. Eleanor and I left the house together and we walked out the door just after four forty-five. I remember it distinctly. We both commented on what an odd time it was for high tea."

"Were you a guest at the party, sir?" Barnes asked. "Your name wasn't on the guest list."

"The tea was for members of the wedding party," Eleanor interjected. "I wasn't, of course. Rosemary's attendants are all young ladies. But Mrs. Evans asked me to come to the tea for her own reasons."

"What would those reasons be?" Witherspoon prodded. Getting information out of some people was as difficult as getting a cat to fetch.

"Really, Inspector." Eleanor frowned irritably. "I don't see what that has to do with your investigation."

"Mrs. Evans was exhausted," Tobias Sutton offered. "She invited my fiancée to help her act as hostess."

"Tobias," Eleanor snapped.

"Now, now, dear," he said soothingly. "You're trying to protect Mrs. Evans' social reputation, but the police are hardly likely to tell anyone that she needed help with the hostessing duties."

"I suppose you're right." She smiled at him, then turned her attention to Witherspoon. "Mrs. Evans invited me because there were so many guests and she wanted to insure that everyone had a nice time."

"Wouldn't her daughter have acted as a hostess?" Barnes asked.

She laughed. "Of course, but Rosemary would naturally have spent most of her time with the young ladies."

"Mrs. North, why do you think someone is claiming they saw you coming into the back door of the Evans home at twenty past five?"

"I've no idea." She smiled smugly. "But as Mr. Sutton has just said, we left here at the very same time. Just after four forty-five."

"Did Mr. Sutton walk you to the Evanses' front door?" Barnes looked at Sutton as he asked the question.

They both spoke at the same time.

"Of course he did," she replied. "He's a gentleman."

He said, "Oh no, I went the other way, toward the hansom stand. I was going home."

CHAPTER 7

As she'd done half a dozen times in the last ten minutes, Mrs. Jeffries craned her neck and peeked out from her hiding place. She wanted to make sure there weren't any constables patrolling the area. Agatha Moran was a murder victim; it was possible the inspector had instructed the local police to keep an eye on the neighborhood, and if one of them spotted her lurking in the lower ground-floor doorway of an empty house, she'd be hard-pressed to explain herself.

But she saw no one on the street except for a passing hansom cab and an elderly woman carrying a shopping basket.

She sagged against the doorframe and wondered if this was worth the effort. She'd been staring at the Moran place for a good fifteen minutes now, and only one person had crossed the threshold. A woman swathed in black from head to toe had gone into the house a few minutes ago, and for a brief moment, Mrs. Jeffries had felt the excitement of the hunt surging through her veins, but her elation had been short-lived as she'd realized the visitor wasn't a visitor at all, but most likely one of the hotel residents. The lady had been dressed in mourning out of respect for her dead landlady.

Straightening away from the doorway, she sighed and rubbed her cold hands together. She really ought to go home. There was so much to do. Coming here had been a foolish mistake. She started toward the tiny staircase when she heard the church bells strike the quarter hour. She eased back into her hiding place; it wouldn't hurt to stay another fifteen minutes. She'd come here because her pride had been wounded, but now that she was here, there was a slight chance she might learn something useful.

At their afternoon meeting the other day, the others had more or less implied she didn't have the wits to avoid being spotted by the inspector or one of the many constables that knew her on sight. Their comments had stung, so much so that she'd determined to prove them all wrong. This, of course, just goes to show that pride goeth before a fall; by the time she got home today, she'd have wasted the whole morning and have nothing to show for it.

Just then, the front door of the Moran house opened and the lady in black appeared. She hovered in the doorway for a moment, talking to someone in the house, but just then a hansom went by and Mrs. Jeffries couldn't hear a word that was said.

The woman came out onto the street and turned toward Hemmingford Road. Mrs. Jeffries took a swift look around to make sure she wasn't being watched, and then dashed up the stairwell. She raced across the pavement as the lady disappeared around the corner. She kept back a bit, not wanting her quarry to know she was being followed, but then quickened her pace when she realized the woman was heading for the train station.

Mrs. Jeffries rushed into the ticket office just as the lady reached the window. Throwing caution to the wind, she ran across the small room just in time to hear the woman say, "A single to King's Cross, please."

When it was her turn, Mrs. Jeffries purchased the same. "When's the next train?" she asked the ticket seller.

"Comin' in now, ma'am." He jerked his thumb to his right, indicating she was to go in that direction.

The carriage doors were opening when she came onto the platform, and Mrs. Jeffries saw the lady in black disappear into a car at the far end. Taking a deep breath, she ran for the car, leapt in, and slammed the door behind her just as the whistle blew.

There were three people in the compartment. Two men reading newspapers were sitting next to the windows, and her quarry had taken the spot by the door. Mrs. Jeffries had no choice but to take the seat opposite.

The lady leaned toward her, and for one, brief, horrifying moment, Mrs. Jeffries was sure she'd been caught. But instead of "Why have you been following me?" the woman asked, "Excuse me, madam, but is it possible to get from King's Cross Station to Victoria? Your English trains are very confusing to me and I have a Channel crossing today."

Mrs. Jeffries couldn't believe her good luck. She'd not been caught, and even better, the lady was a foreigner, a stranger to London. "Of course it is. When we get to King's Cross, I'll show you exactly what you must do. Are you French?"

"Oui, madam," she replied with a smile. "I came to London to attend a funeral."

"Oh dear," Mrs. Jeffries said sympathetically. "I'm so very sorry."

The woman was attractive and appeared to be in her late thirties. Her hair was light brown, her complexion smooth and unlined, and her eyes a light shade of green.

"It was expected." She shrugged, causing her voluminous black coat to gape open. Beneath it, she wore a gray blouse with mother-of-pearl buttons and a black wool skirt. On her head was a high-crowned black felt hat swathed in so much veiling it reached the tip of her gloved fingers. "My uncle was very old. I am Madame Deloffre and I so appreciate your assistance. I've been in London for several days now taking care of my uncle's business, and it's such a confusing place."

Mrs. Jeffries' heart sank as she realized she'd let her enthusiasm overcome her common sense. Agatha Moran had just come back from a trip to the continent, and though it was supposed to have been a holiday for her, no sensible businesswoman would pass up an opportunity to advertise her own establishment. She'd probably passed out brochures and cards everywhere. No doubt Madame Deloffre had found one of those cards and decided it would be a perfect place for a lone female traveler to stay while she was in London. Blast, she'd probably made another mistake, and this one was going to cost her the rest of the morning. Still, she'd do her best to help the woman.

"I'm"—she started to use her real name and then thought better of it—"Mrs. Johnson," she finished.

"How do you do, madame." She inclined her head. "One of these days I'd like to come back to your country under better circumstances."

The train pulled into the next station and one of the two men got out. The other one didn't look up from his paper.

"A death in the family is always a sad occasion," Mrs. Jeffries said as the carriage door slammed and the train started off again.

"It wasn't just that," Madame Deloffre explained. "I expected my uncle to die; he was ninety-four and had a bad heart. Mais non, what was most upsetting was that I stopped to see my English friend and I found out she'd been murdered."

From the corner of her eye, Mrs. Jeffries saw the man stick his head out from behind the newspaper. She ignored him. "Murdered. Oh my gracious, that's terrible." She felt her spirits rise. Perhaps this wasn't to be a wasted morning after all.

"She was stabbed to death." Madame Deloffre's eyes were as big as saucers. "I couldn't believe it when her housekeeper told me what happened. Mon Dieu—" She broke off with a shake of her head.

"Were you close friends?" Mrs. Jeffries asked softly.

"Not really, I only met her a time or two in Paris. But I liked her very much. She hired me to do some translating work for her. Well, that's not quite true. I only translated a few documents and a . . . I can't think how to say it in English . . . but you know, the words on the stones of the dead."

It took a moment before Mrs. Jeffries understood. "You mean headstones or tombstones. You translated tombstones for your friend?"

"Oui." Madame Deloffre shrugged slightly. "That's how we met. We were both in Le Cimetiere de Grenelle, a . . . what you would call a cemetery, and she heard me speaking English to one of my students. She asked me what some words on a . . . a . . . tombstone meant and I translated them for her. After that, she hired me to translate some official documents."

By this time, the man by the window had given up all pretense of reading his newspaper. He was openly staring at them, but both women pretended not to notice.

"That's a very interesting way to make someone's acquaintance. You'll forgive my impertinence I hope, but what did the words on the tombstone say?"

Madame Deloffre looked out the window as the train rumbled into King's Cross Station. "It said the usual words one would expect to see on the stone of the dead. 'Here lies Delphine Odette Aimee, beloved wife of Sir Madison Lowery. Gone but never forgotten in our hearts.'"

Betsy stopped and stared at the greengrocer's and tried to decide if it was worth going inside and having a chat with the clerk. She'd been to every shop along High Street and found out nothing they didn't already know about the Evans family. But she wanted to learn something before she went back to Upper Edmonton Gardens for their afternoon meeting.

She pulled her cloak tighter against a sudden blast of cold wind and hurried toward the entrance.

The clerk smiled at her as she entered. "Can I help you, miss?"

Betsy returned his smile with one of her own. He was no more than twenty, with brown hair, a thin face, and a scattering of spots along his cheeks. "I'd like a pound of carrots." She pointed to a bin.

"Very good, miss." He picked out the carrots and tossed them onto the scales hanging from the center rafter.

"I don't suppose you know a family named Evans?" she asked. "I've a note for Mrs. Evans from my mistress and I've lost the address. She'll get really angry if I don't deliver it."

"They live just up the road." He pointed to his left. "Chepstow Villas. My sister works there. Is there anything else, miss?" He pulled a sheet of old newspaper from the shelf beneath the bins, held it under the scales, and tipped the carrots onto the page without spilling a single one.

"Do you have any apples that aren't too expensive?" She wanted to keep him talking.

"Sorry, miss, but we don't."

"What's the address on Chepstow Villas?" she asked.

"I'm not sure." He frowned. "Oh wait, I know how you can tell which house it is; it's the one with the half-built conservatory on the end. My sister showed it to me when I walked her home from her afternoon off last Monday." He grinned broadly. "We had a bit of a celebration at the pub that afternoon."

"What were you celebrating?" Betsy asked.

"The daughter of the house, Miss Rosemary Evans, is getting married." He laughed. "And as it was the last time before the wedding that the servants had their afternoon off together, Miss Rosemary gave the butler coin to buy everyone a bit of cheer."

"That's a lovely idea!" Betsy exclaimed.

"My sister says that Miss Rosemary is the decent one in that household. They're all going to miss her when she moves away to live with her new husband." He leaned forward and dropped his voice. "And just between you and me and the lamppost, once the staff is stuck working for just Mr. and Mrs. Evans, I've heard they'll be looking for new positions."

"Mr. Sutton isn't going to have an easy time of it," Barnes said as he and the inspector stepped into a hansom cab. He banged on the ceiling and they started forward with a jerk. "There's nothing worse than when one of the fairer sex goes all quiet like she did. She was so furious with the poor fellow, she didn't even trust herself to have a good shout at him. My wife has only been that angry at me once, and I shudder when I think about it."

Witherspoon couldn't help himself—he had to ask. "Er, if you don't mind my asking, why was your wife . . ."

"Ready to club me in my sleep." Barnes chuckled. "It was when we were first married, sir. A gang of thugs roughed me up pretty badly and it scared her. She'd have not been so angry except that I had a chance at another position; her cousin had offered me a foreman's job in a shoe factory in Barwell. The wages were good, but I didn't want to move to Leicestershire so I turned the job down. I liked being a policeman."

"How long did she stay angry at you?" Witherspoon asked. He wondered if Lady Cannonberry would ever want him to give up his position. He didn't think so; she seemed quite enthusiastic about his cases.

Barnes grinned. "A good two weeks, sir, and I don't mind admitting, it was the longest two weeks of my life. She barely spoke to me. My missus isn't just my wife, she's my dearest companion."

"You're a lucky man, Constable. From what I've observed of matrimony, there are many couples that can't stand the sight of each other." Witherspoon pushed his spectacles back up his nose. "As for Mrs. North, unless we can find any evidence connecting her to Agatha Moran, she wouldn't have a reason to want her dead. But we'll keep looking at the situation and see what turns up."

"It's Mrs. North's word against the maid's." Barnes sighed. "But if I was a betting man, I'd put my money on the servant. She's no reason to lie."

They discussed the case as the hansom made its way to Islington. By the time the cab pulled up at the curb in front of the house, it was raining hard. They got out, and while Barnes paid the driver, Witherspoon made a run for it.

The constable arrived on the stoop just as Jane Middleton opened up. "Hello, sirs, I was wondering when you'd return." She stepped back and opened the door wider, ushering them inside. "Do come in and dry off a bit."

"Thank you, Mrs. Middleton, you're most kind," Witherspoon replied. "Is Miss Farley in? I'd like to have another word with her."

"She's upstairs in her room," Mrs. Middleton said. "I'll fetch her after you have a decent cup of tea."

Witherspoon started to protest and then changed his mind. "Thank you, ma'am, we'd both very much appreciate something hot to drink."

"Come along then." She shooed them into the kitchen. "Make yourselves comfortable," she ordered as she set about making tea.

"If it's agreeable with you," Witherspoon said, "we'd like to have a look at Miss Moran's office before I interview Miss Farley."

"I thought you might want to go in and have a look 'round. No one's been in or out since . . ." Her voice broke, but she recovered quickly. "I've kept the office locked for just that reason." She pulled a key out of her apron pocket, put the kettle on the cooker, and came toward them. Handing it to Witherspoon, she said, "Here, you and your constable take as long a look as you like. I'll bring the tea in there when it's brewed."

Twenty minutes later, Witherspoon sighed and put the stack of newspapers to one side. "Honestly, why does anyone save old newspapers! These go back to June."

"Old papers can be very useful." Barnes looked up from the stack of invoices he was doggedly working his way through. "I use mine to polish my boots and start the fire."

The inspector shook his head in disbelief. "Surely they have newspapers on the continent . . ." He stopped as the door opened and the housekeeper stuck her head into the small, cramped office.

"Would you like more tea?" she asked.

"No thank you, I've just finished the first one you gave me," Witherspoon said.

"I'm still working on mine," Barnes added. "Mrs. Middleton, is there a reason you saved all the newspapers for Miss Moran? Did she ask you to?"

Jane nodded vigorously. "Indeed. She wouldn't tell me why; she simply asked me to keep them until she returned. There's a newsagent just up the road. She asked me to buy a *London Daily Tattler* every day. I've no idea why she liked the thing. It wasn't like her at all." She pointed to the stack in front of the inspector. "There's nothing of real interest in them, just gossip and silliness."

"What about these invoices and receipts?" Barnes asked. "Was there anything special about any of them?"

Jane shook her head. "Everything was in order. Miss Moran and I kept in contact by letter. She knew every penny that came into the hotel and every penny that went out. She didn't even ask me anything about the receipts when she went flying out of here on Monday afternoon. She just said she had urgent business to see about, but she wouldn't say what it was."

"Had she been in contact with the Evans family anytime in the past year?" Witherspoon pushed his chair away from the desk.

"I couldn't say if she'd been in direct contact with them or not, but I know she kept an eye on them," Jane declared. "Every month or two she went to Bayswater and had a bit of snoop around their neighborhood. I know I should have told you this, but it seemed such an ugly bit of pettiness, and I didn't want you thinking ill of her. She was a good and decent woman."

Witherspoon sighed audibly. "I do wish you'd mentioned this before—" he began.

"I know," she interrupted. "I should have. But I kept hoping you'd find out who killed her without me having to tell you. Miss Moran watching the family she used to work for and snooping around their neighborhood doesn't make her sound very nice."

Barnes straightened up from the file cabinet he'd been using as a desktop and dusted off his hands. "How long had she been spying on them?"

"She wasn't spying." She crossed her arms over her chest and glared at him. "She was keeping an eye on them, and she's been doing it for as long as I've worked here."

"Do you have any idea why she did such a thing?" Barnes asked.

Jane hesitated. "I don't know. For a long time, I thought it might be because she was enamored of Mr. Evans, but I don't think that's what it was. Honestly, if I knew, I'd tell you. Much as I hate the idea of her good name being bandied about by gossips, I'd rather that than having her killer get clean away."

Mrs. Goodge put the plate of scones down on the table next to the teapot and then slipped into her chair. She'd barely had time to get tea on the table before they'd begun coming in for their afternoon meeting. She'd had a brief word with Mrs. Jeffries about hiring Phyllis and had been quite relieved when the housekeeper had thought it quite a good idea. "We could do with some extra help," she'd murmured as she'd dashed off to do the upstairs dusting.

"Goodness, everyone was here on time. All of you must have learned quite a bit today." Mrs. Jeffries smiled confidently. For once, she had quite a bit to report as well.

"I'd like to go first, if I may," Mrs. Goodge volunteered. "I've two roast chickens in the oven and I'll need to baste them a time or two before we're finished here. It'll not do us a bit of good if I burn up the inspector's supper."

"By all means, go ahead." Mrs. Jeffries poured herself a cup of tea.

"One of my sources today was a young lady who used to work for Sir Madison Lowery," she announced with a triumphant smile.

"Cor blimey, that is a bit of good luck!" Wiggins exclaimed.

"Indeed it was," she agreed hastily. She didn't want them asking too many questions about how Phyllis happened to end up in her kitchen. "Phyllis worked as a housemaid for him for almost four years. She was recently let go." She told them everything she'd learned.

"She was let go because Sir Madison couldn't afford to keep her on." Luty pursed her lips. "That pretty much fits with what my sources have told me about Lowery's finances. He's broke and desperate to find a rich wife."

"You can say that about half the aristocrats in London," Ruth said. She was thinking about Lydia Mortmain.

"I think his wife dyin' is more useful to us than his bein' broke," Smythe interjected. "And from the way Mrs. Goodge heard it, it sounds like he took his sweet time gettin' a doctor there to help the poor woman."

"I heard that, too!" Ruth gasped. "Oh sorry." She flashed the cook an apologetic smile. "I'll wait my turn."

"That's alright. I was finished."

Mrs. Jeffries had no idea what any of this meant, but she had the feeling that they were finally making a bit of progress. "Do go on, Ruth. What did you learn?"

"As you all know, yesterday I had to leave early because I had a friend coming to supper. She knew quite a bit about Sir Madison Lowery." Ruth took a quick sip from her cup. "According to my source, despite his aristocratic heritage, most of the wealthy families in London did their best to keep their marriageable daughters well away from the man." She told them everything she'd learned from Lydia Mortmain. Because of her frequent absences from London, Ruth was sensitive to the fact that she'd not always participated in the inspector's cases, so she took great care to recall every detail. When she'd finished, she sat back in her chair.

"So the Trents thought there was something suspicious about her death?" Mrs. Jeffries clarified. She wanted to make sure she understood the situation before she started dropping hints in the inspector's ear.

"Apparently Mr. Trent was prepared to go to the police but didn't because of his wife's health and the damage it might do to her friendship with Margaret Porter Hains."

"But why should the woman who introduced them feel responsible?" Wiggins looked confused.

"Because Margaret Hains vouched for his character," Ruth explained. "Which means there shouldn't have been even a shadow of doubt about Lowery, but apparently, there was."

"And Sir Madison?" Mrs. Jeffries pressed. "He was ill as well?"

"Not very," Ruth replied. "He had mild symptoms which cleared up quickly. His poor wife suffered for two days before she finally passed away."

"How long was she sick before he called in a doctor?" Smythe asked.

"From the way Phyllis told it, it was long enough that she didn't have a morsel of anythin' left in her," Mrs. Goodge added. She glanced at Ruth, her expression sheepish. "Now I'm doin' it. I'm sorry."

"That's alright," Ruth replied. "My source didn't know exactly how long it was, but it was long enough to get tongues wagging. Furthermore, he inherited quite a bit of money from her as well as the house. But he's apparently spent most of it, as he's reduced to selling the fittings and fixtures and taking in a lodger."

"But what does the first wife's death have to do with Agatha Moran?" Wiggins asked. "Seems like Sir Madison didn't even know our victim."

"We're not certain about that fact," Betsy said quickly. "There may be a connection we just haven't seen as yet."

"We'll just have to keep digging until we do find it," Ruth declared.

"But was Lowery desperate enough to commit murder?" Hatchet murmured. "I suppose we'll never know the truth about his first wife."

"I'd not be too sure of that," Luty said. "The truth has a way of wiggling to the surface. Anyways, we'd best get movin' on. It's gettin' late."

Mrs. Jeffries nodded in agreement. "Would you care to go next?"

"Didn't learn a danged thing today." Luty shrugged philosophically. "But there's always tomorrow."

"You're in good company, Luty," Smythe said. "I didn't learn much today either. But like you said, tomorrow's another day."

Hatchet grinned broadly at his employer. "I've learned a few interesting tidbits."

"Humph," Luty snorted.

"Do go on," Mrs. Jeffries encouraged. "Luty's right. It is getting late."

"I had a very interesting conversation with two people who knew quite a bit about some of the people involved in our case," he said. He told them about his meeting with Reginald and Myra Manley.

"Eleanor North"—Wiggins' brow furrowed—"isn't she the next-door neighbor?"

"That is correct."

"But why would she have any reason to stab Miss Moran?" he pressed. "They didn't even know each other."

"But maybe they did," Betsy said. "If her fiancé had once known Agatha Moran, maybe she knew her, too."

"Is there anything else you'd like to report?" Mrs. Jeffries asked Hatchet.

"No, that's all."

She glanced at Betsy. "Did you have any luck today?"

"Just a bit." Betsy smiled. "I talked to some shopkeepers on the high street near the Evans house. But the only thing I found out was that the Evanses' servants were all off on Monday afternoon." She told them about the tiny bit of information she'd learned from the greengrocer. "But I'm going back out tomorrow."

"Don't you have the final fittin' for your dress tomorrow?" Mrs. Goodge asked as she got up from the table. She kept her attention on the maid as she walked over to the cooker and opened the oven door.

"Yes, but that's at nine in the morning."

"Aren't you goin' to spend the rest of the day with your family?" Smythe interjected. "You don't want them gettin' their feelin's hurt right before the weddin'."

"I can do it all," she protested. "I've got all day. Norah and Leo have other things to do in London besides sit and hold my hand."

"That's fine, Betsy," Mrs. Jeffries said quickly. She glanced at Wiggins. "How did you do?"

Wiggins shrugged. "I don't know that what I heard is goin' to be particularly useful, but I did meet up with a footman from the Evans household." He repeated what he'd learned from Mickey Dobbs. "It's not much." He smiled sheepishly. "Maybe I'll hear more tomorrow."

"It's fine, Wiggins," Mrs. Jeffries assured him. "Now, I've

got something to report." She told them about her meeting with Madame Deloffre. She took her time in the telling, giving them a blow-by-blow account of her every action, from her hiding place in front of the Moran house to the final good-bye with Madame Deloffre at King's Cross railway station.

"So Beatrice Trent wasn't his first wife. She was his second." Mrs. Goodge spooned liquid over the chickens.

"Do you think the Evans family knows he was married twice before?" Luty asked, her expression thoughtful.

"I doubt it," Hatchet said. "We've all been trying to get the goods on all of the people who were at that party, but none of us picked up this particular fact."

"It can't be common knowledge," Mrs. Goodge said flatly. She shoved the birds back in the oven and closed the door. "That's not the sort of gossip that people keep to themselves, so one of us would have heard by now."

"It's a good thing Mrs. Jeffries went to the Moran house today." Wiggins reached for another piece of bread. "Otherwise we'd still be in the dark as well. Seems to me she's found us a motive for Sir Madison. He might have killed her to keep her from tellin' the Evans family their soon-to-be son-in-law had two dead wives."

"Why thank you, Wiggins." Mrs. Jeffries beamed.

"But how did Lowery know that Miss Moran had found out his big secret?" Smythe asked.

"Maybe she told him," Betsy suggested. "You know, to scare him off and try to keep him from marrying her former charge."

"We can speculate all day, but it'll not do us any good at this point in the case," Mrs. Jeffries said. "Lowery does seem to have a reason to have murdered Miss Moran, but we mustn't jump to conclusions just yet."

"What were the papers that your Madame Deloffre translated for Miss Moran?" Wiggins asked as he slathered butter on his bread.

"A death certificate for Delphine Lowery," she replied.

"How did that one die?" Smythe asked.

"Don't tell us," Luty said. "I'll bet it was food poisonin'."

"And you would be correct." Mrs. Jeffries smiled. "The first Mrs. Lowery died three days after she'd eaten a batch of oysters."

Mrs. Jeffries managed to corner the inspector as soon as he stepped through the front door. Within moments, she had him ensconced in his favorite chair and drinking a nice glass of sherry.

"I do hope your day was productive, sir," Mrs. Jeffries said as she sank down on the settee opposite him.

"I'm never sure if I've been productive or not," he admitted. "But one thing is for certain: The constable and I worked very hard today. We learned quite a bit."

"Do begin at the beginning, sir," she pleaded. "You know how much I love hearing all the details of your day. We've plenty of time. Mrs. Goodge says dinner won't be ready for another forty-five minutes."

"Are we having roast chicken?"

"That's right, sir."

He took a sip of sherry. "Constable Barnes and I started off with a visit to the Evans household. We needed to go back, you see. The constable wanted to verify something the maid had mentioned, and I wanted to have another word with Mrs. Evans."

She listened carefully as he spoke, sometimes asking a question or making a comment. By the time he'd finished his recitation, their glasses were empty and she was trying to come up with a way to pass on some of the information the staff had learned. "Have you decided then, to focus your attention on the Evans household?"

He sighed and looked off into the distance. "Well, they have acted oddly. Mrs. Evans has been less than truthful with us and . . . oh, I don't know. We found out so much information today and I can't make sense of any of it."

"It's early days yet and you must give yourself time to see the pattern and the connections among these divergent facts."

"But what if I don't?" he wondered mournfully.

"Nonsense, sir. Your instincts have always served you well on your other cases," she assured him. "There's no reason to believe they won't serve you equally well on this one. As you've often said, sir, 'One can't go wrong listening to one's inner voice.' In this instance, you must give your voice a bit of time. Gracious, sir, who knows what other facts you'll turn up now that you're on the hunt, so to speak."

She knew that Witherspoon had very little faith in his own abilities, so she took every opportunity she could to bolster his confidence in himself and his "inner voice."

"You're very kind, Mrs. Jeffries." He gave her a grateful smile.

"Kindness has nothing to do with it, sir. You always do your duty, and you'll do your duty here and catch this killer."

"I hope so," he replied.

"As I said earlier, sir, you've excellent instincts." She had to tread carefully here. They'd learned so much today that she didn't want to push him in the wrong direction. She hesitated for a brief moment and then plunged ahead. "As it happens, over tea this afternoon, Mrs. Goodge mentioned that she'd heard quite a bit of gossip about Sir Madison Lowery."

* * *

Mrs. Jeffries stared through her bedroom window at the mist gathering outside. It was almost midnight and the house was silent, but she couldn't sleep. She pulled her shawl tighter against the night chill and kept her gaze on the gas lamp across the road. Her mind kept going over and over everything they'd found out. She didn't like forming an opinion so early in the investigation, but the evidence against Sir Madison Lowery was beginning to mount up. But was it? His motive was very questionable. Surely he'd not have committed murder merely because Agatha Moran threatened to expose his first marriage? Exposure could only be a threat to him if he knew that the Evanses would insist their daughter break off her engagement, and from what they'd learned about the character of Mrs. Evans, she'd not let a bit of gossip stop her from marrying off her only child to an aristocrat, even a minor one. But perhaps Mr. Evans wouldn't be so eager for the match and would put a halt to the marriage.

She'd drop a hint in the inspector's ear tomorrow at breakfast. He needed to pay Sir Madison another visit. She'd have a word with Constable Barnes as well, just to make certain the right kind of questions were asked.

Taking off her shawl, she draped it over the back of her rocking chair and went to her bed. Pulling the bedclothes aside, she got in and yanked the covers up to her chin. But what if Lowery wasn't the killer? she asked herself as other bits and pieces began to whirl about in her mind. Eleanor North had lied about being late, and one had to ask why she'd do so about such a petty thing unless she had something to hide. Arabella Evans had disappeared for a long period of time as well. But did either of them have a genuine motive for wanting Agatha Moran dead? And what about Miss Moran's longtime tenant? Perhaps Ellen Crowe finally decided to exact a bit of vengeance for old betrayals.

They'd had cases in the past where rage and hatred seethed for decades in a human heart before erupting in murder.

She flopped over onto her side. They'd learned a surprisingly large number of facts today, but what did they really know? She thought for a moment and then sighed. When one actually considered all the information they had about the crime, it didn't add up to very much. Just past dark on a public London street, Miss Moran had been stabbed to death. There were half a dozen spots where someone, anyone, might have witnessed the killing, but so far, no one had come forth. A house-to-house of the neighborhood hadn't yielded any clues either.

She rolled onto her back and stared up at the ceiling. She gave up trying to make sense out of what they'd learned thus far and let her mind wander off of its own accord. Snatches of conversation drifted through her head, sparking thoughts that lasted less than a blink of an eye. Finally, just as she was drifting to sleep, one idea grabbed hold and wouldn't let go. What if they were wrong? What if the murder really was simply the result of Agatha Moran being at the wrong place at the wrong time? What if the killing was simply a random act of violence?

"I've already told you everything I know." Sir Madison Lowery's handsome features contorted in a heavy frown as he confronted the two policemen on his doorstep.

"We understand that, sir," Witherspoon said politely, "but we've a few more questions. May we come in?"

Lowery hesitated, and for an instant, the inspector was sure he was going to slam the door in their faces, but he stepped back and motioned them inside. "My housekeeper is off this afternoon. Otherwise, she'd be tending to unwanted visitors."

They stepped inside the foyer. The floors were a white

and black tile set in a pattern of alternating rows. Opposite the front door, a plant stand with a three-foot-tall blue and white Chinese vase sitting on it stood at the base of the staircase.

"This way." Lowery gestured for them to follow him down the hallway. He led them through a set of double doors and into the drawing room. The bottom half of the walls were paneled in a dark wood, above which were cream-colored walls. Blue and cream drapes hung at the windows and a huge portrait of Lowery dominated the wall over the mantelpiece. Despite the cold, no fire blazed in the hearth.

"You might as well have a seat," he offered ungraciously as he pointed to a blue upholstered settee. "But do be quick. I'm due at my fiancée's shortly." He walked over and stood by the fireplace.

They sat down. Barnes took out his notebook and looked at the inspector expectantly. They had a lot of questions that needed answers.

Witherspoon wasn't sure where to begin. "Mr. Lowery," he began.

"I have a title, Inspector," Lowery interrupted. "I'd like you to use it."

"Sorry, sir," the inspector replied. "You said earlier that you were late in getting to the tea party."

"We've been over all that." Lowery leaned against the mantelpiece and crossed his arms over his chest. "I really see no point in repeating myself. You've got my statement."

Witherspoon simply stared at him. He'd learned that sometimes, saying nothing actually got quite good results. People talked to fill the silence.

"Oh alright." He uncrossed his arms and straightened up. "I suppose one of the servants must have seen me. I didn't come in through the back. I came in through the conservatory."

"Why didn't you tell us this before, sir?" Barnes asked softly.

"Because my soon-to-be mother-in-law is a stickler for propriety." He came toward them. "If she knew I'd come in by shoving aside an oilcloth and climbing through the window, she'd have been terribly upset."

"Exactly what time was it that you shoved the oilcloth aside?" Witherspoon asked.

Lowery sighed heavily and flopped into the chair. "I don't know what time it was, only that I was very, very late. The truth of the matter is, I was playing cards at my club and I lost track of the time. But by slipping in the way I did, I managed to avoid having to answer any of Mrs. Evans' questions about why I was late."

"You were concerned about Mrs. Evans," Witherspoon pressed. "Not your fiancée?"

"Rosemary barely notices whether I'm there or not," he admitted. "Sometimes I'm amazed she even agreed to marry me."

The door to the drawing room flew open and a dark-haired young man stuck his head into the room. His eyes widened in surprise when he saw them. "I'm sorry, I didn't realize you had guests . . ." He started to withdraw.

"They're not guests, they're the police," Lowery said quickly.

The fellow smiled uncertainly. "Er, uh, yes, I can see that . . ."

Barnes stared at the newcomer. He was every inch a young English gentleman. He wore a pristine white shirt and navy blue vest, red cravat, and navy blue trousers. His eyes were blue, his features unremarkable, and his build slender. "Who are you, sir?" the constable asked.

"Christopher Selby, I'm Sir Madison's—"

"Cousin," Lowery finished for him. "Mr. Selby is my

cousin. He's staying with me." He turned his attention to the newcomer. "Did you want something?"

Selby shook his head. "It can wait. I'll see you later." He bowed to the policemen and withdrew.

"Have you ever met Miss Agatha Moran?" Witherspoon suddenly asked.

Taken aback, Lowery sputtered, "I've already told you I've never seen the woman before."

"Were the police already out front when you slipped in through the conservatory window?" Barnes kept the pressure up. "Even with the oilcloth up, you can easily see the front of the house from just about any part of the conservatory."

"I don't know . . ." He hesitated.

"Nonsense, sir. You've got eyes in your head. You know what you saw. It was only a couple of days ago."

"I don't remember . . ."

"I'd be careful how you answer, sir," Barnes warned. "We have spoken at great length to all the servants, and as you well know, there are a goodly number of them in the Evans household." He was on a fishing expedition, but this one wasn't to know that.

"Oh, very well." Lowery's shoulders slumped. "They were already there when I got to the house. I could see the commotion outside, but honest to God, I'd no idea anyone had been murdered. I thought there'd been an accident or a robbery. The truth of the matter was that I was hoping that whatever had happened would distract Arabella Evans from realizing just how late I was. It was my hard luck that the curtains were closed so most of the guests had no idea anything untoward was happening right outside the house."

"You were married previously?" Witherspoon asked. He knew the fellow had been married before.

Lowery's eyes widened in surprise. "I'm a widower, but I don't see what that's got to do with this situation."

"Have you ever been to France, sir?" Barnes asked. He glanced at the inspector. He'd tried to mention the French wife on the ride over this morning, but by the time they'd gotten through all the other bits and pieces the inspector insisted on talking about, they were on Lowery's doorstep. But he was relieved to see that Witherspoon didn't look surprised by his question. Good, Mrs. Jeffries' hints must have gotten through to him.

"What kind of a question is that?" Lowery blustered. "Of course I've been to France. Many times."

"Did you live there, sir?" Barnes continued. He kept his attention on his notebook, flipping through the pages as though he were looking for something.

"I did," Lowery admitted. "I lived in Paris for several years."

"Were you married when you lived in France, sir?" Witherspoon asked.

The color drained from Lowery's face. "I don't suppose there's any point in my denying it—someone's already told you the whole story."

Witherspoon felt a surge of confidence. He wasn't quite certain what had led him to ask Lowery this question, but his instincts were right! His inner voice was working again.

"Did your wife die?" Barnes asked.

"Yes, I'm a widower twice over." Lowery got up and began to pace. "My first wife died of accidental food poisoning."

"And your second wife, sir?" Witherspoon pressed. "The former Miss Beatrice Trent, how did she die?"

Lowery stopped and turned his back to them, focusing his attention on the window. "You already know the answer to that, Inspector."

"She died of food poisoning as well," Witherspoon said softly. "Goodness, sir, you are unlucky in your wives."

He whirled around to face them. "Lots of people die of food poisoning," he charged. "I almost died of it myself, both times."

"Was there an inquest?" Barnes pressed.

"Of course not, Beatrice was properly treated by a doctor," Lowery snapped. "And Odette was seen by a physician as well. Both their deaths were accidents. I'm not answering any more questions about either of my wives. I loved them both." He stopped and took a deep breath. "Unless you're going to arrest me, Inspector, I'd like you and the constable to get the hell out of my home."

CHAPTER 8

Wiggins walked slowly down Marsdale Street, keeping his eyes open for a likely soul who could spare a few moments for a chat. As he strolled past number three, he took a good look at the four-story brown brick house. The cream-colored façade on the ground floor was pitted with gouges where the plaster had crumbled, the gutters sagged, and the stairs were riddled with cracks. The front door could use another coat of paint as well, he thought. This was Tobias Sutton's home, and from the looks of it, the fellow wasn't much of a success.

At their meeting this morning, Luty had commented that she'd heard from one of her sources that Sutton hadn't won a case in years and that his career was just about finished. The only reason Sutton hadn't been asked to leave his chambers was because he'd gotten himself engaged to Mrs. North.

He'd decided to have a closer look at Tobias Sutton not because he thought the man had anything to do with the murder, but because it had been a good excuse to get out of the house this morning. Wiggins reached the end of the street and paused, trying to decide if it was worth the effort to turn around and try again. He decided it wasn't. In this cold weather, he could do with a cup of tea, and he'd spotted a nice café around the corner.

He stifled a shaft of guilt and continued walking. He'd come to Shepherds Bush because he was a coward. Cor blimey, he should have followed Betsy when she left the house. He could tell she was upset, but he didn't have a clue as to why. Betsy was like a sister to him, but for the life of him, he'd never understand her or any other woman.

The day had started off well enough; everyone had come to the meeting all bright eyed and raring to go. Luty had told everyone what'd she found out last night about Sutton, Hatchet had passed along a tidbit he'd heard about Rosemary Evans, and then Mrs. Jeffries had announced they were hiring someone to help out and that the girl would be coming at ten o'clock.

Everyone started talking at once, asking how they could have their meetings with a stranger about the place, but Mrs. Jeffries had assured them that wouldn't be a problem. Phyllis Thomlinson would be working from half past nine, which was after their morning meeting, until four, which was before their afternoon meeting. She'd explained that Mrs. Goodge had vouched for the girl and that with the wedding, Christmas, and the murder, they simply had to have more help.

After the meeting, Smythe had gone off on some mysterious errand of his own, Mrs. Jeffries had announced she was going to St. Thomas' Hospital to have a word with their friend Dr. Bosworth, and Mrs. Goodge had shooed everyone out of the kitchen. It was then that he'd seen Betsy slip into the dry larder. He'd grabbed his coat and hat off the coat tree and then hurried out to catch up with her. He'd thought they might walk to the omnibus stop together. But just as he reached the larder door, he heard her crying. He'd no idea what to do so he'd stood there like a ninny, listening to her sob and wishing he were anywhere but the back hall of Upper Edmonton Gardens. About then, one of Mrs. Goodge's sources had pounded on the back door, and after he'd let the laundry boy in, Wiggins had run like the coward he was. He couldn't stand to see Betsy cry.

He opened the door of the café, stepped inside, and went to the counter. "Good mornin'." The counterman gave him a friendly grin.

"Good mornin'," Wiggins replied. "I'd like tea, please."

A few moments later, the counterman put a cup in front of him. "Cold out there, isn't it?"

"One of the worst days we've 'ad all winter," Wiggins said with a grateful nod. He was desperate to have someone, anyone, to chat with. The more words that filled the air, the easier it was to forget the sound of Betsy's crying. "Mind you, it's not as bad as it was last week when it was rainin' so 'ard."

"I like the rain." The man grinned broadly. "It's good for business. Do you work around here?"

"No, I'm lookin' for a friend," Wiggins lied easily. "He works as a footman for a barrister named Sutton, but I've lost the ruddy address."

The counterman's heavy brows drew together. "You mean Tobias Sutton? That couldn't be right. That fellow could no more pay a footman's wages than he could sprout wings and fly."

"Are ya jokin'?" Wiggins feigned surprise. "But that's who Jimmy told me 'e worked for. Said the feller had a house on Marsdale Street. 'E give me the address and I've gone up and down the street twice now, thinkin' that seein' the numbers might jog my memory, but it didn't. You're sayin' this Sutton fellow hasn't got a footman?"

He laughed. "He can barely afford my Lorna's wages, and she only goes in to clean for him on Tuesday mornings for a few hours." He turned and called, "Lorna, come out here and tell this poor lad he's wasting his time."

Wiggins blinked as a chubby red-haired woman stepped out from behind a curtain that he'd not noticed. Apparently, there was a back room behind the counter.

She gave the counterman a sour look. "For God's sake, Reg, can't a person have any peace? What are you wanting now? I'm dead on my feet and I've got to go to the Hubbards' this afternoon."

"It's my fault, ma'am," Wiggins said quickly. He gave the hapless Reg a quick smile. "I was askin' questions about a barrister named Sutton—"

"You mean Tobias Sutton," she interrupted with a sneer. "I've a good mind not to go back again. Stupid sod didn't pay me for last Tuesday."

"You told me you didn't work on Tuesday," Reg interjected. "You were back here twenty minutes after you left."

"Leavin' weren't my idea. He's the one who made me go. But he still should 'ave paid me," Lorna declared. "I went 'round there just as I always do. It wasn't my fault some woman showed up. She was probably someone who hired him to go to court. She looked angry enough to skin him alive. I'll bet she was wantin' her money back because he did such a terrible job. You know, he's not won a case in years."

Wiggins knew he had to be careful here. He didn't want to arouse their suspicions by asking too much, but on the other hand, he had to find out the identity of Sutton's mysterious visitor. "Cor blimey, Jimmy said his guv was a quiet sort, you know, one of them old bachelors that spend their time readin' and writin'. But your Mr. Sutton sounds like he's got a right excitin' life if he's got young women . . ."

"She wasn't young, she was middle-aged." Lorna gave a derisive snort. She helped herself to a cup of tea from the urn on the counter. "Sutton's life is about as excitin' as watching paint dry. The only thing he's done since I've been his cleaner is to get himself engaged."

"Engaged? How old is 'e then?"

She stared at him for few seconds, her expression speculative. "Why do you care how old the man is?"

Wiggins shrugged, smiled, and took a sip of tea. Lorna was obviously a lot more suspicious than Reg. "I'm just wonderin' if I've got the right barrister. Are you sure there isn't someone else in the neighborhood with that name, an older man? I've got to find Jimmy. 'E owes me money."

"Your Jimmy is pulling a fast one on you." Lorna burst out laughing. "Take my word for it, your friend doesn't work for Tobias Sutton. He's middle-aged, not old, and there's no one else by that name in the neighborhood."

"But he said he worked on Marsdale Street. He give me the address. He even wrote it on a bit of paper and slipped it in my coat pocket. I must 'ave lost it 'cause when I looked for it, all I found was a scrap of a soap advertisement." Wiggins bit his lip. "What about the lady who come to see this Mr. Sutton? Was she from around 'ere? Maybe that's where Jimmy works?"

Lorna looked at him as if he were pitiful. "I've never seen her before. When she arrived, I was at the window, doing the ledges, and I saw her gettin' out of a hansom cab. She's not from around here."

"You're grasping at straws, lad." Reg shook his head in sympathy. "I hope Jimmy didn't owe you a lot of money, because I don't think you're going to be getting any of it back."

"I'm sure you'll do just fine, Phyllis," Mrs. Jeffries said as she escorted Phyllis down the back stairs toward the kitchen. She skidded to a halt as she spotted Mrs. Goodge serving tea to the man from the gasworks. "Come along, then, Mrs. Goodge is busy at the moment." She ushered her back up the stairs they'd just descended and pointed toward the front of the house. "Please give this floor a thorough cleaning. You don't need to polish the silver in the dining room; that's one of Wiggins' tasks. Be sure and dust the bookcases in the inspector's study, but don't bother beating the rugs. That was done last week."

Phyllis bobbed a quick curtsy. "Yes ma'am. Shall I use the Adams furniture polish on the wood or do you want it rubbed with oil?"

"Use the Adams, please. This is a very modern household," Mrs. Jeffries replied. "Oh, and Phyllis, you don't need to curtsy to anyone here, including Inspector Witherspoon."

Phyllis started to bob, caught herself, and giggled. "Thank you, ma'am, I'll try to remember, but it's such a habit. We had to curtsy at my last place. Sir Madison would get very angry if anyone forgot. Right before he let me go, I was in a rush and I didn't bob and weave properly to Mr. Selby, who I don't think even cared, but Sir Madison saw it and spent ten minutes giving me a lecture about proper servants' behavior."

"Sir Madison doesn't sound like a very nice person. But as long as you are respectful and do your duties, you'll do just fine here." Mrs. Jeffries nodded a good-bye to the girl as she headed for the back stairs. There were dozens of questions she'd like to ask Phyllis, but right now she was in a rush. She had to go to St. Thomas' Hospital, and that trip took ages. She hoped Dr. Bosworth wasn't too busy and would have time to speak with her. She'd been very remiss in waiting this long to avail herself of their friend's expertise.

She hurried down the stairs and into the kitchen. The man from the gasworks was gone, and the cook was at the worktable with a sugar hammer in one hand and a cone of sugar in the other. Samson, Mrs. Goodge's ill-tempered tabby cat, was sitting on a stool by the door. He hissed at her as she went past on her way to the coat tree.

"Phyllis is in the dining room if you need her," she said to the cook. She put on her hat and started tying the ribbon under her chin. "If she can get that floor cleaned, that'll be a great help."

"Did Betsy seem upset?" Mrs. Goodge put down the cone and the hammer. "She was awfully quiet when she left today, and her eyes were red."

Mrs. Jeffries fingers stilled. "I think she might be worrying that Phyllis is going to take her place." She finished her task and reached for her cloak. "But I don't know what we can do about the situation. We need the help, and like it or not, once she and Smythe are married, things are going to change around here. I hate to see her upset and thought that everyone understood Phyllis is only here on a temporary basis."

"I don't think it's just that we've hired more help," Mrs. Goodge said. "I don't think she's havin' a case of nerves. Before breakfast I heard her askin' Smythe about where they'd be livin' and where they were goin' on their weddin' trip. But he just laughed and told her to trust him. But I think he's wrong: I think she needs a bit of security right now, you know, like my Samson does sometimes when he crawls into my lap for a cuddle. He does that when somethin' scares him. Right now Betsy's a bit frightened."

Mrs. Jeffries glanced at Samson. A pack of wild dogs wouldn't scare that wretched cat, but the cook was blind to his nasty disposition and considered him her baby. "You're probably right. Do you think one of us should have a word with Smythe?"

Mrs. Goodge shrugged, picked up the hammer, and took a whack at the sugar cone. "I don't know. He might have figured it out for himself; he's not totally dense. You off to see Dr. Bosworth?"

"Yes." She slipped on her cloak. "I've no idea how long I'll be gone. But I will definitely be back for our afternoon meeting. Oh, that reminds me, what are we to do about Phyllis when you're with one of your sources? We almost barged in when you were chatting with the gasman."

"Don't worry about that." Mrs. Goodge grinned. "I thought and thought about it and the answer was right under my nose. All I do with my sources is get them talkin' about the people involved in our cases. Now unless Phyllis is actually at our meetin's, she'll not know who our suspects might be. So if she happens to hear me chattin' with someone, she'll simply think I'm a terrible old gossip."

Smythe was leaning against the pub when Betsy came hurrying around the corner. He pushed away from the wall. "Where've you been?"

"The dressmaker's," she explained. She'd also gone for a walk to get herself under control before she had to face anyone. Learning that they'd hired another maid had taken the wind out of her sails. She knew she was being silly; Mrs. Jeffries had made it perfectly clear that the girl was only there to help out until she and Smythe were back from their wedding trip. Which was another thing that was worrying her—she'd no idea where she was to live and no idea where they were going after the vows and the reception. To top it off, she was certain Norah and Leo regretted coming back to England. "I had a final fitting."

He pulled her into his arms, but instead of kissing her, he stared at her with an anxious, worried frown. "Are you alright? Your eyes are red. Have you been cryin'?"

"It's the wind." She gave him an overly bright smile that didn't fool him for a minute. "It makes my eyes water. Come on, let's go upstairs and get this over with." She pulled away, grabbed the handle of the door that led to the second floor of the pub, and flew up the stairs.

Norah was waiting for them when they came into the sitting room. "I wondered when you'd get here." She smiled as she said it, but the smile didn't mask the irritation in her eyes.

Leo stepped out of the bedroom, a welcoming smile on his face. "Hello, I'm glad you've come. We've not had near enough time to visit. Can you stay for lunch?"

"Of course," Betsy said. She went to the couch and sat down across from her sister. "That's why we've come." She patted the seat next to her. "Sit here, Smythe." When he slipped into the spot next to her, she grabbed his hand and hung on for dear life.

Leo took the chair next to Norah, and for a few seconds, the four of them stared at one another. Then everyone began to speak at once, then stopped, and all of them erupted in laughter.

"You go first," Betsy said to Norah. "After all, you're the oldest."

"Why you cheeky monkey." Norah giggled. "And all I was going to say was that I hope you both like pork roast, because that's what I've ordered for lunch."

After that, everyone seemed to relax. Smythe and Leo got into an intense discussion about the best wood to use for cabinetry while Betsy and Norah talked about the wedding lunch menu, Betsy's dress, Norah's dress, and whether or not the bride and groom had to leave before any of the guests.

By the time Betsy and Smythe were ready to take their leave after lunch, Betsy felt much better than when she'd arrived. She was ashamed of herself. She shouldn't have dreaded spending a few hours with Norah; she and her sister were finally getting to know each other again.

Luty wished she'd worn something a bit more subdued than her bright green cloak with its shiny brass buttons, but she'd no idea she was going to be following Eleanor North's housekeeper down a busy Bayswater street. She increased her pace as the black-garbed figure ahead of her rounded a corner. Luty doubled her efforts to keep up with the woman. She had no idea what she'd do once she caught up with her, but she was sure she'd think of something. Hoping that she wouldn't see anyone she knew, she continued following her prey down Westbourne Grove. She stopped and leaned against a postbox as the woman went into the L & C Bank.

She thought for a moment and suddenly had an idea. Even by her standards, it was a pretty pathetic one, but it was all she could come up with at short notice. The truth of the matter was that she was desperate to contribute something. So far, all she'd managed to find out was that Lowery was broke, the Evanses were rich, and Tobias Sutton was a lousy lawyer.

She moved closer to the bank building and positioned herself by the front door and waited there. Luty took a deep breath as the door opened and an elderly woman, not dressed in black, stepped out onto the pavement. She gave Luty a cursory glance, nodded politely, and walked on. The door opened again, and this time, it was the one she'd been waiting for. Keeping her head down, Luty launched herself at the figure in black, slamming into the woman hard enough to send her reeling back against the door and sliding to the ground.

"Oh my gracious me," Luty cried. "I'm so sorry. I was in such a hurry to git into that bank I almost killed ya."

Dazed, the woman stared at her. She had gray hair and there were deep lines etched around her mouth and eyes. Her brown straw hat was askew, her coat gaped open, and her black bombazine skirt had hitched up to her knees. She scrambled to her feet as several passersby began to take an interest in the scene.

"You really should watch where you're going," she snapped, giving Luty a good glare.

"I am so sorry, ma'am." Luty sniffled and looked away. She couldn't cry at will but she could make her voice tremble. "It . . . it . . . was all my fault. I do hope you're not hurt any."

"I'm fine, thank you. There's no real harm done, but you did give me a terrible fright."

Luty sniffled again. "I'm sorry," she whispered.

"Oh dear, look ma'am, please, don't upset yourself. I'm perfectly fine. I shouldn't have lost control of my tongue."

Luty kept her head down a moment longer. "No, you've every right to be angry. I was in a hurry and I wasn't payin' attention." She dabbed at her cheeks and then looked up. "If you're not in a terrible hurry, there's a hotel that serves a nice tea just up the road. Please let me make this up to you."

"I couldn't possibly allow you to do that." The woman smiled briefly as she straightened her hat. Then her eyes narrowed thoughtfully as she studied Luty from head to toe. "Well, if it would make you feel better—"

"Oh it most definitely would," Luty interrupted. She wasn't stupid; she knew the woman had changed her mind because she'd noticed the expensive cut of her coat and realized the muff she carried was sable. "Come on, then, the hotel isn't very far."

"I know the place," the woman replied. "I've never been inside but it looks very expensive."

"I've been there lots of times," Luty said quickly. "After the scare I gave the both of us, I need somethin' to wet my whistle. You look like you could use somethin' to put the color back into yer cheeks, too. You're as white as a goat's hind end." She was deliberately playing the part of the rich, uncouth American.

People were a lot less likely to watch their tongues when they thought you were a fool.

Five minutes later, she was ensconced in a secluded corner of the Imperial Hotel. Mrs. Enid Jones, housekeeper to Eleanor North, was sitting in the leather chair opposite her. A huge fern kept them nicely hidden from any prying eyes and insured they'd have privacy.

"I thought we'd go into the tearoom," Enid murmured.

"Oh, we'll be more comfortable here." Luty waved a bellman over.

The bellman smiled in recognition. "Good day, Mrs. Crookshank. It's lovely to see you again. What can I bring you and your guest?"

Luty hadn't been lying when she said they knew her here. They ought to; she was one of their biggest investors. "A nice pot of tea and a tray of pastries." She glanced at Enid. "Is that alright with you?"

Enid nodded.

"I do hope you're not in too much of a hurry. The pastries here are delicious and you'll want to enjoy them."

"I'm sure I will." Enid Jones took a deep breath and pulled her coat tighter.

"Do you live around here?" Luty asked conversationally.

"Mrs. North lives on Chepstow Villas." She smiled uncertainly. "As I said, I'm just the housekeeper."

"That's an important job," Luty replied. "I used to do housekeepin' back in Colorado. Mind you, that was before I married my late husband and we went to prospectin' for silver."

"You were a housekeeper?" Enid asked eagerly.

"Well, not a proper one like you," she said. "Back in those days it was more like ridin' roughshod over a herd of bad-tempered cowpokes. The place I worked at was more a hotel than house, but I did the cleanin' and the cookin' and saw that everythin' was right clean and tidy."

Enid cocked her head to one side. "You Americans are an odd lot. A rich English person would die before they'd admit to being a domestic servant."

"Why? Honest work ain't anythin' to be ashamed of," Luty said.

"I didn't say it was." Enid laughed.

Their tea arrived, and before long, the two women were chatting as if they were old friends.

"Mrs. North can throw a tantrum as well." Enid picked up a cream puff. "Everyone used to say it was her husband who had the bad temper, but that's not true. You should have heard her a few days ago. She was screaming like a fishwife, and poor Mr. Sutton hadn't done anything wrong."

"Then what got her so het up?" Luty helped herself to a lemon tart.

"Jealousy." Enid shook her head in disgust. "At her age, can you believe it? She's almost fifty and here she was screaming at poor Mr. Sutton because she'd found out some woman had been to his house. He kept trying to explain, to tell her that she'd just appeared at his doorstep, but she wouldn't listen."

Luty swallowed the bite of tart she'd just put in her

mouth. "Goodness, you'd think a woman of that age should be able to control her feelings. Then again, you'd think a feller like Mr. Sutton would have better sense than to tell his fiancée he'd been havin' female visitors."

"Oh, he didn't tell her," Enid countered.

"I just assumed he musta told her. But if he didn't tell her, how'd she find out? She bribin' his servants to keep an eye on him?"

Enid laughed heartily. "He doesn't have any servants, just a cleaning woman who comes once a week." She leaned toward Luty and dropped her voice to a whisper. "She hired a private inquiry agent. Well, you can't blame the woman after what she went through with that awful Mr. North. She and Mr. Sutton are to marry next month. This time, she wanted to be sure about the character of the man before she let him put the ring on her finger."

The Evans Import and Export Company was located in a modern brick building on Fenchurch Street. Barnes pulled open one of the heavy double doors and held it open for Witherspoon. They'd been discussing the case on the hansom ride here from the station. "The constable we sent to Putney did confirm some of what Ellen Crowe told you," Barnes said as they stepped into the lobby. "Ellen Crowe was visiting Miss Whitley, but she wouldn't confirm exactly when Mrs. Crowe left. She said she wasn't sure of the actual time."

"How can she not know what time a guest left?" Witherspoon shook his head in disbelief. He marched across the shiny wood floor to the staircase.

"According to her statement, she fell asleep when Mrs. Crowe left. Apparently they'd had a glass of wine or two. She didn't awaken until her maid announced that dinner was ready."

They started up the stairs to the first floor. "So for all we know, she could have left Putney at four o'clock, taken the train to Waterloo, and been able to get to Notting Hill easily by five fifteen."

"It does seem possible, sir," Barnes replied. They'd reached the first-floor landing and the inspector stopped and rested against the banister. He was slightly out of breath.

Barnes, grateful for a chance to recover himself, leaned against the opposite wall. "I thought that Sir Madison Lowery was our prime suspect."

Witherspoon straightened up. "He is, but we've no real evidence against him. Were you able to send the request to the Paris police?"

"I did, sir. But if his first wife's death was an accident and there was no inquiry or suspicion of foul play, I don't see what the Paris police can tell us."

"Probably nothing, but it doesn't hurt to ask. Furthermore, we don't know that her family wasn't suspicious of their English son-in-law. According to the information we've heard, the Trents were certainly skeptical of the man."

"Not enough to call us in when their daughter died," Barnes pointed out as they started down the hallway.

"True," the inspector said. "But they were faced with the same situation we face, and they had no evidence that her death was anything but an accident."

"Come on, sir," Barnes scoffed. "The fellow isn't even thirty-five and he's buried two wives and both of them dead by food poisoning."

They'd reached the last office in the corridor. Witherspoon put his hand on the doorknob but didn't turn it. He looked at the constable. "I have a feeling the Trents weren't aware he'd been married previously. We only found out because my cook heard a bit of gossip from one of her old colleagues."

"True, sir," Barnes replied. He glanced to the other side of the hall and noted it was a shipping agent's office.

The inspector opened the door and the two men stepped into the office. The room was a huge, cavernous place. One wall was covered by shelves filled with mechanical devices, old-fashioned oil lamps, china figurines, bags of coffee, brightly colored miniature carriages, boxes of different sizes, and an entire row of children's toys. On the far wall, there was a door leading to an inner office, and directly in front of the inspector and Barnes were two long, narrow windows with their shades up to let in the pale morning light.

Two young men sat at the desks in front of the shelves. When the door opened, both of them looked up from their ledgers. One of them rose to his feet, his mouth gaping open slightly in surprise as he stared at the two policemen, while the other simply sat in his chair, gawking at them with wide, curious eyes.

The first one turned his head slightly. "Mr. Branson, the police are here," he called over his shoulder.

A head popped up from behind a stack of black box files piled on the desk in front of the inner office. He had wispy gray hair, an elfin face, spectacles, and he wore an old-fashioned wing tip collar. "I'm afraid if you're looking for Mr. Evans, he isn't here," he said as he scurried toward them.

"We're aware of that, sir," Witherspoon said politely. "Are you Mr. Evans' chief clerk?"

"I am." He held out his hand. "Douglas Branson."

The two men shook and the inspector introduced Constable Barnes. "It's you we've come to see," he said. "And if you don't mind, the constable would like to have a word with your junior clerks."

Branson hesitated. "Of course, but if you're here about the day of the er . . . unfortunate incident, the juniors won't be much use. They weren't here. Mr. Evans sent them both to the dock to inspect a shipment of heavy equipment before we took custody of it."

"We'd still like to speak to them." Witherspoon inclined his head toward the inner office door. "May we use that office? I'd like to take your statement, please."

"I suppose it'll be alright," Branson muttered. "But we mustn't touch anything. Mr. Evans is very particular." He pushed open the door and motioned for the inspector to follow.

Barnes waited till they disappeared before turning his attention to the two clerks. There didn't seem any point in interviewing them separately. "What's all that on the shelves?" He pointed to the row of toys. He was both curious and wanted to get them talking.

"That's the bits we get stuck with when the shippers and consignees get into a tiff over who owes what," the one who was standing replied. He was tall and lanky, with a headful of thick blond hair and bushy eyebrows.

"What do you do with it?" Barnes moved closer to have a better look. "Just let it sit here?"

"When the shelves get too full, we sell it off," the one still sitting at his desk replied.

"What's in those boxes?" Barnes asked.

The blond one pointed to a big box at the far end of the top shelf. "That's full of defective cutlery—the consignee refused it as the forks only have two prongs—the one next to it is from America and it's filled with goose down feathers, and the little box on the end is tins of chili peppers from Mexico. We get all sorts of things. Some of it doesn't sell very well in England."

Barnes laughed. "What's your name, sir?"

"John Banning. I've been a clerk here for two years."

"I'm Harold Hartman," the other clerk volunteered. "I've worked here for three years. Mr. Branson was telling the truth, Constable. We were both gone on Wednesday afternoon. Mr. Evans sent us off before lunchtime."

"It was an important shipment," Banning added. "It was coming in on the *American Star*. She docked right on time, but we had to wait for customs clearance before we could get onboard and inspect the goods."

"What dock, and what time did you get on board?" Barnes asked.

"Tilbury and it was half past two before she was cleared," Hartman said. "It was nice for us; we had a good lunch at the Seaman's Inn."

"And how long did it take you to do the inspection?" He leaned against the wall and took out his notebook.

"We were finished by four o'clock," he replied. "So we went on home. Mr. Evans had told us we could leave for the day when we'd finished. Like I said, it was nice for us. We usually have to report back to the office no matter how late it is."

"Do you do inspections often?" Barnes asked them.

It was Banning who answered. "I'd say it isn't more than once a month. We only do it when we're bringing in something very expensive."

Inside Jeremy Evans' office, Inspector Witherspoon was doing his best to keep Douglas Branson from meandering off the subject. "Now, back to Wednesday afternoon. What time was it you left the office?"

Branson sat behind Mr. Evans' desk. The inspector was in the straight backed visitor's chair opposite him.

"Mr. Evans sent me to the customs house just before lunch. I had six shipments to clear."

"And he instructed you not to come back here when you'd finished, is that correct?"

"He didn't instruct me," Branson said defensively. "He told me I could have the rest of the afternoon off. After all, it is the Christmas season and Mr. Evans knew I wanted to do some shopping. My wife has been hinting that she wants to take violin lessons, though I honestly don't know why as she's tone-deaf, and I've two daughters who are expecting presents as well. Furthermore, Mr. Evans wanted some peace and quiet. He wanted to go over the ledgers. Year-end is coming and he wanted to insure all the accounts were in order."

"Is it his habit to do this every year?"

"Of course. Mr. Evans is very methodical and he does everything correctly. Why, years ago, before Miss Rosemary was even born, our agent in Argentina died unexpectedly, and instead of sending me there, he went himself. He was gone for over six months, but that didn't matter. What mattered was insuring that we got the best possible agency to represent the firm." Branson smiled triumphantly. "For twenty years, the Allende Brothers have been our agents and we've never had cause to complain. That's the sort of person Mr. Evans is. He knows his duty and he certainly wouldn't be involved in anything as sordid as a murder."

Witherspoon forced himself to stay calm. Branson seemed incapable of giving a simple, straightforward answer. "Nonetheless, it's my duty to confirm his statement. Mr. Evans was alone in the office that afternoon, is that correct?"

"I've already told you we were all gone," Branson replied. "I'll admit I was surprised when Mr. Evans told the juniors they could go home when they'd finished, but in retrospect, it shouldn't have been in the least surprising. Mr. Evans had a terrible headache that day. As a matter of fact, I almost offered to loan him my bottle of peppermint oil, as it's awfully good for headaches. You just rub it on your forehead and within a few minutes, you're feeling much better. Mind you, it does sting a bit—"

Witherspoon interrupted. "Mr. Branson, did Mr. Evans tell you he was feeling poorly?" He knew it was a silly question, but his own head was starting to ache and he couldn't think what to ask next.

"Of course not, that wasn't the sort of question one could ask Mr. Evans. He didn't encourage comments on personal matters."

"You've worked for him for over twenty years and you'd consider asking if his head hurt a personal matter?" Witherspoon stared at him in disbelief. Douglas Branson didn't seem to be able to stick to the subject nor to control his tongue.

"Mr. Evans wasn't one to invite any sort of personal comment," Branson explained again. "Everyone thinks he's very taciturn and rather cold, but I know that isn't the case. Though he'd never admit it, he feels things very deeply. There was an old cat that used to hang around the back of the building; Mr. Evans took a liking to it and brought it in. He called him Billy Boy and made him a bed under his desk. He claimed he'd brought the creature in to keep the vermin away, but this is a modern building, and there aren't any rats. Billy was here for over five years, but he was old and one day he died. Mr. Evans was his usual self, didn't bat an eye, just said he was sorry to lose such a good mouser. But later that day, when he thought the office was empty, I slipped back to get my spectacles. I'd forgotten them, but that's neither here nor there. Well, as I said, he thought he was alone, but I peeked into this office and I saw him sitting by Billy's little makeshift bed and he was crying." Branson's eyes filled with tears as he told the story. "He was sobbing fit to break a heart."

Despite the fact that he had dozens of witnesses to interview, including a trip to Lowery's club to verify his statement, Witherspoon didn't have the heart to shut the fellow up.

"It was frightening, Inspector, seeing him like that. He'd skin me alive if he knew I'd told what I saw that day, but I'll not have you thinking he could commit murder." Branson swiped at his eyes. "He's a good man. He's kept me on all these years even though I can't control my tongue. He knows I need the job."

Witherspoon nodded sympathetically. "Your secret is safe." He got up and backed toward the door. "I appreciate your cooperation." He escaped and dashed out to the outer office, but Barnes wasn't there.

"The constable's gone across the hall," the blond one told him. "He said he'd be just a few minutes."

Witherspoon heard Branson coming out of Evans' office. He made a run for it. "Thanks very much, I'll go over and find him. Good day to all of you."

Barnes was coming out of the shipping agent's office as Witherspoon stepped into the corridor.

"I thought I'd have a word with the neighbors and see if they could verify Mr. Evans' statement," Barnes said.

"Good thinking, Constable. What did you find out?"

"The clerk told me that Evans was in his office that afternoon." He pointed at the glass transom above Evans' office doorway. "He saw light coming out there when he left here that day. Are we going to Lowery's club next?"

Witherspoon smiled faintly. "I think that's a good idea. Constable Barnes, forgive me if I'm wrong, but it appears to me as if you've already tried and convicted Sir Madison."

Barnes laughed. "The evidence against him is mounting.

He'd not want the Evans family to know he has two dead wives, and Agatha Moran was in France. She might have stumbled across his dirty little secret."

"True." Witherspoon started down the corridor. "But we don't know she had found out about Odette Lowery."

Barnes fell into step next to him. He knew good and well that Agatha Moran had known the whole story. Mrs. Jeffries had given him all the details. But he couldn't admit that he knew. "You're a brilliant detective, sir. I've no doubt you'll keep digging and eventually we'll find the proof we need to catch the bastard."

Ruth stood on the pavement and peeked through the tiny window into the shop. But all she could see was a table covered with laces and two dressmaker's dummies. She took a deep breath and wondered if what she was about to do would be helpful to their case. After all, she told herself, no one else had seen fit to chase after this clue, and they were all far more experienced than she.

But somehow, she had the feeling that this piece was important. It was the sort of thing a man might overlook, but it had been preying on her mind. But perhaps she was being foolish. Perhaps none of the others had pursued it because they knew it wasn't going to be useful.

Don't be such a ninny, she told herself. The worst that could happen was she might embarrass herself, and that certainly didn't frighten her. Any woman who was willing to fight for women's suffrage certainly wasn't averse to a bit of humiliation. Why, just last year she'd been tempted to chain herself to the fence in front of Parliament along with several of the more radical women in her group. She'd only been dissuaded from such a course of action by knowing how it might upset Gerald if he had to arrest her.

She remembered Mrs. Jeffries' words: "Rosemary Evans

heard her mother arguing with someone. Mrs. Evans said the girl had heard her having words with her dressmaker."

She took another deep breath and reached for the door handle. On principle, she'd avoided establishments like this, preferring to give her custom to a cooperative sewing society and a local shop around the corner from where she lived. But now she opened the door and stepped inside Corbiers.

CHAPTER 9

The inspector had been past Webster's dozens of times over the course of the years, but he'd never really paid any attention to the place until now. It was one of the newer gentlemen's clubs in London, built in the 1830s in the Greek Revival style that was so popular in those days. But now there was enough city dust on the white stone walls to turn them gray, and the elegant columns were chipped and gouged.

"It's not the most exclusive of clubs," Barnes commented. "The majority of the members are aristocrats that have lost most of their cash and gentry that are trying to move up a rung or two on the social ladder."

Witherspoon sighed. "Blast, that just means they'll put up a fuss just to show that they can."

Barnes grinned. Sometimes his inspector surprised him with his insights. That was exactly what this lot would do. "Shall we go in, sir?"

They climbed the wide, broad staircase and went in through the front door. A potted fern held pride of place on a marble-topped table in the foyer. A portrait of a man in early nineteenth-century dress hung on the wall and a set of dress swords were mounted over the open double doorway leading to the main room. Sitting on a chair by the door was a uniformed porter. He leapt up when he caught sight of Barnes.

"What do you want?" he challenged. "This is a private club."

"And we're the police," the constable replied. "Who is in charge here?"

"Mr. Gregg is the club secretary. He's in his office."

"Then please go and get him," Witherspoon ordered softly.

The porter nodded hastily and ran down the hallway to the very end. He knocked once, opened a door, and stepped inside. They could hear him speaking, but they were too far away to hear what was said. Seconds later, a slender gray-haired man dressed in a black frock coat appeared. He hurried up the corridor toward them.

"I'm Justin Gregg. What is it you require?" he asked. His gaze flicked back and forth between the open doorway of the main room and the two policemen.

"We would like to speak to some of your members," Witherspoon explained.

Gregg raised an eyebrow. "Which members?"

"Anyone who might have been playing cards with Sir Madison Lowery on this past Wednesday afternoon." Barnes deliberately raised his voice as he spoke. Nothing got cooperation from these toffs faster than a bit of uncouth behavior.

Gregg's eyes widened in alarm. "Please wait here. I'll go to the card room and see if any of those gentlemen might be able to help with your inquiries."

The constable wasn't having any of that. There were too many exits from these old buildings, and one thing he knew about the upper class, they stuck together. "We'll go with you, sir," Barnes said in a tone that brooked no argument.

Witherspoon flicked a quick glance at his constable but said nothing.

Gregg opened his mouth as though he wanted to argue, then clamped it shut and nodded curtly. "This way."

He didn't lead them through the double doors into the main room; instead, he took them to a door halfway down the corridor, opened it, and motioned for them to follow.

There were three tables in the room but only one had card players. Gregg started for the occupied table, but Barnes stepped in front of him. "We'll take it from here, sir." he said. By this time, the men at the table had stopped their game.

"Gregg, what's wrong?" One of the men stood up and frowned at the two policemen. He was bald, portly, but elegantly dressed in a gray waistcoat, white shirt, and red cravat.

"We'd like to ask you a few questions," Witherspoon said as he moved toward their table. "It won't take long and then you can get back to your game."

"You can go now, sir," Barnes said to the club secretary. Gregg hesitated for a moment, then shrugged and left.

"What's this about?" a dark-haired man asked. He tossed his cards facedown on the table.

"Were any of you here on Wednesday afternoon?" the constable asked.

"I was," the dark-haired man said. "So were Jacobs, McNalley, and Westmorland." He pointed to three other men, including the tall one who'd spoken first. "What of it?"

"Was Sir Madison Lowery here that afternoon?" Witherspoon shifted his weight. He wished someone had offered them a chair. It was wet outside and his knee was starting to hurt.

One of the others laughed. "He was here. He was in a foul mood. He lost."

"How much did he lose?" Barnes knew it probably wasn't relevant to the Moran murder, but additional information couldn't hurt.

"Three hundred pounds." The thin-faced one fixed the constable with a sneering smile. "That's more than you make in a year, isn't it?"

"The constable's income is none of your affair." Witherspoon gave the fellow a hard stare. "What is your name, sir?"

"Lord Westmorland. What's yours?"

"Inspector Gerald Witherspoon. My immediate superior is Chief Inspector Barrows, and I'm assigned to the Ladbroke Road Police Station. Now, as you were here on Wednesday, a few simple questions shouldn't be too difficult, even for you."

Barnes ducked his head to hide a smile. Witherspoon didn't lose his temper very often, but he was a tiger in defense of his men.

Westmorland gasped at the insult. "How dare you speak to me like that."

"You can either answer the questions here, sir," Witherspoon continued, "or we'll assume you have something to hide, in which case we'll need to ask you to come down to the station to help us with our inquiries."

The redheaded man sitting next to Westmorland leaned over and whispered in his ear. He closed his eyes briefly and then fixed the inspector with a sour smile. "My apologies, I didn't realize you were the great Inspector Witherspoon. Apparently you've solved more murders than anyone in the history of the Metropolitan Police. Ask your questions."

Witherspoon felt his cheeks grow hot. Westmorland's comment was calculated to embarrass him, but he wasn't going to allow a silly remark to stop him from his duty. "What time did Sir Madison arrive?"

Westmorland shrugged. "I didn't look at a clock, Inspector. But it was after lunch."

"Was it just the four of you playing?" Barnes asked. "Or did anyone else join the table?"

"It was mainly the four of us," the dark-haired man replied. "I think Carrington joined us for a few hands, but he's the only one."

"What's your name, sir?" Witherspoon asked.

"I'm Fielding Spencer." He pointed to the other men at the table.

"That's Paul Jacobs and Horace McNalley."

"What time did Sir Madison Lowery leave that afternoon?" Barnes took out his pencil and notebook. He flipped it open, balanced it on the back of an empty chair, and began scribbling names.

"The last game broke up a few minutes before five," Spencer answered. "We walked out together and Lowery got into a hansom."

"And you're absolutely sure about the time," Witherspoon clarified. "You're positive it was after five when you left?"

Spencer nodded. "Very sure, Inspector. I looked at my watch as I left the building. If you don't believe me, you can get confirmation from the porter—he hailed the cab."

Ruth stopped and surveyed the shop. The peek she'd had through the window didn't do Corbiers justice. Shelves of fabric in every color and hue filled one wall. An elegant Regency desk and two matching chairs occupied one corner. Next to the desk was a table draped with a white satin skirt on top of which was a small evergreen tree in a blue ceramic pot. Red velvet bows and white and gold ceramic ornaments in the shapes of stars and bells were tied to its branches, and streamers of brightly colored braided ribbons were draped in loops around it.

A familiar voice boomed across the shop, snapping Ruth out of her examination of the Christmas tree. "Why Lady Cannonberry, I had no idea you were one of Madame Corbier's customers."

Ruth's gaze shifted to the other side of the shop. A short, blonde-haired woman wearing a gray and green striped dress stood in the open doorway. Behind her, Ruth could see a large worktable surrounded by seamstresses cutting and sewing.

"Hello, Mrs. Corry. It's lovely to see you again." She smiled politely. Blast, Edwina Corry was a dreadful hidebound old snob who actively tried to dissuade women from joining the women's suffrage groups.

Edwina Corry stepped out into the shop, carefully fitting an elaborate hat with trailing gray and green veiling onto her head. "How long have you been coming to Corbiers? Frankly, considering your political and social attitudes, I should have thought this would be the last place I'd run into you."

Ruth forced another polite smile to her lips. "I've heard that this establishment does excellent work and . . ." She trailed off as a dark-haired woman emerged from the workroom.

"Why thank you, Lady Cannonberry. I'm Catherine Corbier. Welcome to my humble shop," she said in a voice with a lovely French accent. She continued across the room to a coat tree hidden behind the evergreen. She took a gray cloak off the peg. "Would you like me to send our footman out to hail you a cab?" she asked Edwina Corry as she draped it around the woman's shoulders.

"That's not necessary." She gave the Frenchwoman a brief

smile. "I've more shopping to do. I trust my dress will be ready by Friday?"

"But of course," Madame Corbier replied as she escorted her to the door. "It will be delivered by noon."

Edwina Corry gave Ruth a curt nod and stepped outside. Madame Corbier closed the door behind her and then turned to give Ruth a dazzling smile. "And now, madam, what can I do for you?"

"I'd like to see some dress patterns, please." She started over to the Regency desk. "My best traveling outfit is completely worn out and I need a new one."

"Very good, madam." She gestured toward the chair in front of the desk. "Please take a seat and I'll get the pattern book." She turned toward the shelves of fabric and opened a drawer located near the floor. Pulling out a large book, she came back to the desk, put it down, and flipped open the pages. "This model is very popular." She pointed to a drawing of a beautifully cut suit in mulberry red. "May I ask who recommended my establishment?"

Ruth thought about lying but decided against it. Telling the truth was simply much easier. "I happened to see someone in one of your creations and it was exquisite. I know I've a reputation for not being overly concerned with fashion, but Mrs. Evans' outfit was so lovely I asked some of my friends and found out that she'd had it made here."

"That is most flattering." Madame Corbier inclined her head graciously. "What dress was it that you noticed? The blue serge with the gray overskirt?"

Ruth started to nod affirmatively but thought better of it. "No, the dress I'm referring to is a green day dress with a peacock blue striped bodice."

"Oh that one." Madame Corbier smiled broadly. "I made that last season; I'm surprised Mrs. Evans still wears it. She's very fashion conscious."

Ruth was glad she'd stopped and had a word with one of her more fashionable friends before she'd come here today. Getting a description of one of Arabella Evans' outfits had been very easy. "I don't know Mrs. Evans personally, but every time I've seen her she's beautifully dressed. She must spend a good number of hours in your shop, but from the results, it's certainly worth it for her."

"I haven't seen her in ages." Madame Corbier turned the page. "This outfit is popular as well. As you can see, it's the very latest fashion from Paris. See how the cloak collar stands up? That means you can wrap a wool cravat under it without damaging the lines of the suit."

Ruth looked at the picture. It was a lovely traveling suit and she really did need a new one. "I like it very much, but I'm not overly fond of the color. Orange red doesn't compliment my skin."

"We've this fabric in both a brown and a blue herringbone tweed and also in pale lavender and blue stripe." She drew back and studied Ruth thoughtfully. "If I may be so bold, Lady Cannonberry, with your lovely skin, I'd recommend the blue herringbone."

"I agree," Ruth declared. "I don't suppose you've time to do a fitting now? I know I didn't make an appointment . . ."

"I can do a fitting now." Leaving the pattern book on the desk, she rose to her feet and headed for the workroom. "If you'll step in here, I'll take your measurements."

"That's very kind of you, madame," she said as she trailed after her. She'd already found out what she needed to know. Madame Corbier had said she hadn't seen Mrs. Evans in ages, so she wouldn't have been arguing with her a few days ago. But there might be more information to be had, and if it took buying what would probably be a ridiculously expensive outfit, so be it. It was a small price to pay for helping to catch a killer.

* * *

Hatchet got in the back of the badly dressed, destitute men and women lined up outside the rectory door of St. Matthew's Church. He was here to see his old friend, Emery Richards, who was one of the good souls helping to serve the hungry people who had no place else to go for a hot meal.

"What are you doin' here?" The man in front of him turned and gave him a good glare. "You're a toff."

Hatchet raised an eyebrow. He knew his shiny black top hat, exquisitely tailored greatcoat, and polished shoes set him apart from everyone else here, but nonetheless, even well-dressed men could be unemployed and hungry. "I'm not here for food; I'm here to see someone."

"That's alright then." The man sniffed and wiped his nose on the grimy sleeve of his threadbare brown coat. "Sometimes they run out of food."

The door to the rectory kitchen opened and the line began to move. Hatchet stepped aside every time someone walked up behind him, letting them go ahead of him. By the time he crossed the threshold and made his way to where Emery was ladling out a gray-looking stew concoction, everyone had been served.

Emery looked up and saw him. He was a small, slender man about the same age as Hatchet. He had a head of iron gray hair, piercing blue eyes, and a long, straight nose. "Hello, old friend, give me a few minutes to help with the clearing up."

"I can lend a hand as well," Hatchet offered as he slipped out of his coat.

Emery picked up the empty serving bowl. "Good, we can use one. We're short today."

Hatchet tossed his coat on the back of a chair, put his hat on the seat, and got to work carrying empty serving platters, bread baskets, and water jugs into the small kitchen. An hour later, after the dishes were all washed, the tablecloths shook and tucked into drawers, and every crumb swept up, he and Emery stepped out into the street.

"Alright, Hatchet." Emery slapped his cap onto his head and slipped on his gloves. "What is it you need to know?"

Hatchet didn't bother to come up with a story. He and Emery were old friends, and like Hatchet, Emery had ended up in domestic service. He was retired now and living a quiet life, but he'd spent a number of years as a butler to the rich and powerful. He still had numerous sources of information, and that's why Hatchet often came to visit him.

"Have you ever heard of Sir Madison Lowery or a family named Evans?" Hatchet adjusted his stride to match Emery's shorter one.

"Ah, so Inspector Witherspoon got that case." Emery chuckled. "This is your lucky day, my good man. I'm several steps ahead of you."

"Really?" Hatchet grinned in delight. Sometimes it was like the old days, when he and Emery had been out in the world together. They'd traveled from one place to the next: to Europe, South America, and Australia, splitting up only when Hatchet went off to the United States and Emery went to Hong Kong. But despite their foolishness, they'd both survived. "You always were good at thinking ahead."

"Thank you." Emery grinned broadly. "When I read about the Moran murder and noted where the poor woman was killed, I was pretty sure your inspector would catch the case and you'd soon be showing up on my doorstep."

"Not fair, I tracked you down at St. Matthew's . . ."

"Stop splitting hairs; you know what I mean." Emery tipped his cap to a passing matron. "Good day, Mrs. Dorian. Lovely to see you looking so well."

"Good day, Mr. Richards." She inclined her head in acknowledgment.

"That's Mrs. Dorian. She's the head of the Ladies League at St. Matthew's," Emery said. "Incredible woman—the vicar's terrified of her. Apparently she read the Gospel and took the adage to feed the poor literally. She's the one who led the drive to feed the destitute twice a week. Believe me, if it had been up to the vicar, the poor and the hungry would still be hungry. But I digress. Let's get back to your case. I put out a few discreet inquiries about its principals. At least the ones that I could identify."

"What did you find out?" Hatchet asked. They stopped as they reached the corner and waited till there was a break in the traffic before venturing across.

"Not very much," Emery admitted. "I'm sure you've already heard the gossip surrounding Sir Madison Lowery. He's a bad gambler, hasn't worked a day in his life, and lives on the money he inherited from his first wife, and from what I hear, that well is almost dry. Lucky for him, he's made a match with the Evans girl. That family has more money than the Bank of England."

"Are you sure? They live well, but their home isn't particularly ostentatious."

"Of course I'm sure. Much to the chagrin and annoyance of his wife, Jeremy Evans has made it a point to deliberately downplay the family's wealth. Considering how much money he's accumulated over the years, he lives quite modestly. She's a social climber if there ever was one, not that I fault her for that; social climbing of one form or another has been the national sport since the Conqueror crossed the Channel. But Jeremy Evans isn't interested and I rather admire him for that."

"Perhaps he knows his wife is doing the climbing for him," Hatchet suggested.

"No, he lets her do what she wants because of their daughter. The marriage hasn't been a particularly happy one. At one point, the gossip was that he was going to divorce her but she convinced him to think about it and sent him off on a business trip to South America. Six months later, when he got back, his good lady had just given birth to Rosemary, so for the sake of the child, he abandoned the plans for divorce."

"Divorce? Are you certain? That would ruin them socially. No one would have anything to do with either of them." Hatchet stopped in his tracks. This was one piece of gossip no one had reported.

"Divorce might be social suicide"—Emery looked amused—"but there are some who prefer that to being shackled to someone they loathe."

"How did you find this out?"

"I've got excellent sources." Emery started walking again. "As a matter of fact, that good lady we just passed is one of them, and she ought to know all about the Evans family. Her sister used to work for them when they lived in Portsmouth."

Hatchet was the last to arrive at their afternoon meeting. "I'm so sorry to be late," he apologized, "but as I was getting information that might be helpful to our case, I do hope I'm forgiven."

"Show-off," Luty muttered under her breath.

"Of course you're forgiven," Mrs. Jeffries said. "Besides, you're only a few minutes late." She wasn't in the best of moods herself. "And as you're here, why don't you go first."

Hatchet beamed. "Thank you. I met up with an old friend today, and luckily, he knew quite a bit about the people involved in our case." Without mentioning any names, he told them everything he'd learned from Emery

Richards. "And apparently, at that point in their lives, the relationship between Arabella and Jeremy Evans was so bad, she was the one who insisted he go to Argentina."

Mrs. Goodge, her expression incredulous, said, "He was actually goin' to divorce her?"

"According to my source, he was," Hatchet confirmed. "The marriage wasn't very happy. But when he returned, she'd given birth to Rosemary so he decided to stick it out."

"I wonder if he's still unhappy," Smythe murmured.

Betsy poked him in the ribs. "What about her? Maybe the misery wasn't all one-sided. Maybe she was unhappy, too."

"I expect she was, love," he agreed. "But that's not goin' to happen to us. In a few short days, we'll be happily married."

"Can I go next?" Luty asked. She shot Hatchet a sour look. "You ain't the only one to find out somethin'."

"By all means," Mrs. Jeffries said.

Luty told them about her meeting with Enid Jones. She took her time in the telling, drawing out the details and making sure she repeated everything she'd heard word for word. When she'd finished, she smiled smugly at Hatchet and helped herself to another piece of seed cake.

"Cor blimey," Wiggins exclaimed. "Why's she marryin' Sutton if she don't trust him? Imagine, hirin' a private inquiry agent to spy like that. It's disgustin'."

"Well, from her point of view, it made sense," Ruth pointed out. "We've heard that she was miserable with her first husband."

"Then she shouldn't have agreed to Sutton's proposal if she wasn't certain of his character," Mrs. Goodge argued.

"I wonder if this private inquiry agent was the fellow that Eddie Butcher saw followin' Agatha Moran," Smythe suggested. "I mean, if Mrs. North knew that he'd seen another woman at his home, perhaps he was told to find out what he could about her."

Mrs. Jeffries thought about that. "I suppose that's possible. But until you find Eddie Butcher and we get a description of the man, we won't know."

Smythe nodded in agreement and made a mental note to pass everything along to Blimpey.

"Then we're sure it was Agatha Moran who went to Sutton's home?" Wiggins asked. "I mean, I know for certain a lady came to visit him, but do we really know it was Miss Moran?" He told them what he'd learned at the café. "But Lorna didn't give me much of a description exceptin' to say the woman come by hansom cab and that she was middle-aged."

When he'd finished, no one said anything for a few moments. Finally, Mrs. Jeffries spoke up. "We know that Tobias Sutton was acquainted with Agatha Moran. What we don't know is why she would have had reason to go see him. Wiggins is right—without a description, we can't be sure who the woman might have been."

"I think it was Agatha Moran," Mrs. Goodge declared. "Who else would it have been?"

"I agree," Ruth put in. "From what we know of Mr. Sutton, he doesn't sound as if he has many relationships of the female persuasion, and he did know her, even if it was a long time ago."

Mrs. Jeffries nodded. "Would you like to go next?" she said to Ruth.

"Thank you, yes. Arabella Evans lied to Inspector Witherspoon," she blurted. "On the Monday before the murder, Rosemary overheard her mother arguing with someone and Mrs. Evans claimed it was her dressmaker. But I went to Corbiers and had a very interesting conversation with the proprietress, and no one from there has seen Mrs. Evans in ages."

"But how can that be?" Betsy asked. "Isn't she doing Rosemary's wedding dress and the trousseau?"

"It's finished," Ruth replied. "Madame Corbier said that Mrs. Evans was terrified there would be a problem at the last minute so she insisted everything had to be done by the first of December. She wants the wedding to be perfect. Madame Corbier said it will be one of the biggest social events of the year. Apparently, a member of the royal family has been invited and hasn't sent regrets."

Mrs. Goodge snorted. "That doesn't mean they're goin' to attend. Believe me, I know. But why would Mrs. Evans say somethin' that is so easily shown to be a lie? That's what I don't understand. What if the inspector asks about it?"

"I don't think Madame Corbier would have been quite as forthright with him," Ruth explained.

"You think she would have lied to the police to protect one of her customers?" Mrs. Jeffries asked.

Ruth entwined her fingers together and brought her hands up to her chin as she thought about how to answer. "Well, I don't wish to cast aspersions on her character, but I think if she had to choose whether to tell the truth to a policeman or whether to offend a customer who brings her hundreds of pounds every year, I think she'd have lied. Oh dear, that makes her sound a terrible person, and she isn't. She's very nice."

"But she told you the truth," Smythe pointed out.

"Only because I didn't ask the question directly. I got my information very indirectly," Ruth explained. "And I'm not a policeman. That's my report."

"And a very good one it was, too," Mrs. Jeffries said.

"I'll go next," Betsy volunteered. "Not that there's much for me to say. I spent most of the afternoon asking about the

Evans family but all I managed to learn was that Mr. Evans had popped into the chemist's after lunch on Monday and purchased a tin of headache powder. He mentioned to the clerk that as the staff was off on Monday afternoon, he might be able to slip into the house and have a bit of peace and quiet. Sorry, I know it's not very much."

"You found out more than I did," Mrs. Goodge charged. "All I heard was that a scullery maid at the Evans house accused the tweeny of stealin' off with an old carpetbag that the housekeeper had promised to her. Oh, and someone in the household sneaks outside and smokes those uh . . . dear." She broke off with a frown. "What are those things called? They're little papers with tobacco inside them, but I can't think of their name. They're not cigars."

"Cigarettes?" Wiggins said. "Someone in the house smokes cigarettes?"

"That's what the scullery maid claims." Mrs. Goodge laughed. "She keeps findin' the end bits on the walkway leadin' to the servants' privy. But no one will own up to it."

"That's an expensive habit for a servant," Hatchet murmured. "They're not cheap, and from what we know about the Evans household, I don't see Mrs. Evans tolerating any of her staff sneaking off for a smoke."

"Maybe it's Mr. Evans," Mrs. Jeffries suggested.

"He'd not have to sneak out to the walkway by the servants' privy," Luty said dryly. "He could just go into his study." She glanced at the housekeeper. "Did you see Dr. Bosworth today?"

Mrs. Jeffries made a face. "No, I went all the way over there and it was a wasted trip. He wasn't there, and like a fool, instead of finding out he wasn't available as soon as I got to the hospital, I spent two hours looking for him instead of having the good sense to check with one of the matrons."

"He's not gone back to America, has he?" Hatchet asked.

Dr. Bosworth was one of their special friends. The household had made his acquaintance on one of the inspector's earlier cases, and his expertise had been instrumental in tracking down the killer. He did postmortems for the Metropolitan Police, not in the inspector's district but one closer to St. Thomas' Hospital.

Bosworth knew weapons, especially firearms. He understood the kind of damage a specific type of gun could do to flesh and bone. He'd had plenty of experience in such matters as he'd spent several years practicing medicine in San Francisco, where, he assured them, there were plenty of bullet-ridden bodies. He also had some very progressive, some would even say radical, theories about how an in-depth examination of the crime scene and the victim's body could yield a number of clues to the discerning viewer. Unfortunately, except for the inspector's household and one or two of his colleagues, he couldn't get anyone else to listen to his ideas. Mrs. Jeffries had made it a point to seek Bosworth's opinion whenever they had a case.

"No, don't worry, he'll be back soon," she replied with a laugh. "He's gone to Wales to visit friends."

"We ought to ask him how likely it is to get food poisonin' from oysters," Luty said.

"I can answer that," Mrs. Goodge offered. "You've got to be careful with oysters. That's why people only go to a fishmonger's they can trust. Mind you, I've known of a few cases of food poisonin' from eatin' bad oysters, but I've never heard of anyone dyin' from it."

"Maybe it wasn't food poisoning that killed Sir Madison Lowery's two wives," Betsy suggested. "Maybe we ought to ask Dr. Bosworth if there's a kind of poison that's deadly and produces the same symptoms as food poisoning. That would be a clever way to get rid of a wife you didn't want. Bring her home some fancy oysters but poison her with something else."

Mrs. Jeffries had the inspector's sherry waiting when he came home that evening. "Was your day successful, sir?" she asked as she handed him his glass.

"It was successful in the sense that we learned a number of interesting facts," he replied. "The lad we sent to Putney to verify Ellen Crowe's alibi reported back to Constable Barnes, but unfortunately, the two ladies had a glass of wine over lunch and Miss Whitley had no idea what time it was that Mrs. Crowe left."

"So she might have left earlier than she claimed and had time to get to Notting Hill," Mrs. Jeffries speculated. She didn't believe it for a second. How would Ellen Crowe know that Agatha Moran was going to be in front of the Evans house that afternoon? No, even if the woman had harbored a grudge for years, why would she wait till now to kill her?

In her experience, murder usually needed a trigger of some sort, and thus far, there was no evidence the victim had done or said anything that was going to have any bearing on Ellen Crowe's life.

"We went to Fenchurch Street," Witherspoon continued. "I wanted to have a word with Jeremy Evans' staff. They more or less confirm his story that he was there alone that day going over the accounts." He took a sip of his sherry and told her about the chat Barnes had with the two clerks. He described the shelves filled with exotic products that no one wanted and laughed as he recounted seeing Douglas Branson's head coming up from behind a stack of files. He repeated everything the chief clerk had said, but his expression sobered when he got to the part about Jeremy Evans weeping over his dead cat.

Mrs. Jeffries listened closely, nodding in encouragement as he spoke and occasionally breaking in to ask for more details.

"And after we finished at Fenchurch Street," Witherspoon continued, "we went to Webster's."

"Webster's?"

"That's Sir Madison Lowery's club." He put his glass on the table. "And as you can imagine, the whole experience left much to be desired. Some of those people were very reluctant to speak to us. Constable Barnes had to get quite firm with the club secretary and several of the members. You'd think they'd be more concerned about lawlessness and murderers wandering the streets, but they're not. They seem to think speaking to a policeman is most inconvenient. Getting information out of any them is very difficult."

She smiled sympathetically, knowing that the inspector had had a miserable time of it. "I suppose you weren't able to find anyone who could verify Lowery's statement that he was playing cards until late that afternoon."

"On the contrary," he answered. "As I said, Constable Barnes can be quite firm when the occasion calls for it, and I, too, can hold the line, as they say, when necessary. After we both made it clear that we weren't larking about, we found half a dozen people who confirmed his statement. Lowery didn't leave Webster's until just after five o'clock. He couldn't have traveled across town to Notting Hill in time to have murdered Agatha Moran."

Mrs. Jeffries rose early the next morning and slipped down the back stairs to the kitchen. Moving quietly so she wouldn't awaken Mrs. Goodge, she put on the kettle, stood by the cooker until it boiled, and made herself a pot of tea. While she waited for it to brew, she went to the wet larder for the cream.

Going to the cupboard, she didn't bother with a cup and saucer, but got down the bit mug a workman had left. She poured the tea, added cream and two sugars, picked up the mug, and wandered over to the kitchen sink so she could stare out the window.

It was still dark. That suited her mood perfectly. She was so depressed that if she weren't a responsible adult, she'd stamp her foot and scream just to make herself feel better. After their meeting yesterday afternoon, she'd been excited. They'd found out so much information, she'd been sure the case was practically solved. She had dozens of hints at the ready to drop into the inspector's ear while he drank his sherry and ate his supper.

But after what he'd told her, her ideas had evaporated faster than a puddle of water on a hot, dry day. She'd almost choked on her sherry when he'd insisted that Sir Madison Lowery couldn't have gone from his club to the Evans house in time to murder Agatha Moran.

Ye gods, Lowery was their prime suspect. She knew he was the killer, she just knew it. "Are you sure the gentlemen in the card room were telling you the truth?" she'd asked. "Aristocrats have been known to stick together, sir."

But he'd assured her he'd doubled-checked with the porter and he, too, verified that it was after five when Lowery headed home. As they were leaving the club, Barnes had stopped and spoken to the hansom cab drivers lined up waiting for a fare and had found the cabbie who'd taken Lowery to Notting Hill.

The driver remembered him easily: All the way across town, Lowery kept yelling at him to go faster.

She heard a noise behind her and whirled about. Mrs. Goodge was standing in the doorway watching her. She held Samson in her arms. "What's wrong?"

"Lowery isn't the killer," she replied.

Samson squirmed and Mrs. Goodge put him on the stool. "I take it you'd already decided he was guilty."

"All the evidence pointed to him, and now I've no idea who it is." She sighed audibly. "Betsy's getting married in a few days and they'll be off on their wedding trip. Right after that Christmas will be here and the chief inspector and the Home Office won't be pleased that the murder hasn't been solved."

She walked to the cupboard and got a cup and saucer, went to the table, and poured some tea for Mrs. Goodge.

The cook petted Samson across his broad back and then came to the table. She slipped into her chair and nodded her thanks as she reached for her tea. "No one expects you to have the answer at your fingertips," she told the housekeeper. "Give it a day or two, and you'll soon figure it out."

"I'm not so sure that I will," she said morosely. "I spent most of the night thinking about the case. I went over and over everything we've learned and I haven't a clue who murdered that poor woman."

"You don't have to come up with the solution right this minute." Mrs. Goodge added sugar to her cup. "Do what you always do; let all the bits and pieces simmer and boil in that brain of yours. You'll figure it out. You always do."

Mrs. Jeffries looked down at the table. She felt like such a fraud.

They all had such faith in her, were all so certain she'd put the puzzle together and come up with the right answer. And that was the problem, Mrs. Jeffries thought. She knew that one of these days, she couldn't do it. One of these times, the killer's identity would elude her and she'd fail them. She'd fail them all.

CHAPTER 10

Even though the following days were busy for everyone, no one in the household forgot they had a case. But despite their best efforts, they'd found out practically nothing they didn't already know.

Mrs. Goodge tried her best to dig up a few more tidbits, but with everything happening at Upper Edmonton Gardens, it was very difficult. Smythe and Betsy had refused to allow the cook to do the catering for the wedding reception; they insisted she was to be an honored guest and spend the day enjoying herself. Nonetheless, Mrs. Goodge considered it a matter of pride that some of her best recipes be on the table celebrating the nuptial meal.

So in between cooking her black currant cream and baking her special tea scones and two Battenberg cakes, Mrs. Goodge questioned her sources as best she could. But it appeared that providence was against her finding out anything new about the principals in the case. The butcher's lad was useless, as was the rag and bone man, the laundryman, three different fruit vendors, and even a bootblack boy she'd brought in to shine everyone's shoes.

Luty and Hatchet had no luck, either. All of Luty's contacts seemed to have left town for Christmas, and the individuals Hatchet tapped for information had never heard of anyone connected to the case.

Betsy was the busiest of all. Between spending time with her relatives, packing for her wedding trip, and helping Phyllis clean the rooms for the reception, she'd barely had a free moment. Add to that, she'd only seen Smythe at mealtimes because he kept disappearing on one mysterious errand or another.

Smythe, for his part, had barely had time to breathe, let alone find out any information about their case. He'd wasted more hours than he cared to count harassing the builders to finish their flat, and even though his wedding clothes were ready and hanging in his cupboard, he'd had to go to his tailor because he'd forgotten to get a decent traveling suit made. He'd paid extra to have it prepared in time. Then he'd stood in line for half a day to get a special license because they'd not had the banns read at their local parish church. Just when he thought he'd be able to get back to the case, he'd received a note from his solicitor telling him the new will was ready and could he come and sign it? On his way home, he'd passed the wine merchant's, so he'd stopped and made sure they'd ordered the champagne he wanted for their reception.

He was determined to do his Betsy proud. But he was a bit worried about the flat. The others, even Wiggins, had done a good job of keeping the secret, but now he wished he'd asked Mrs. Jeffries or Mrs. Goodge to have a look at the paint and wallpaper he'd chosen. A woman's point of view might have been a good idea.

Perhaps it would have been an even better idea to let Betsy have a say in how her new home was to be decorated. It was too late now—the die, as they say, was cast. But he'd comforted himself with the thought that if she hated the colors, they could always change them. He was going to spend the rest of his life making her happy and giving her anything she wanted.

Wiggins hadn't fared any better than the others. He'd done his best to get out on the hunt, but one thing after another had cropped up. He was the best man, and his new suit had needed two alterations before it fit properly. Mrs. Jeffries had put him in charge of hiring the men from the domestic agency who were to be waiters at the reception, and that had taken ages. He'd never have thought that answering a few simple questions about the proper way to carry a serving tray or open a bottle of champagne would be so hard for some lads.

Lady Cannonberry hadn't found out anything, either. She'd had high tea with a woman she didn't like very much and dined out two evenings straight with nothing to show for her efforts except a bad case of indigestion.

But it was Mrs. Jeffries who suffered the most. In the three days that had passed since she'd realized her prime suspect was out of the running, so to speak, she'd not come up with any other ideas about the identity of the killer.

She wasn't certain if it was because her time was taken up with supervising the overall preparations for the wedding and Christmas, or whether it was because something terrible had happened to her reasoning abilities. But she was now frightened that she was no longer capable of putting facts together to form a useful theory.

As the days had passed, they had less and less to report and their meetings had become shorter and shorter. At their morning meeting on the day before the wedding, Mrs. Jeffries was downright desperate.

"I know we've all been very busy," she told them. "But we really must try and learn a bit more. In the past three days, we don't appear to have made very much progress—"

"We've made no progress at all," Mrs. Goodge interrupted. "We've not found out a bloomin' thing we didn't know already. Time is movin' past us here. If we don't get a few more bits and pieces to add to what we know about this case, Mrs. Jeffries will never put the puzzle together and this one won't get solved."

Betsy put down her cup. "Norah and Leo are going out to see his grandmother today so I'm free."

"Today should be better," Smythe said. "I'll 'ave a bit of time and I've got a source I'm goin' to see. Maybe that'll help."

He'd already sent word to Blimpey that he'd be stopping by the Dirty Duck. For the price he was paying, Groggins better have something useful for him to bring back. Mrs. Goodge was trying to be tactful, but her words had hit home. They were running out of time. Tomorrow, he and Betsy would be out of this one. They'd be leaving for their wedding trip right after the reception.

Mrs. Jeffries forced a smile. "Of course we're all doing our best." The cook wasn't deliberately trying to make her feel bad, but her words had stung. If she didn't come up with a solution before the wedding, everyone would feel she'd let them down. Working on this case wouldn't be the same without Betsy and Smythe. "And we'll keep on doing our best until we've got this case solved."

"I'm not certain what I ought to do," Ruth complained. "You'd think that with this case still on the front page of all the newspapers, someone would know something useful, but no one does. Every time I'm out socially, I make inquiries, but the only gossip I hear is what we already know." She sighed. "I do so want to help Gerald. He'll feel terrible if he doesn't solve this murder before Christmas."

"Even if 'e doesn't catch the killer, our inspector shouldn't feel bad," Wiggins stated. "He's got more to his credit than anyone else."

"We'll solve the case," Mrs. Jeffries said quickly. "And he'll have this one to his credit as well."

Wiggins pushed his empty cup toward the housekeeper. "Can I have more, please? It's right cold today. At least Inspector Nivens isn't snoopin' about and makin' trouble. This mornin', I overheard the inspector tellin' Constable Barnes that Nivens is in Scotland and not due back till the New Year. That's a bit of luck."

"I wondered where that varmint was," Luty said. "It ain't like him to keep his nose out of the inspector's business."

All of them disliked the overly ambitious Inspector Nigel Nivens. He'd been a thorn in their sides from the very beginning. Nivens was jealous of their inspector's success as a homicide detective, and he was always trying to prove that Witherspoon had help with his cases, which, of course, was true. They were all of the opinion that he was a self-centered toad of a man who used his many political and social connections to bully his way up the chain of command in the Metropolitan Police.

"No, it isn't like him at all." Mrs. Jeffries poured Wiggins more tea. "That reminds me, I suppose we have learned something new. Constable Barnes told me he and the inspector went back to Putney yesterday afternoon. They spoke to Olivia Whitley's servants. Unlike her mistress, the maid remembered when Ellen Crowe left that afternoon. It was close to five o'clock."

"So unless Mrs. Crowe sprouted wings and flew across the Thames," Hatchet said, "she'd not have been able to get to Chepstow Villas in time to murder Agatha Moran."

"So we can strike another person off our suspect list," Luty muttered. "Well nells bells, that's two now. If we keep losin' the ones that had a reason to want the woman dead, we'll never catch this killer."

Mrs. Jeffries cringed inwardly. That's precisely what she'd been thinking.

Smythe pushed his way through the crowd and slipped onto the empty stool next to Blimpey Groggins.

"It's about time you showed up." Blimpey lifted his glass of beer, pointed at Smythe, and nodded to the barmaid. "I was beginnin' to wonder if you'd gotten scared of the approachin' nuptials and made a run for it."

"You don't know what it's been like," Smythe protested. "I've not 'ad a bloomin' minute to myself. There's been one thing after another. It took 'alf a day of standin' in line just to get the special license."

"You'd have saved yourself time and cash if you'd 'ad the banns properly read." Blimpey frowned at him. "You'll not stay rich throwin' your money away like that."

"Betsy didn't want to." Smythe shrugged. "She said it was too embarrassin'. We've had the banns read twice before, and both times, the weddin' got pushed back. I wasn't goin' to cross her on that topic, believe me."

"Since you put it like that, I don't much blame ya." Blimpey gave an agreeable nod and leaned back as the barmaid approached. She put two glasses of bitter on the table. "Thanks, love." He waited till she'd gone before he spoke. "Right then, let's get to business. First of all, yer lot's not the only one snoopin' about the persons of this case."

Smythe took a small sip of beer. "Who else is nosin'

about then?" He was fairly sure he already knew the answer, but he was paying Blimpey a pretty penny, so he might as well get all the details.

"A private inquiry agent named Milo Callahan. He was watchin' Agatha Moran's house on the day she died," Blimpey replied.

"You know for certain this Callahan was at her house that day?" Smythe pressed. That was probably the man that Eddie Butcher had bragged about seeing.

Blimpey looked askance. "You doubt me? Corse I'm sure. He was hired by Eleanor North. Apparently, Mrs. North's current fiancé, one Mr. Tobias Sutton, was once involved with Miss Moran."

"Involved how?" Smythe asked.

Blimpey chuckled. "Now don't rush me. Let me tell it as it should be told. Callahan's not very good at his job but he works cheap. He'll probably not be able to help much even though he was there that day."

"But if he was there . . ."

"He was and my people 'ave already spoken to him. The only thing he saw was Miss Moran leavin'. He tried fol-lowin' her, but it was rainin' and she walks faster than he does. He lost her."

"What time did she leave?" Smythe asked.

"Callahan doesn't 'ave a pocket watch." Blimpey grinned. "He didn't know the exact time, only that it was later in the afternoon. Like I said, he's not very good at what he does."

"Blast a Spaniard, could this case get any worse?" Smythe sighed heavily.

"Listen to the rest of what I've got to tell before you start pissin' and moanin'," Blimpey retorted.

"Sorry, it's just we've all got a feelin' that time is movin' on and we're no closer to an answer. Everyone's gettin' a bit nervous. Go on, what else 'ave you got for me?"

"The reason that Agatha Moran was murdered." Blimpey paused dramatically. "Twenty years ago, while she was workin' as a governess on the Isle of Wight, Agatha Moran fell in love and had a child out of wedlock. The father refused to marry her, and she lost her position as a governess. The father was Tobias Sutton."

"Bloomin' Ada, that's goin' to put the cat among the pigeons," Smythe muttered. "Does Eleanor North know that Sutton had an illegitimate child?"

"I don't know that she knows for certain," Blimpey replied. "But she was suspicious enough that she hired Callahan to watch the Moran house. But that's not all I've got. I've saved the best for last."

"I'd say this was pretty good—we've got another suspect now and Eleanor North doesn't 'ave an alibi for the time of the murder." Smythe grinned. "But go on, tell me the rest."

"Agatha Moran left the Isle of Wight and went to Portsmouth. She went into hidin' and gave birth to a baby girl. That child is Rosemary Evans."

Betsy smiled at the maid as she led her into the Angel Arms Pub. She silently prayed that no one she knew would pop in for a quick pint right at this moment. Coming up with a likely reason to be swilling gin at this time of the morning would be difficult at best. But she'd spotted the maid coming out the servants' entrance of the Evans house, followed her, and made contact. She was determined to find out something more on this case. She was getting married tomorrow and this might be her last chance.

"I'll have a gin, please," the maid told the barman. She pointed to Betsy. "She's paying so make it a large one."

He looked at Betsy. She reached into the inside pocket of her cloak and pulled out some coins. "Bring her whatever she wants and bring me one as well," she instructed as she handed him the money. She waited till he'd turned away to pour their drinks before she spoke. "Thanks very much for coming with me. My name is Laura Kingsley."

"I'm Adelaide Smith." She kept her attention on the barman as he poured gin into their glasses.

"Very pleased to meet you, Miss Smith," Betsy said politely. The woman was gray-haired and hard-faced. She wore the uniform of a housemaid rather than a housekeeper or a cook, which meant she'd not moved up in the pecking order. "As I said earlier, I'm looking for some information. I'm willing to pay you for your time."

"Just keep the gin poured nice and tall." Adelaide broke into a smile as the barman put two glasses in front of them. "And I'll tell you anything you want about the mistress."

"How long have you worked for the Evans family?" Betsy heard the door open behind her and risked a quick glance over her shoulder. This pub was entirely too close to her own neighborhood for her liking. But she didn't recognize the lad making his way to the bar.

"Two weeks." Adelaide picked up her glass and drained it.

"Two weeks," Betsy repeated. Blast, this woman probably wouldn't know much of anything. She was wasting her time and her money.

Adelaide signaled the barman for another. "That's right, I came from an agency. The daughter in the family is getting married and the mistress wants everything to be perfect." She broke off with a derisive snort. "Stupid woman, she's got me cleaning the ruddy attic. Now I ask you, how many people eating a wedding breakfast go up and look at the attic. Miserable job it is, too, dusting them cobwebs and half freezing to death because the silly cow keeps the windows open so no one will know she sneaks up there to smoke her cigarettes. Thanks, luv," she said as he put another gin in front of her.

Betsy gave him more money and then turned to Adelaide. "Who's the silly cow? One of the servants? Miss Evans?"

Adelaide laughed. "One of the servants? Are you joking? If we were caught doin' something like that, we'd be sacked on the spot. No, it's her nibs, Mrs. Evans, that sneaks up there to smoke her cigarettes." She leaned closer to Betsy. "Corse, she doesn't know that I know about it. If she did, I reckon she'd send me back to the agency. She's right sneaky about her habit, and I think she'd just about die if any of her fancy friends found out about it."

"How did you find out?" Betsy asked. The information was amusing but hardly the clue that was going to solve the case.

"I'd left the duster up there and I nipped back up to get it. I saw her sitting by the open window, puffing away." Adelaide shrugged. "I just thanked my lucky stars that she hadn't seen me. Mind you, I think one or two of the others know about her as well. The scullery maid was complaining about finding the cigarette ends outside and having to pick them up, and I heard the cook telling her to hold her tongue, and we know what that means."

"Yes, we do," Betsy agreed. "Rich people like to pretend they're better than they are. If one of us servants sees their weakness, we'd best be quiet about it or we'll find ourselves on the street with no references."

"That's the truth." Adelaide tossed back the rest of her drink and, when Betsy started to wave at the barman, she stopped her. "I've had enough, thank you. The cow's got me scrubbing down the wet larder this afternoon, and I've got to be sober enough to drag the sand in and out of the back."

Betsy reached into her cloak again and pulled out a pound note. She felt sorry for this woman. A saying that Mrs. Henderson, a nice Quaker lady who used to come to the East End and distribute bread to the poor, used to say went through her mind, and for the first time in her life, she really understood what it meant.

"There but for the grace of God go I," Mrs. Henderson would say if people sneered at those down on their luck and standing in the queue for the free loaves.

When Betsy looked at Adelaide's careworn face, she realized that if she'd not collapsed on the inspector's doorstep, if she'd not met Smythe and Mrs. Jeffries and all those who had come to mean so much to her, this woman's life could have been her fate. "Here, take this." She handed her the money.

Adelaide's mouth gaped open. "Blooming Ada, this is a whole pound."

Betsy didn't want her to think it was charity. "You earned it. You've done me a great service by telling me what you know."

"You'll not tell anyone you found out from me about Mrs. Evans' little habit, will you?" She grabbed the note and stuffed it into the pocket of her faded brown jacket. "It's only a temporary position, but I'm there for two more days and I need the money."

"Don't worry," Betsy replied. "I won't say a word."

"You promise?" she asked. "If I stay on until the daughter's wedding, the agency said they'd be able to send me out somewhere else and I'd not lose any days of work. My son is sick and I'm the one keepin' a roof over our heads."

Betsy's heart broke at the raw desperation in the woman's eyes. "I promise. Your secret is safe with me. No one will ever know that you spoke to me."

By the time the others had returned for their afternoon meeting, Mrs. Jeffries' mood had improved a bit, but not by much. "Goodness, this is lovely," she commented as she slipped into her seat. "Mrs. Goodge has outdone herself."

The cook had put out scones, seed cake, and freshly made brown bread. There was also a pot of her fancy damson plum preserves.

"I thought the occasion called for somethin' a bit special." The cook smiled at Betsy and Smythe. "Tomorrow's your big day. It never hurts to start the celebratin' a bit early. Besides, everythin' else is done. Phyllis has done a wonderful job of gettin' the upstairs rooms ready for the reception, Wiggins has the waiters at the ready, and the entire house is clean as a whistle."

"All we need is the bride, groom, and food." Wiggins reached for the jam, took off the top, and spooned it onto his plate.

Betsy giggled. "We'll be there this time for sure. I can't wait to see all my friends in church." She looked at Mrs. Jeffries. "The inspector does remember that he's to walk me down the aisle at half past two?"

"Of course he does," Mrs. Jeffries replied. She'd remind him again when he got home this evening.

"Don't worry, Betsy. I'm meeting him here at two o'clock," Ruth added. "And the carriage taking the both of you to the church will be here at two twenty, just in case there's a lot of traffic on Holland Park Road."

"I don't need a carriage." Betsy blushed. "The church is just across the garden."

"Of course you need a ride." Smythe helped himself to a slice of cake. "You'll not want to get your new shoes dirty walkin' across the garden, and besides, it might rain."

Betsy narrowed her eyes. "Don't even joke about that . . ." She broke off as they heard a pounding at the back door.

"Who in the dickens is that?" Luty looked around curiously. "We're all here."

Wiggins was already on his feet and racing for the hall. Fred trailed along at his heels.

The door opened and they heard the footman say, "Cor blimey, you're a sight for sore eyes. We've all wondered if you'd get back in time for the weddin'."

"I wouldn't miss that for the world," a familiar voice said. "Hello, Fred, old boy."

A few moments later, Wiggins, with a bouncing Fred at his heels, came back into the kitchen, followed by a tall, pale-faced man with auburn hair.

"Dr. Bosworth," Mrs. Jeffries cried in delight. "How wonderful to see you."

She started to rise, but he waved her back into her chair.

"It's wonderful to see all of you." He'd been to the house many times, so he headed for the empty chair next to Lady Cannonberry. He nodded at each of them as he came to the table.

"Let me get you a plate." Betsy got up. "You'll not want to miss tasting Mrs. Goodge's scones."

"When did you get back?" Hatchet asked. "We heard you were in Wales."

"My train got back this morning, and I stopped in at St. Thomas'." He grinned at Mrs. Jeffries. "Matron told me you'd been there looking for me."

Betsy slipped a plate, a serviette, and silverware in front of him and went back to her seat.

"Indeed I was." She poured him a cup of tea and passed it along to him. "I wanted your opinion on several topics."

"I heard about your murder." Bosworth reached for a scone. "It was in the Cardiff newspapers. Poor woman, stabbing is a messy way to die. I hope she went quickly. Unfortunately, there's not much I can tell you about her death. I've not had time to track down the postmortem report."

"As you've only just returned, that is understandable,"

Mrs. Jeffries said. "Let me tell you what we know. Agatha Moran was stabbed through the heart. The police report estimated that there were two or three thrusts of the knife. Inspector Witherspoon told me that the postmortem said the murder weapon was probably an ordinary kitchen knife."

Bosworth swallowed the bite he'd just put in his mouth. "Did he mention how long the blade might have been?"

She shook her head. "I'm afraid not."

"That's too bad," he replied. "The papers say she was found on a public street just after dark. Apparently, she was found by a passerby right after she'd been stabbed. That leads me to believe her death must have been very quick."

"That's what we think, too," Luty said. She told him the rest of the details.

He ate his scone as he listened. When she'd finished, he took a sip of tea. "It sounds like the poor woman didn't lay there suffering while she bled to death. Still, it's an ugly way to die, but I'll know more after I get my hands on the report."

"Dr. Bosworth, is there a poison that looks like food poisoning but is really something bad enough to make sure you die?" Betsy asked. "I know it's an odd question, but we've a reason for asking."

"We think someone connected to the case might have murdered two wives with fake food poisonin'," Mrs. Goodge added. She told him about Sir Madison Lowery.

Bosworth crossed his arms over his chest and leaned back in his seat. "There are a number of poisons that produce the same symptoms. The fact of the matter is, if the attending doctor was treating both husband and wife and they'd both become ill after eating bad seafood, he'd probably have diagnosed food poisoning and wouldn't have checked for anything else."

"And if only one of them died, he wouldn't have insisted on a postmortem," Hatchet stated. "Correct?"

"Most likely not, especially if the husband were a member of the aristocracy. But it's odd that your killer would switch from poison to a knife—"

Mrs. Jeffries interrupted. "He's not our killer. He couldn't be. He's got a very good alibi. We've no idea who murdered poor Miss Moran."

"Maybe what I found out today will help a bit," Smythe offered. "My source told me somethin' very interestin'." He relayed what he'd learned from Blimpey Groggins, making sure he didn't leave anything out of his recitation.

When he'd finished, no one commented. Then Mrs. Jeffries said, "So Arabella Evans took Agatha Moran's child and raised it as her own."

"But how could she fool a man like that?" Mrs. Goodge asked. "Wouldn't he notice she wasn't with child?"

"Not if he was in Argentina," Mrs. Jeffries mused, her expression thoughtful. "And according to the gossip, Jeremy Evans was going to divorce her and that would have ruined her socially. So she gets him to agree to go off on a business trip halfway around the world, and when he returns, she presents him with a child. It's one thing for Evans not to care how a divorce might affect either of them, but he knew something like that would ruin a child's life."

Mrs. Goodge still looked confused. "But how could they have done it? Mrs. Evans didn't grow a belly and Miss Moran did."

"It would be easy," Bosworth interjected. "This was twenty years ago, Mrs. Goodge, and back then, many women of a certain class wouldn't venture out of their homes when they were expecting."

"But there would be servants . . ."

"Who were bribed to keep their mouths shut," Smythe

said. "How do you think my source got his information? When Jeremy Evans boarded the ship to Argentina, Arabella Evans hired Miss Moran to be a companion, and the two women moved to a cottage out in the country, away from all those pryin' eyes."

"Agatha Moran made a deal with Arabella Evans that she could stay with the family and be the girl's nurse and then her governess," Smythe continued. "But it looks like Mrs. Evans sent the girl off to school and paid Miss Moran off."

"That's probably where she got the money to buy the house in Islington and open the hotel," Luty surmised.

"And Mrs. Evans pulling a nasty trick like that would explain Miss Moran throwing a fit when she found out," Betsy added. "But she took the money."

"And kept an eye on her daughter." Ruth took a dainty bite of brown bread. "Mrs. Middleton admitted to Gerald that Agatha Moran frequently went to Bayswater to have a look at the Evans house. She must have been trying to watch out for the girl."

"And when she found out that Lowery was a probable murderer, she must have gone to see Sutton to enlist his help in making sure the marriage didn't take place," Hatchet said excitedly.

"Does that mean that Sutton murdered Miss Moran?" Luty asked. "You know, to keep her from spillin' the beans about him bein' Rosemary's papa. He'd not have wanted Eleanor North to find out he'd fathered a child and abandoned the mother."

Mrs. Jeffries wasn't sure. "I don't know. According to Mrs. North's second statement, Sutton turned the other way and went home before she went to the Evans house that evening."

"He could have come back," Smythe said. "He could

have waited for her to go inside and then come back, spotted Miss Moran, and shoved a knife in her heart."

"Which would mean he'd have had the knife on his person and been prepared to commit murder," Mrs. Jeffries commented. Something didn't make sense, but she couldn't put her finger on it. What she needed was a bit of peace and quiet so she could absorb this new information.

"And he'd have had to have known that Rosemary Evans was his daughter," Hatchet said softly.

"I'll bet he did know," Luty murmured.

"What makes you say that?" Mrs. Goodge asked.

"Remember how he and Eleanor North met? He was walkin' past her house," she explained. "Now why in tarnation would he be in that neighborhood if it wasn't to try and catch a glimpse of his daughter?"

Mrs. Jeffries really wished she could have just a few moments to think this through.

"I'll bet that Mrs. Evans is the killer." Wiggins helped himself to another slice of cake. "Let's look at it logically. Miss Moran comes back from holiday and finds out her daughter is goin' to marry a murderer. She hurries along to the Evans household and tells Mrs. Evans she's got to stop the weddin'. I'll bet it was Miss Moran that Rosemary Evans overheard arguin' with her mother on that Monday afternoon."

"And we know that Arabella Evans is such a social climber, she'd die before she'd stop Rosemary's marriage to an aristocrat," Ruth pointed out.

"That's right." Wiggins waved his fork for emphasis. "And we know that Mrs. Evans was gone for a good long while durin' the tea, so she could have nipped down to the kitchen, snatched up a knife, and hurried outside to stab it into poor Miss Moran's heart."

"Did Mrs. Evans have blood on her clothes?" Dr. Bosworth asked. "If she was stabbed in the heart, the blood would have spurted and the killer would have gotten some of it on his person."

"And Mrs. Evans couldn't have had time to murder Agatha Moran," Betsy said. "When she disappeared during the tea, she sneaked off to smoke a cigarette."

Witherspoon was so tired when he got home that evening that he asked Mrs. Jeffries to send his dinner up to his room on a tray. "I think I'll just have a quick bite to eat and then go right to bed. I don't want to eat in the dining room; I might get food on those lovely lace runners on the table."

"We can move them off, sir," Mrs. Jeffries argued.

"No, no, everyone's worked very hard to get the house in order for the reception, and we all want it to be perfect." He yawned and started up the staircase.

"Would you like a quick glass of sherry before you go up, sir?" She hurried after him. "We can have it in your study." She'd come up with a clever way to pass along the information they'd learned today. Tomorrow wasn't just Betsy's wedding; it was Rosemary Evans' wedding as well. The Evans wedding and the killer were tied together, but for the life of her, she couldn't determine the murderer's identity. Not until she had some time to herself.

"I don't want one, but please feel free to have a nice drink yourself." He turned and gave her a winsome smile as he reached the first-floor landing. "All I want is a quick supper and then I'm off to bed. Send Wiggins up with a tray. I'll leave it in the hall when I'm done. I want to get plenty of rest. I've a big responsibility tomorrow."

Upstairs, Smythe and Betsy sat on the couch in the small sitting room and held hands. "Are you nervous?" she asked.

"No, I've been waitin' for this day for a long time." He took a deep breath. He'd wanted the flat to be a surprise, but he'd changed his mind and decided it might make her happier if she knew their plans. "When we come back from our weddin' trip, we're movin' into our own flat. It's close by so we can stay on here. And well . . . I've bought the buildin', but I've put it in your name so you'd have somethin'. If you don't like the colors and the wallpapers, we can change them, and I've changed my will so that if somethin' happens to me, I've left everythin' to you."

She put her hand over his mouth, stopping the rush of words. "Don't say such things, not on the night before our wedding. I've come close to losing you before, but nothing is going to happen to either of us . . . and you didn't have to change your will. I don't have anything to give to you except my love and my trust, so not another word."

"Your love was all I ever wanted." He grinned. "And by the way, we're goin' to Paris for our weddin' trip. You can tell Norah and Leo tomorrow before the weddin'. I know she's been pesterin' you about it."

Betsy's eyes filled with tears, but they were tears of happiness. "She's been pestering me about everything, but she's my sister. I'm so glad we've gotten to know each other again. By the way, I told her that you weren't poor, but she'd already figured that out on her own."

"Of course she did." He laughed and dropped a kiss on the top of her head. "She's a smart one, just like her sister."

Mrs. Jeffries closed the double doors behind her as she stepped into the dining room. It looked wonderful. White lace runners were draped over the dining table, now with the additional leaves added so that it ran the length of the room. Elegant green and white bunting, courtesy of Ruth, had been draped over the windows, and net streamers, also in green and white, were looped from the chandelier to all four corners, forming a festive crown over the room. Polished silver serving platters, cut glass crystal, and the household's best china were lined up on the sideboard. Mrs. Jeffries nodded in satisfaction. Phyllis had done them proud. Betsy was going to have a wonderful reception.

Next she went into the drawing room and smiled in sheer delight as she stepped inside. More bunting at the windows, more streamers crisscrossing the ceiling, lace runners on all the cabinets and tables, and to top it off, a beautifully decorated Christmas tree with the wedding presents tucked safely beneath the branches. That had been Wiggins' idea.

She spent the next ten minutes turning off the lamps and locking up the house. It was late and she was tired, but she knew she'd never sleep. Not with all the ideas racing through her head. Picking up one lantern, she went back upstairs and into the dining room, where she helped herself to a sherry before going into the drawing room. She put the lantern on the table and sank down on the settee.

Closing her eyes, she put her head back against the cushion and took several long, deep breaths. She'd found that relaxing her body helped to free her mind. She didn't try to make sense out of any of the facts of the case; she simply breathed and let her mind go where it would.

Snatches of conversation drifted in and out of her mind. *The scullery maid complained that someone had stolen a carpetbag promised to her.* She relaxed her shoulders into the cushions. *"He told her they'd covered everything, includin' her ruddy table, and what's more, them cloths cost good money and if they all weren't accounted for, he'd add it to her bill. You could hear them shoutin' at each other all the way down in the kitchen."* Mrs. Jeffries opened her eyes and reached for her sherry. She took a sip and closed them again. *"They confirmed the light was burning when they left that day."* Her eyes flew open and she sat up. *He described the shelves filled with exotic products that no one wanted and laughed as he recounted seeing Douglas Branson's head coming up from behind a stack of files. He repeated everything the chief clerk had said, but his expression sobered when he got to the part about Jeremy Evans weeping over his dead cat.*

A pattern formed in her mind. For one brief moment, the entire sequence of events was crystal clear, but before she could rally the individual parts into some semblance of order, it disappeared. But she knew she was right—she knew who killed Agatha Moran.

But had she figured it out too late? How was she to prove it? The evidence was circumstantial at best, and tomorrow, of all days, was the worst possible time to set any course of action in motion. What if she was wrong? What if she had lost the ability to put the puzzle pieces together?

She got up and began to pace the room. No, she might doubt herself sometimes, but she knew she was right. This solution was the only one that made sense. She heard the hall clock strike the hour and knew she ought to go upstairs. Sleep would be impossible, but perhaps in the privacy of her room she could think through all her options and decide the best way to proceed. Picking up her lantern, she went upstairs.

She closed the door as quietly as possible and blew out the flame. Darkness descended, but she'd left her blind up and there was enough light for her to see. Putting the lantern on her desk, she made her way to the window. She had to think.

She eased herself into her rocker and fixed her gaze on the gas lamp across the road. She kept her eyes wide open, letting her vision blur and shift as she concentrated on the faint light. The idea she'd had earlier came quickly, and this time, her mind paid attention to the details. She sat there for over an hour.

Mrs. Jeffries gave herself a small shake and stood up. She no longer had any doubts about the identity of the killer.

But the question was, could an arrest wait a day or two? That was the real quandary. Tomorrow was the biggest day in Betsy's life, and she wanted everything to be perfect. Inspector Witherspoon was giving her away in marriage. If an arrest was made tomorrow, he'd be stuck for hours at the station, questioning the suspect and filling out paperwork. Could she do that to Betsy? Could she do that to Witherspoon?

But if she didn't, she had a horrible feeling that something awful was going to happen.

CHAPTER 11

Wiggins smiled cheerfully as he came into the kitchen. "You're up already, Mrs. Jeffries. Cor blimey, you've even got the tea ready." He walked toward the table, slipping on the suspender that had been hanging loose over his shoulder.

"We're the early birds," she replied. She poured his tea and put it in front of the chair next to hers. "Sit here. I want to talk to you before the others get up." She couldn't believe her good luck. Wiggins was usually the last one up in the mornings.

Mrs. Jeffries hadn't slept very well. She couldn't shake the feeling that if she waited until after the wedding to nudge the inspector toward an arrest, it might be too late. On the other hand, she didn't want to take any action that might damage the wedding plans.

In the wee hours of the morning, she'd come up with

what she hoped was a solution to her dilemma, but it would involve a bit of subterfuge on her part. She'd realized she couldn't let any of them, except for Wiggins, know she'd come up with a solution to this case.

Everyone in the household was already excited and nervous about the wedding, and the last thing they needed was any additional conflict about whether or not they should act now or wait until the reception was over.

"What's wrong?" His face creased with worry as he sat down.

"Nothing is wrong," she assured him hastily. "I just need you to do something for me today. Something you can't tell the others about." She reached over and touched his hand. "This might be difficult for you, because I know you don't like keeping secrets from the people you care about."

Wiggins' eyes widened in alarm. "You're scarin' me, Mrs. Jeffries. What's this about?"

She pulled back. "You have to promise that you'll do what I ask and not say anything to anyone, especially Betsy or Smythe. Can you do that? I could be wrong about this course of action, and if I am, we'll have worried them for nothing."

"Alright." He took a drink of tea. "I promise I'll hold my tongue. What do you want me to do?"

"Your wedding clothes are upstairs, right?"

"They're in the cupboard. Why do you want me to put them on now? It's a bit early. The weddin's not till two thirty."

"No, I just wanted to be sure you had them at the ready. If I'm correct in my assumptions, when you come back, you might be a bit pressed for time." She took a deep breath, then told him what she suspected might happen today and what she needed him to do.

"Corse I'll do it." He nodded his head for emphasis. "But

what are you goin' to tell the others when they get up and I'm gone?"

"I'll think of something," she replied airily. "And if I'm wrong, if you see . . ."

"I'll come home quick as a wink," he finished as he got to his feet. "Let me get my coat and hat. It's cold out there."

"You'll miss your breakfast. I'll wrap some scones for you to take with you." She got up. "But do hurry. Mrs. Goodge will be up any minute now, and if she sees you leaving, they'll be no end of questions."

"Where's Wiggins?" Smythe asked for the tenth time. "'E should be here. He's my best man."

"I've told you," Mrs. Jeffries said calmly, "I've sent him out on an errand for me. Besides, it's only gone nine o'clock. You've plenty of time before the wedding."

Smythe paced across the kitchen and stared out the window onto the road. "I know I'm actin' like a ninny, but I'd thought Betsy would be here this mornin'."

"It's bad luck for the groom to see the bride before the weddin'," Mrs. Goodge said. "That's why we sent her off to stay with her sister and brother-in-law today. She's havin' breakfast with them and gettin' dressed there. They're leavin' tomorrow so this is her last chance to spend any time with them."

"What time will she be back?" He swung around and came back to the table.

Mrs. Jeffries rolled her eyes. They'd been over this half a dozen times. "Norah and Leo are bringing her here in a hansom this afternoon. She'll be back at two fifteen at the earliest. By then, you and Wiggins will be on your way to the church. At two twenty, Ruth will send her carriage here and Betsy and the inspector will get in and drive around to the church. Mrs. Goodge, Lady Cannonberry, and I will be walking across the garden to the church, and Phyllis will be left in charge to supervise the waiters and insure that all is ready for the reception."

Smythe took a deep breath. Blast a Spaniard, he was as nervous as a kitten in a room full of bulldogs. "So I won't be seein' 'er before the weddin'."

"That's the whole point," Mrs. Goodge snapped. "Again, I'll say it slowly so you'll understand. It's bad luck for the bride and groom to see each other before the weddin'." The cook wasn't in the best of moods. She knew that Mrs. Jeffries was up to something. Wiggins was missing, she wouldn't say where she'd sent him, and she kept watching the clock as though she expected something to happen.

"Why don't you go to Howards? You can take some carrots or an apple to the horses," Mrs. Jeffries suggested. "I'm sure Bow and Arrow would like a wedding day treat. They'll not see you for the next week. They'll miss you."

"That'd get me out of the house," Smythe muttered, more to himself than to them. "I'm goin' to walk a hole in the floor if I stay here." He grabbed his coat off the peg and started for the back door. "Right then, I'll go. The horses always calm me down when I'm het up. You tell Wiggins when he gets back to wait 'ere for me. We need to walk to the church together. I want to make sure 'e's there on time. I don't like 'im disappearin' like this."

"He hasn't disappeared. He's running a small errand for me. But I will make sure he stays here," Mrs. Jeffries reassured him.

He nodded and headed off down the corridor. A moment later, the back door slammed.

"Alright." Mrs. Goodge, who'd been standing by the cooker, turned and faced her. "What's goin' on? Don't try to tell me you've sent Wiggins off on an errand, either. I can see that's somethin's happened. You've been watchin' the clock and you've got that look in your eye. You've sussed it out, haven't you?"

"I think so," Mrs. Jeffries replied. "But I wasn't sure what to do about it. I suspect that Tobias Sutton might try and stop Rosemary Evans' wedding. That's why I sent Wiggins off—I sent him to the Evans house. If Sutton does try to stop it, he'll probably go there first rather than the church."

"Why would he do that?" The cook came back to the table and sat down in her spot.

"Remember yesterday when Luty said she believed Sutton knew that Rosemary was his daughter?"

Mrs. Goodge nodded. "That's why Sutton was hangin' around the neighborhood when he slipped and fell on that crack in the pavement and got rescued by Eleanor North. It sounds reasonable enough. But what's that got to do with it? From what we've heard about the man, he's a spineless sort."

"I agree that he treated Agatha Moran very badly. But the fact that he was trying to keep an eye on his daughter leads me to believe he cares about the girl. That being said, if he cares, he'll not let her marry a monster like Sir Madison Lowery."

"Is Sutton our killer then?"

"I'm not completely sure of that," she answered. "I think it might be someone else, but I could be wrong. Oh dear, one moment I'm sure I'm right and the next I'm riddled with doubt. Let me tell you what I've come up with. I want to hear your opinion." She relayed her theory about the killer and how she'd come to the conclusion that it might be best to wait until tomorrow to mention anything to the inspector.

"I'm sure Betsy would appreciate not havin' her weddin' ruined," the cook said dryly, "but what I don't understand is why you didn't tell the rest of us what you suspected."

"You saw how Smythe was acting," Mrs. Jeffries said defensively. "He's so nervous about the wedding he can't remember anything for more than two seconds, and I certainly wasn't going to say anything to Betsy. This is her big day."

"You could have told me earlier. I shouldn't have had to pry it out of you," Mrs. Goodge charged. "I thought we were friends . . ."

"We are friends," Mrs. Jeffries retorted, "and I am telling you." She broke off as the back door slammed and they heard footsteps pounding up the hallway. Both women stood up as Wiggins came running into the kitchen.

"We've got trouble," he announced. "Jeremy Evans is missin'. Tobias Sutton barged in to see him, and twenty minutes later, Evans just walked out the front door. Somethin' bad is going to 'appen. I can feel it. I was standin' right there on the pavement when he come chargin' down the walkway. Mrs. Evans come runnin' after 'im, screamin' that he'd better not do anythin' to ruin the weddin', and he just yelled back for her not to worry, there wasn't goin' to be a weddin'."

"Oh my Lord," Mrs. Jeffries exclaimed as she realized exactly what was going to happen. "He's going to the Lowery house. He's going to kill Sir Madison . . ."

"Sutton must have told Evans the truth about the blackguard." Mrs. Goodge frowned in confusion. "But why would Evans have murdered Agatha Moran? That's the part I don't understand."

"Because he thought she was going to ruin his daughter's life," Mrs. Jeffries said.

"What if he only heard part of the conversation between Agatha and Arabella Evans on that Monday afternoon? What if he didn't realize why Agatha wanted the weddin' stopped? But we don't have time for speculatin' about who did what. We've got to do somethin'."

"What?" Wiggins cried. "The only thing that makes any sense is gettin' the inspector to the Lowery house before someone else is killed, but I don't see how we're goin' to do that."

Mrs. Jeffries stopped and stood stock-still. Her mind worked furiously to come up with a solution to this sudden turn of events. "We'll have to use the anonymous note trick." She hurried over to the pine sideboard and pulled open the top drawer. "Luckily, the inspector has become so famous, an anonymous letter shoved under the front door is a reasonable way for someone who wished to keep their identity secret to communicate with him."

"You think it'll work?" Mrs. Goodge asked worriedly. She glanced toward the back hall as she spoke, making sure the inspector hadn't come down to the kitchen. "I know we've used it before, but . . ."

"But we don't have a lot of choice right now," Wiggins cried. "Someone's goin' to die if we don't get our inspector movin'."

Mrs. Jeffries pulled out a piece of paper and a pencil. She propped the paper on the sideboard, wrote out a short message in crude block letters, folded the sheet in half, and then handed it to Wiggins. "Run upstairs with this, tell the inspector we just found it, that someone just shoved this under the front door this morning."

Wiggins grabbed the note and raced out of the kitchen.

"I hope this works," Mrs. Goodge muttered.

"So do I," the housekeeper replied. "I'm going upstairs. I may need to do a bit of encouraging to get the inspector out of the house this close to the wedding time."

She reached the foyer just as the inspector and Wiggins came down from the upper floors. Witherspoon turned and stared quizzically at Mrs. Jeffries. "Wiggins said someone shoved this note under the door."

"Yes sir, I know. I was there when he found it. We looked outside, but we didn't see anyone. When I saw what it said, I told him to take it right up to you."

Witherspoon sighed heavily. "I do hope this isn't a hoax or someone's idea of a joke. I can't in good conscience ignore it, not when it says Sir Madison Lowery is going to be murdered this morning."

"Of course not, sir," she agreed. "But you can't go alone, sir. If the message in the note is correct, there could well be violence. You must take some constables with you."

"I'll get some lads from the station. It's on the way," he replied as he went to the coat tree. "We can get a hansom from there to Bayswater. I say, this is decidedly bad timing."

"It certainly is, sir," she agreed.

"Do tell Betsy that no matter what happens, I'll be back here by two twenty." Witherspoon grabbed his coat and hat and hurried out the front door.

Mrs. Jeffries turned to Wiggins. She wasn't going to take any chances with the inspector's safety. "You know where Sir Madison lives, right?"

"Corse I do. He lives on Monmouth Road. I've been there twice in the last week tryin' to find a servant or someone to get a bit of information out of, but I've 'ad no luck. You want me to go there?"

She was thinking fast. "How far is Lowery's home from Luty's?"

"They're in Knightsbridge, so it's less than a mile," he replied. He looked down the staircase and saw the cook mounting the stairs. "Here comes Mrs. Goodge."

"Go to Luty's. Have her and Hatchet drive you to Lowery's house. When you get there, simply tell him that you went to the Crookshank house to borrow a punch bowl. When you told them about the note, they insisted on driving over to see if the inspector would need a ride back to the house so he could get to the wedding on time."

Wiggins nodded and was out the front door like a shot. By this time, Mrs. Goodge had made it to the top of the stairs. "Did it work?"

"Yes, he's on his way there now. But he's going to stop by the station first and get some constables to go along. Let's hope they get there in time . . ." She started down the stairs. "Come on, there's no time to lose. We've got to get to Ruth's. I'll explain what we've got to do on the way over."

"What are we goin' there for?" The cook trudged after her.

"We've got to call in a few favors from the lads at the police station," Mrs. Jeffries called over her shoulder. "And we'll need Ruth's carriage so we can get to Constable Barnes as quickly as possible."

Witherspoon and two police constables piled into a four-wheeler that one of the constables flagged down on Holland Park Road.

"Where to, guv?" the driver asked.

"Number three Monmouth Road," Witherspoon replied. "And get there as quickly as you can. I'll pay you double if you hurry. It's a matter of life and death."

The driver took him at his word, let off the brake, and cracked the whip in the air. The carriage lunged forward, slamming the two policemen against the back of the seat and causing Witherspoon, who was sitting opposite them, to grab the handhold hanging above the window and hang on for dear life.

The four-wheeler raced through the streets of London and got to Bayswater in record time. The three policemen stepped out onto the road, and Witherspoon was paying the driver when they heard a shout come from the house. He charged for the front door with the two constables close on his heels. The door was ajar and they raced inside, coming to a halt just inside the drawing room.

Witherspoon stared at the scene. Christopher Selby, blood running from his mouth, was on the floor slumped against the drapes, and Lowery was on the settee, a look of terror on his face as he stared at the gun that Jeremy Evans had pointed at his head.

Evans looked from Selby to Lowery. "Tell your friend not to be a fool. The next time he comes at me, I'll not just knock him down, I'll shoot him."

Witherspoon's heart sank. He knew this wasn't going to end well. "Mr. Evans, please put the gun down. You don't want to commit murder."

Evans laughed harshly but didn't take his gaze off Lowery. "I shouldn't worry about that if I were you, Inspector. If you've done it once, the second time is no effort at all."

"You've killed before?" Witherspoon's heart sank even further. He was fairly certain he knew what Evans' answer was going to be, but he needed to ask the question in front of witnesses. "May I ask who you murdered?"

"You know that already, Inspector," he replied. "I'm the one who killed Agatha Moran, and she certainly didn't deserve to die." He waved the gun at Lowery. "Her murder was a mistake, but this one won't be. I won't hesitate to shoot this scum. He's killed two innocent women for the basest of reasons: money."

"That's a lie." Lowery dragged his gaze away from the weapon and looked at the inspector. His face was drained of color and his eyes were frantic with fear. "I've killed no one. I'm innocent. He's insane. He's mad. He doesn't know what he's talking about."

"You've murdered two women and gotten away with it,"

Evans charged. "And that's what you had planned for my daughter, isn't it? But you'll not hurt her. You'll never get your filthy hands on her."

"Cancel the damned wedding, then," Lowery cried. "But for God's sake, don't kill me."

"You know my wife wouldn't stand for that, and she'd die before she'd cancel the wedding." Evans shrugged. "She wouldn't give a toss if you'd killed ten wives. As long as you're a 'Sir' you'd be acceptable to her, and I can't take that risk. That's why you've got to die."

Lowery's eyes filled with tears. "Don't just stand there." He looked at Witherspoon. "Do something. You're the police. You can't just let him murder me."

The constables started to move forward, but the inspector stopped them with a raised hand. A frontal assault would mean immediate death for Lowery. He'd try reason first.

"Mr. Evans, I'm sure you think you're justified in what you're doing," Witherspoon said, "but if this man has committed murder, you must let the law deal with him. He must stand trial. You've no right to be judge, jury, and executioner."

Evans laughed but didn't take his gaze or his gun off Lowery. "Don't be a fool, Inspector. This country doesn't hang men with a 'Sir' in front of their name. Agatha tried to warn my bitch of a wife, but she wouldn't listen. Lowery's a killer. He marries them and murders them with poison—calls it food poisoning from oysters. But Agatha Moran was onto him and she did what any mother would do; she tried to protect her child." He shifted his weight but kept the weapon's aim steady and focused. "My wife didn't realize I knew about their little deal, but I did. I knew from the beginning that she hadn't given birth to Rosemary, but I love my daughter as much as I could love a child from my own body. My only real regret in this whole mess is that I murdered the real mother, the one who was trying to save my daughter's life."

"Why did you kill her?" Witherspoon wanted to keep him talking. "You claim that she was trying to protect Rosemary from this man, so why did you murder her?"

"Because I only heard half of what she said to Arabella on that Monday," Evans admitted. "Ironic, isn't it? I'd come home early that afternoon. I had a headache and was just going to slip up the stairs and lie down. Then I heard her arguing with Arabella. But I didn't hear the entire conversation. All I heard her say was, 'If you don't stop this marriage, I'll tell everyone she's a bastard.'" He gave a bitter, ugly laugh. "I thought Agatha Moran wanted more money. Years ago, Arabella paid her to go away and leave us alone. My wife didn't think I knew about that, either, but I did. Then this morning, Tobias Sutton told me the truth: He's Rosemary's biological father and Agatha had gone to him for help in getting the marriage stopped. She found out that Lowery had married and murdered a woman in France, just like he murdered Beatrice Trent."

"Why didn't Mr. Sutton come to us with this information?" Witherspoon asked.

"Because he was afraid Eleanor would call off their engagement if she found out he'd fathered a child out of wedlock," Evans said. "But he finally realized he had to do something, that he couldn't let this fiend get his hands on Rosemary, so he came to see me this morning and told me everything."

"For God's sake, arrest this lunatic before he hurts someone," Lowery sobbed.

Evans made a growling sound deep in his throat and started toward him.

"Sir Madison, do be quiet," Witherspoon said quickly. "Mr. Evans is telling us something very important. Do go on, Mr. Evans. Tell me what happened the day Miss Moran was murdered." He was stalling for time: As long as Evans was answering questions, he wasn't pulling the trigger.

Evans halted but kept his gaze locked on Lowery. "I followed her that day. The deadline she'd given Arabella was up, you see, so I had to do something. I took a knife out of one of the cutlery boxes on the shelf in my office, stuck it in my coat, and went to Islington. When she came out her front door, I knew she was going to my house. I knew she was going to barge in to that wretched tea party and ruin my child's life." He sighed. "At least that's what I thought at the time. It was only today that I learned she was trying to save Rosemary, not hurt her."

"When you stabbed her, how did you manage to keep the blood off your clothing, sir?" Witherspoon asked the question casually, as though they were having a conversation.

"I knew where she was going, so I took a shortcut through the mews and climbed through one of the empty window frames in the conservatory. I grabbed the oilcloth from that fancy Spanish table my wife ordered. It's ruined now and I'm glad," he replied. "I held the cloth in front of me when I stabbed her."

Suddenly, there was a commotion from the hallway. Footsteps pounded across the floor and everything happened at once.

"No!" Witherspoon cried out a warning, but it was too late.

Three constables charged into the room. Evans looked over his shoulder, saw them rushing at him, and fired off two shots at Lowery just as the policemen tackled him. Witherspoon and the other constables joined the fray. The inspector got his hand around the gun before Evans got off the third shot.

"Let me go!" Evans cried. "I missed, I missed. He's got to

die." He fought like a wild man, bucking and screaming as they wrestled him to the ground.

Witherspoon rose from the floor and handed the gun to a constable. He rushed to Lowery. The man was curled into a ball, crying, and blood was soaking through his shirt. "I'm shot," he moaned as tears ran down his face. "You let that lunatic shoot me."

Witherspoon knelt beside him, lifted his shirt collar, and examined the wound. "You'll be fine, sir. The bullet barely grazed you."

The constables hauled Evans to his feet. He said nothing as they put the handcuffs on him and led him off.

"You mean I'm not going to die?" Lowery straightened up and dabbed at his cheeks.

Witherspoon thought the fellow might eventually hang, but he didn't want to tip his hand about that matter. "Not just yet."

"What if the inspector isn't back in time?" Mrs. Goodge glanced at the clock, her expression anxious. "What'll we do? It's almost two fifteen." The cook's new pearl gray bombazine dress rustled softly as she paced in front of the hallway door. Samson was perched on his stool, watching her as she moved back and forth.

"We'll ask Betsy's brother-in-law to walk her down the aisle," Mrs. Jeffries replied. She was dressed in an elegant rust-colored day dress, matching hat, and new kid shoes. "But let's keep our fingers crossed that all will be well."

Wiggins, Luty, and Hatchet had gone to Lowery's home, but they'd arrived after Evans was under arrest and the inspector had taken him to the station. A neighbor had reported that Lowery's housekeeper had slipped out a side door and gotten help when Evans had come barging into the house waving a gun.

Now they had to hope that the inspector could get away long enough to do his duty and get Betsy married off properly. Betsy and Smythe were both completely in the dark about the events of the morning. They'd discussed the matter and decided they'd tell them the whole story when they returned from their wedding trip.

"Ruth dropped Constable Barnes off at the station hours ago," Luty added. "He told her he'd do his best to get the inspector out of there and back here on time, and the lads have agreed to help with the paperwork. She went on home to change for the weddin'."

"Where's Smythe?" Hatchet asked.

"He and Wiggins have already gone over to the church. Betsy should be here any minute," Mrs. Jeffries said. "I think I hear the carriage . . ." She dashed to the window. "Thank goodness, we're in luck, it's Ruth . . . oh, and she's got the inspector with her. We're going to make it. We're going to have a wedding!"

A few moments later, Ruth and the inspector appeared in the kitchen. "Gerald's made an arrest," she announced brightly. She winked at Luty. Mrs. Jeffries gave Ruth a quick, grateful smile. "How wonderful, sir. We knew you'd get this case solved."

Witherspoon smiled modestly. "Thank you all, but I wasn't sure myself that we'd have a happy ending to this day. I'll tell you all about it later. Right now, I'd better tidy myself up a bit."

"You can use the mirror in my room." Mrs. Goodge put on her new white gloves.

"Thank you, I believe I'll do just that."

Mrs. Jeffries noticed there was a smudge on the edge of his collar and his cravat needed to be straightened. "Betsy will be here any moment. The rest of us had better go. Isn't it a beautiful day for a wedding? We'll see you at the church, sir."

* * *

"You look very lovely, my dear," Witherspoon said to Betsy as they entered the narthex.

She wore a cream-colored lace gown with a high neck, fitted bodice, and long, elegant sleeves. A matching veil was held in place with a garland of pink roses.

"Thank you, sir, and thank you for doing this for me." She blushed with pleasure and then took a deep breath. "You know, walking me down the aisle. You've been so very good to me and I'm so proud to have you by my side."

He patted her hand. "Our household wouldn't be the same without you, and I'm deeply honored that you asked me." He smiled. "Are you ready?"

She nodded and took her place next to him. "Are you alright, sir? It looks like your bottom lip is swollen."

He'd gotten clipped in the mouth during the struggle with Evans, but he wasn't going to mar her wedding by mentioning such an ugly incident. "I had a bit of an accident earlier today, but I'm fine." He gave her his arm and signaled to the lad on the door leading to the sanctuary.

The doors opened, the music started, and he and Betsy walked down the aisle.

"I can't believe they're finally married," Ruth said to Mrs. Jeffries. "I'm so happy for the both of them. Do you think they'll resent the fact that we didn't tell them about Evans?"

They were sitting on chairs in the drawing room. Betsy and Smythe were in the place of honor on the settee. Mrs. Jeffries pulled her foot back to avoid her toes getting trampled by a waiter passing with a tray of canapés.

"This is their special day and it doesn't seem right to discuss murder and mayhem." Mrs. Jeffries shrugged. "We'll tell them what happened when they get back from their wedding trip."

Constable and Mrs. Barnes drifted by; she was laughing and he was holding her hand as they made their way to the happy couple to pay their respects. Smythe got up and introduced them to Norah and Leo, who were occupying the chairs on the other side of the settee.

"How did you figure it out?" Ruth asked. "If you hadn't sent Wiggins to the Evans house this morning . . ." She broke off as Witherspoon came toward them.

"There you are." He beamed at Ruth. "Are you enjoying yourself? Would you like some champagne?"

"I'm having a wonderful time, and I've just had a glass." Ruth patted the empty chair next to her. "Now do sit down and tell us what happened. We're dying of curiosity."

"Well, it was very odd, you see. I expect Mrs. Jeffries told you that someone put a note under our door this morning. The note was very explicit: It said that Sir Madison Lowery was going to be murdered."

"Do you have any idea who might have done such a thing?" she asked.

Witherspoon thought for a moment. "Not as yet. But regardless of who it was, I couldn't ignore it. I couldn't take the chance," he explained as he sat down. "When we arrived at the Lowery house, Jeremy Evans confessed, but as he was holding a gun on Lowery at the time, I was quite worried that things could go badly."

"Gracious, that must have been so frightening," she said.

"Unfortunately, blood was shed and Lowery was wounded, but not seriously." He told them everything that had transpired at the Lowery household.

Mrs. Jeffries listened carefully, and a slow, satisfied smile formed on her lips as he related the details of Evans' confession. She'd been right. She had figured it out in time! She hadn't lost her reasoning ability and she could still put the puzzle pieces together.

"But how did he keep from getting blood on his clothes?" Ruth asked curiously. "After all, didn't Dr.—" She clamped her mouth shut.

"After all what?" Witherspoon repeated.

"Uh, I meant I once heard a doctor say that stabbings are always messy," Ruth said quickly.

"And that doctor would be right." The inspector patted her hand. "Evans kept the blood off his clothes by grabbing one of the oilcloths from the conservatory. He held it in front of him when he stabbed her."

Mrs. Jeffries' spirits soared. She'd been right about that, too. She raised her hand and signaled the waiter. This called for another glass of champagne. Maybe two.

"So if the oilcloth had blood on it, what did he do with it?" Ruth asked.

"He stuffed it in an old carpetbag."

Mrs. Jeffries beamed at the waiter as she helped herself to a glass. They were doing a wonderful job. "Thank you."

Ruth took a glass as well. "But didn't you search the Evans house that night?" she asked the inspector.

Witherspoon pursed his lips. "No, I'm ashamed to say we didn't. We'd no compelling evidence that gave us cause for a thorough search. By the time we realized her murder was directly connected to the Evans household, he'd gotten rid of it. He weighted the bag down with stones and tossed it into the Thames. I doubt we'll ever recover it, but we've no real need to, as he's confessed to the murder."

"Where did he get the knife?" This question came from Mrs. Goodge, who'd come up behind them and been listening.

"From the cutlery kit in his office," Witherspoon replied. "The place is full of all sorts of odd items that his company imported into the country. He took the knife and went to her house. I don't think he'd have gone through with the murder if she hadn't gone to Chepstow Villas."

"You mean, at that point, he thought that Miss Moran was willing to make Rosemary a social pariah rather than see her married to Lowery," Ruth clarified.

"That's right." Witherspoon sighed. "He just didn't know then why she didn't want the girl to wed him. Evans thought she was simply greedy, that she was trying to blackmail Mrs. Evans for more money to keep quiet. He only realized today the real reason behind her determination to keep Rosemary away from the man."

"Are you goin' to arrest Lowery?" Mrs. Goodge waved at Wiggins, who was standing across the room, chatting with Phyllis.

Witherspoon thought for a moment. "I'm not sure we can," he answered. "Even if he did murder two women, they're both long buried, and any evidence of what really caused their deaths is interred with them. However, all of the facts are bound to come out at Evans' trial, and at that point, it will be up to the Home Office as to whether or not we pursue a prosecution of Lowery."

"Once the details get out and into the papers, Sir Madison will be a social pariah himself. He'll be broke and there won't be a family in the entire country that'll let him near one of their daughters," Mrs. Goodge muttered.

Witherspoon laughed and got to his feet. "If you dear ladies will excuse me, I must go and thank Constable Barnes. He's the one who rallied the lads into doing the paperwork and suggested we put Evans in a holding cell so I could get back in time for the wedding. Oh, and Ruth, it was so good of you to bring the carriage to fetch me home. Your timing was impeccable."

Ruth smiled but waited till he'd walked away before she

said, "My timing was the result of a quick message from Constable Barnes."

Mrs. Goodge laughed. "This has been a wonderful day." She glanced at the housekeeper. "You'll have to tell us the rest of the details later."

"We'll have a quick meeting after the reception."

"Luty and Hatchet are dyin' to find out the rest of it," Mrs. Goodge said. She glanced across the room. Their two friends were chatting with the newlyweds. "Seein' those two lovebirds so happy makes me wonder how Rosemary Evans must be feelin' right now."

"I imagine she's relieved not to be marrying Lowery and brokenhearted that her father committed a murder to save her." Mrs. Jeffries sighed. "But they have a lot of money, and I imagine that rather than face the social humiliation of having a murderer in the family, Arabella Evans will probably pack up and leave the country."

"That's what I'd do," Mrs. Goodge said. "I'm goin' to get another plate of food. It's actually very good."

"I'll come with you." Ruth got up as well. "That black currant cream is absolutely delicious."

"I made that dish," the cook said proudly as she led the way to the dining room. "And the Battenberg cakes and the scones. The caterers did the rest."

Mrs. Jeffries sipped her champagne. She'd not lost her touch. She saw Betsy stand up and make her way through the crowd.

"Alright." Betsy stopped in front of her and put her hands on her hips. "What's going on? I know something has happened because you've got an expression on your face like a cat that's just got the canary."

"I'm just happy that you're finally married. It was a beautiful wedding. I was quite surprised to learn that Smythe's Christian name is Goodwin."

"That's right, I'm Mrs. Goodwin Smythe." Betsy's eyes narrowed suspiciously. "You're trying to change the subject, aren't you? Come on, tell me what happened. You know I'll not have a moment's peace until I know."

"Jeremy Evans was arrested today," Mrs. Jeffries said. "We didn't want to say anything to you and Smythe because this is your special day and we didn't want it ruined."

"Ruined? What'll ruin it is if we don't know what's happened."

"Betsy, it's your wedding day and we all want it to be special for— "

"You and the others have already made it the most special day of my life," she interrupted. "I'll never forget what all of you have done for me, for us."

"Then why do you want it tainted with the details of an ugly murder?" Mrs. Jeffries asked softly.

"Because it's not just about the murder. It's about justice!" she exclaimed. "Surely you must know how important our cases are to Smythe and me. They mean everything to both of us. I came from nothing, Mrs. Jeffries, and I got lucky and found myself at Upper Edmonton Gardens. Coming here changed my life in ways you can't imagine. You and the inspector believed in me; you encouraged me to be my best, to learn to speak properly, to read books and newspapers and magazines because I had a right to be a part of the world. But the best thing you ever did for me was to give me a chance to serve the cause of justice. Because justice, doing what's right, making sure that the innocent don't suffer because it's convenient for the rich and the powerful, that's the most important thing anyone can do in their entire life."

"Well said, my love," Smythe commented softly as he came up behind her. He looked at the housekeeper expectantly. "Come on, Wiggins let it slip that there's been an arrest. So you'd best give us the details. We'll not leave for our weddin' trip until you do."

A feeling of great pride swept through Mrs. Jeffries as she listened to Betsy's passionate speech. The girl was right; this wasn't about murder. It had never been about murder.

It was about justice.

Justice that was blind to money, wealth, class, and privilege. Oh, she didn't fool herself that the law in England was perfect as yet. But they were certainly well on their way.

"Alright you two." She motioned to the empty chairs. "Sit yourselves down and I'll tell you everything."